SHIFT

"It's slick and quick with just the right amount of squick (Benjo's lovely and gross), and the central premise unfolds satisfyingly."
   Tom Pollock, author of The City's Son

"It's like the best kind of video game: full of fun, mind-bendy ideas with high stakes, relentless action, and shocking twists!"
   E C Myers, author of Fair Coin

"Scott Tyler thinks joining ARES will fix his problems; instead he finds a frightening and deadly conspiracy. Curran's debut is a fast and funny mind-bending trip. The potentially confusing concept of shifting is nicely handled, and the mystery's reveal is tantalizing. Realistic British teens and a couple of completely creepy villains make this sci-fi thriller a must for genre fans."
   Kirkus Reviews

"A hi-octane, timey-wimey thriller. It'll blow your mind!"
   James Dawson, author of Hollow Pike

KIM CURRAN

S H I F T

STRANGE CHEMISTRY

An Angry Robot imprint
and a member of the Osprey Group

Lace Market House
54-56 High Pavement
Nottingham NG1 1HW
UK

www.strangechemistrybooks.com
Strange Chemistry #2

A Strange Chemistry paperback original 2012
1

A catalogue record for this book is available
from the British Library.

ISBN 978-1-908844-03-3
eBook ISBN: 978-1-908844-05-7

Set in Sabon and Aspirin Refill by THL Design.

Printed and bound by CPI Group (UK) Ltd, Croydon, CR0 4YY

JUBILEEWOODS.ORG.UK

For Chris

PROLOGUE

Take a second and think about all the decisions you've made in your life. The small ones, like which socks to wear in the morning. Do you go for the blue ones with the hole in the toe? Or the pair your gran bought you with the cartoon character on the heel that you secretly really like but know will get your arse kicked if anyone at school sees them? Then there are the big, life-changing decisions, like should you go to university or do you ask that girl out to the cinema even though you're almost certain she'll laugh in your face. Remember that time you chose to walk instead of taking the bus and you ended up getting drenched in a hailstorm and your mum went mental because you'd ruined your new shoes? Or when you put a whoopee cushion on Sharon Connor's chair and everyone laughed so much that she ran out of class crying and you wanted to cry too?

Think about all those fixed pinpoints in the map of your life. The choices that have got you to where you are now. Well, what if you could change them? What if you could undo every decision you've ever made. Unmake every mistake. Would you?

Let me stop you right there. You're probably thinking it would be really cool. You're imagining getting on that bus instead of walking in the rain, right? Thinking about all those lost opportunities taken, all those missed moments seized. Sounds great, yeah? Wrong. It's a nightmare.

And if I'd known that going out that night would have ended up with me being kicked out of home, arrested by a secret government division and hunted by a brain-eating nutjob, I'd have stayed at home.

But then, I'd never have met her. Aubrey Jones. The girl who was going to change everything. The girl who was going to get me killed.

CHAPTER ONE

The withered hand raked across my face, leaving four bloody gashes. Everything went red. I was losing blood, fast, and I'd used up my last med pack an hour ago. My heart slowed to a deafening thud, drowning out the groans of the creature. I kicked out as it came in for a second attack and raised my shotgun.

Click. Empty. Damn.

I ran. Or, rather, I limped. Bent double, holding my stomach, dragging my foot behind me. If I could just reach the door ahead I might be safe. Glancing back I saw the foul thing dragging itself across the floor, a single desire animating its decaying limbs. Flesh.

The door was only steps away. I wrenched it open and dived through. I wasn't alone. The room was filled with the living dead. As one they turned and started shuffling towards me, their arms raised. I tried to open the door again but in my panic I kept missing the handle. I could almost feel their fetid breath on my neck when finally it creaked open.

I was sure I saw the zombie's rotting lips curl in a smile as it lunged. I was drowning in blackness, as gnarled fingers tore at my skin. Two blood-dripping words floated out of the gloom.

You lose!

"That'll be because you, Scott, are a loser," my sister said from the doorway.

"Get out of my room, Katie!" I shouted, throwing the game controller at her. She dodged it with an effortless sidestep and stuck her tongue out at me.

I sighed. She was right. It was Friday night, the last day of term, of the last year of secondary school, and I, Scott Tyler, was sat at home being eaten by a dead guy, while the rest of my class were out there celebrating.

Try Again? flashed at me from the screen. Yeah right, like how about I give the past five years another try?

Five years of mediocrity and mundanity and it wasn't like the future was looking any brighter. In a matter of weeks I would be back at the same school for my A-Levels. Back with the same boys, with the same teachers. The only difference was I would be allowed to wear my own clothes. That's if Mum didn't throw them all out again like she'd done a few years ago because she thought they made me look like a tramp.

As if on cue, Mum started screeching from downstairs. "Scott! Katie! Dinner! Now!"

Perfect. As if my night couldn't get any worse, I would now have to be subjected to my weekly slice of hell, otherwise known as The Tyler Friday Family Dinner. Why

Mum insisted on us all eating together, I had no idea. I guess it was her attempt to pretend we were a normal, functioning family. But there's a reason we never spent any time together. We pretty much hated each other.

I silenced the game with a jab of the remote and somehow found the energy to drag myself out of my room.

Katie was sat in the hallway, her legs dangling between the banisters, her face pressed up against the wood. She flinched at the sound of something being slammed in the kitchen downstairs.

"They at it again?"

She nodded.

I crouched down next to her and leant my back against the wooden rails. "What is it this time?"

"Dad's Christmas party. Again."

"Where he was flirting with the pre-pubescent receptionist?"

"And she was so slobbering drunk she was dancing on the tables by nine. That's the one."

We sat in silence for a bit, listening to Mum and Dad screaming about how they ruined each other's lives.

So far, so Tyler family.

I saw Katie biting her bottom lip and I really didn't know what I'd do if she actually started crying. I hadn't seen Katie cry since she was seven and I made her walk the plank out of our tree house, which was supposed to be a pirate ship, and she broke her leg. She told Mum she'd slipped.

Katie wasn't supposed to be dealing with stuff like

this at her age. Hell, I wasn't supposed to be dealing with this stuff like this and I was five years older. I couldn't stand seeing her like this. Not down to some protective brotherly affection type thing. We don't have that kind of relationship. No, but because it scared me.

Katie's supposed to be the tough one. She might be younger, but she's better at pretty much everything, including football, kick boxing, fencing and playing computer games. Dad once said she was more of a man than I'd ever be. Thanks, Dad. As for Mr Tyler himself, he's what psychologists call a "classic male". Disinterested. Disconnected. And dissatisfied. He works for some crappy solicitors' firm, and blames Mum getting knocked up with me for why he never finished university and made it as a real lawyer. Mum was a housewife until two years ago when she took an assertiveness course, started wearing jeans a size too small and heels three inches too high, and began her own online pottery business, which she runs out of the shed in the back garden. So if she wasn't collecting a triumphant Katie from a fencing competition or whatever, she spent most of her time out in the shed. Pottering. Literally. I guess it was so she could avoid Dad who'd come home from work, plonk in front of the TV, before dragging himself upstairs to snore for eight hours straight. He and Mum didn't even share the same bed any more. I wished they'd just get a divorce, like most of my friends' parents. But oh, no. They had to stick together, for the sake of us kids.

"Hey," I said, nudging her. "At least they wanted you.

You weren't 'The Mistake.'" I made bunny ears over the phrase to try and show that it was supposed to be a joke.

"Hey, at least you weren't the Band-Aid Baby. The one who was supposed to fix everything," Katie said, and her chin went all wrinkly like a walnut.

"Come on." I stood up and offered her my hand. "Let's get this over with."

"It's pasta," she said, refusing my help and pulling herself to her feet using the banisters. We both rolled our eyes.

When we arrived in the kitchen Mum and Dad had descended into a frosty silence. I took my seat next to Katie and pulled a silly face, the one that used to make her really laugh when she was little; my tongue pushed into my upper lip and my eyes rolling back.

"Oh, Scott," she sighed. "Why do you have to be such a twat?"

Swearing was also something Katie did better than me.

Moment of sibling solidarity well and truly over, I punched Katie and she kicked me in the shin, before Mum slopped ladles of soggy conchiglie onto our plates. I held up a wobbling shell and glanced at it. Seeing the expression on Mum's face, I ate it without comment.

Katie pushed her food around her plate, as if looking for some decent cooking under it. I, on the other hand, shovelled mouthful after mouthful into my cheeks. The sooner I finished the ritual torture, the sooner I could be back in the solace of my bedroom.

My mobile buzzed in my pocket. I pulled it out,

careful not to let Mum see, and read the message.

WT U DNG

It was from Hugo. Hugo who had an IQ of 154, who could recite pi to eighty-eight decimal places, but who'd singularly failed to get his head around predictive text so used an impenetrable textspeak of his own devising. He was the closest thing I had to a best friend. Although I'm not sure either of us really liked each other that much. I punched out a reply.

NOTHING. AS ALWAYS.

A few mouthfuls later, my phone buzzed again.

SCRWS R DWN RC. FNCY IT

While I was trying to unravel Hugo's message, I caught my name being mentioned.

"Don't you think, Scott?" Mum was asking me something and I'd totally missed it. I snapped my attention away from the phone under the table and back to my dysfunctional family. She nodded encouragingly, so I picked up my cue.

"Yeah, sure," I said.

Dad laughed. "What would he know about business? And when is he going to get a haircut?"

"He's got an A in GCSE business studies. Which is more than you've got," Mum snapped.

"Well, he'd better have after the amount we're paying for that so-called education of his."

And they were off again. About lost opportunities and how they wished they'd never met.

I scooped up the last of my pasta and piled it into my

mouth, then fired off another text.

SCREW WHAT NOW???

Just as I was cleaning my plate, my phone started playing "The Eye of the Tiger". I really had to get a new ringtone.

"Scott! How many times? Not at the table!" Mum said, interrupting her character assassination of Dad.

"I've finished!" I said through a mouthful of meatballs. I shoved my chair away from the table and looked at my phone. Hugo's squashed face stared up at me from the screen. I slid across the answer button with a greasy thumb.

"Seb's crew!" Hugo's impossibly posh voice said from the other end of the line. "Seb's crew are down the Rec. Would you care to accompany me and see what might be occurring on this fine night?"

"I don't know... I mean, Seb?"

"There may be girls there."

"I'll see you in five."

And that was my first bad decision of the night.

CHAPTER TWO

"Are you sure we're allowed?"

"Allowed?" Hugo said. "The Rectory Grounds are public property, Scott. Of course we're allowed."

"But what about Seb–"

"You're not still angry about when he flushed your Teenage Mutant Ninja Turtle down the loo, are you? That was four years ago, Scott."

"It was five years ago. And I really liked that turtle."

"You really need to learn to let go," he said, patting me on the back. "Always was your problem. I bet Seb doesn't remember."

I wasn't so confident. Up until six weeks ago we would never have dreamt of coming to the Rec on a Friday night. This was the domain of Sebastian Cartwright – St Francis's king of cool – and the rest of his crew. Guys to whom people like Hugo and I were at best invisible and at worst fair game. Then Hugo helped Seb cheat on his History GCSE coursework and a magic door had opened up, letting Hugo, and by proxy myself, into their realm.

It was understood that as long as we didn't get too close, we would be permitted to remain within their orbit.

"Actually, the only thing I'm not sure is allowed is that T-shirt," said Hugo. "What were you thinking, Scott?"

"It's vintage," I said, in indignant defence.

The chatter of laughter floated on the light breeze and managed to overcome my faint terror. Perhaps Seb and the rest of the crew weren't that bad. Besides, school was over now. And with it all those petty definitions of who was in and who was out. Maybe sixth form wouldn't be so bad after all. Maybe our newfound access to the inner echelons of cool would be our passport to a new life, without wedgies and debagging.

Who was I kidding?

The group stopped talking as we approached. I froze, my legs twitching, ready to run if needed. Seb gestured to Hugo with a jerk of his chin and that was it. We'd passed.

Hugo nudged me in the side. "See. We're cool."

"Hugo, we will never be cool," I whispered back as we took our seats on a mossy log.

A beer can was pressed into my hand and instinctively I went to pass it on. But there was no one next to me. I prised the ring pull open and took a glug. It was warm and tasted faintly of old socks. But pretending to like beer was all part of being sixteen, wasn't it? I took a second, smaller sip, and peered around at the group.

Besides Seb there were six other boys, including Seb's

younger and utterly insane brother, Lucas. Lucas had
been in my sister's year at primary school, before he'd
been suspended for setting fire to the caretaker's cupboard. He had a crazy, unhinged look in his eyes, and
was currently hanging upside down from a tree branch,
singing the jingle from an advert for orange juice. Everyone ignored him.

There were also, as Hugo had promised, girls. Three
of them. Girls were still a bit of a mystery to me. Not
helped by the fact I'd gone to an all-boys' school. I'd had
a girlfriend last summer, if holding hands for a couple of
weeks and then being publicly dumped qualified as a
girlfriend. But since then, I'd hardly managed to speak
to a female I wasn't related to. I doubted I'd have
much of a chance with any of these girls either. They were
each firmly attached to one of the guys in the group.
By their lips in one case. I tore my eyes away from the
writhing mass of flesh and slurping noises. And that's
when I saw Her.

A fourth girl, standing alone, she deserved the capital
letter. She wasn't like any girl I'd ever seen before. Her
face was illuminated by the drifting light of her cigarette.
She had cropped blonde hair, heavy, black eyeliner and
crazy mismatched clothes: a blue military-style jacket
with a bright orange hoodie underneath. She stood away
from the group, as if waiting for someone and wanting
to make it very clear she had nothing to do with any of
us, and she was staring right at me.

I checked over my shoulder to make sure it really was

me she was looking at. I've made that mistake before. The scrub grounds stretched out behind me, with no one in sight.

I turned back to her. She had a pale face and perfect cupid lips. They curled upward, amused by something. Her eyes flashed for a moment and then she looked away. It had just been the briefest of glances my way. Just a scan across the group. A glazed expression passed over her face and she watched Lucas, who was now trying to set fire to the tree. Whatever amused her about me seemed long forgotten. Which wasn't surprising. Guys like me did not register to girls like her.

I took another swig of the warm beer and tried to pick up the trail of the conversation.

"No way, you'd get fried," Seb said, his hand absent-mindedly cupping the butt cheek of the red-head next to him. They were talking about the Pylon.

"No you wouldn't," I said, shocked at the sound of my own voice.

"Oh, yeah?" Seb said, standing up and towering over me.

I should have just backed down. Shut up. But the words kept coming. "As long as you don't touch the ground at the same time you'd be OK. It's a current thing. Besides, the Pylon was switched off years ago," I finished lamely, wishing the soggy ground of the Rec would eat me up. I glugged at my beer, hoping they'd all just carry on.

"Prove it."

I coughed. "I'm fine, thanks. I don't want to end up

like Tony. Ha Ha." No one else was laughing. They were all staring at me, grinning. They couldn't seriously think I'd do anything as stupid as Tony Plumber?

Every one of us knew Tony's story. It had passed into our collective urban myth. Six years ago, to this very day, he'd come to the Rectory Grounds and climbed the Pylon. Whether it had been live then or not was still a matter of contention. But what everyone knew was that he'd climbed to the top, thrown his school tie over the wire in an act of defiance, and slipped. But he didn't just fall. He got his trousers tangled in the wires on the way down and tore a testicle clean off. We all knew someone who knew someone who swore they were there that night to see a lone ball dangling from a wire twenty feet up, as Tony writhed on the ground. It had earned him the nickname Tony One-Plumb-er.

"I don't see why that would bother you, Scott," said Hugo from next to me. "It's not like you have any balls to start with."

I gawped at Hugo, my supposed best friend. Oh, so this is how it goes? I thought. A heady hit of life with the cool crowd and you turn on me. Well, he could have them, the Judas. I stood up and threw my empty beer can to the floor. I was off home.

Only I wasn't.

My legs weren't leading me back to the safety of the street. They were, beyond my control, walking me towards the Pylon.

The crew started whooping and laughing and thumping me on the back as if I was a boxer heading for the ring. I tried to tell my limbs to stop, to turn around, but they were taking orders from a different part of my brain. A part that cared what these idiots thought of me, that didn't want to look like a coward in front of them all. As the cheers got louder and the adrenaline started flowing, that stupid, pack-mentality part of my brain took over completely. No one would call me a loser once I'd conquered the Pylon. I wouldn't be called Scotty "Snotty" Tyler any more. I'd be their hero. I'd be one of them. And She would be watching.

"What are you doing?" Hugo hissed at me. I ignored him.

My fingers curled around the wire fence. Behind it stood the Pylon, like a stunted Eiffel Tower, calling to me. The stick-figure man on the *DANGER OF DEATH* sign waved me away. Or maybe it was just his body con-vulsing with the current. Either way he wasn't stopping me. I hefted myself up.

Halfway, my trainers slipped in the loops of wire. There was a gasp as I clung by my fingers, legs pedalling in the air. A thought struck me. I could let go now and fall, what? Six feet? That wouldn't be so bad. An inele-gant end to what had been a stupid idea to start with, but at least it would be over.

But then I heard them chanting my name. They were chanting my goddamned name! My foot found its pur-chase again and I pulled myself up and over the fence. Any thoughts of quitting vanished as I landed on the other side. It was just me and my personal Everest.

I didn't even know if I was right about the Pylon being switched off. I remembered a YouTube video of an elephant wrapping her trunk around a live wire and hitting the ground. If it could do that to a jumbo, what exactly would happen to me? Only one way to find out.

I jumped, leaping up to grab onto the first strut. I waited for the bolts of electricity to send me flying back into the fence. Nothing. I was safe. For now. The crew had fallen into a shocked silence, watching my ascent.

I stepped up to the next rung. And the next one.

"OK, you've made your point," I heard Hugo say. "Now come back down!"

Before I knew what was happening, I was fifteen rungs up, only feet from the very top. A girl's voice cried out in apparent concern. I glanced back, to see if it had been The Girl calling after me. Big mistake.

I couldn't move. As soon as I'd looked down to the ground, everything span and my limbs froze. Oh, now you decide to stop, I said to my treacherous legs. And the worst thing? The Girl was watching. She took a drag on her cigarette, shook her head, and turned away.

What the hell was I doing? I wasn't impressing anyone. The only thing I was going to do was get myself killed.

Sweat prickled on my forehead and it felt as if something was trying to get out of my stomach. I closed my eyes and pressed myself against the metal bar. Just one more, I said, over and over, one more strut and you can go back down.

Without opening my eyes, I stretched up a shaking hand, feeling for the metal rod above. My fingers closed around it, sharp edges cutting into my flesh. I had two hands on the final strut and I lifted my foot up.

The snap of metal was like the sound of a coffin lid slamming shut. The broken strut slipped through my fingers and I was falling, hands grasping at air, legs kicking helplessly.

A single thought flooded through my mind. Why? Why the hell hadn't I given up when I had the chance? Why the hell was I such a complete and utter loser?

Then it happened. Everything went black and I felt a flipping lurch in my stomach, like when you go over a hill in a car and it takes a few seconds for your insides to catch up with you. A strange sense of being suspended between two places at once. My head pounded and I felt hot and cold at the same time.

When the lights came back on, I was lying on my back, gazing up at the Pylon through the fence. I wasn't dead. I wasn't even hurt, apart from a thudding in my backside. Sitting up, a smile stretching my face, I turned to look at the crew. They weren't watching any more. They were sitting back on the logs.

"Is he just going to lie there all night?" one of the girls said.

"Pathetic," said another sneering at me. "He couldn't even make it over the fence."

I sat up and stared at them. What did they mean? I'd

made it all the way to the top, I'd fallen almost forty feet with nothing but a few bruises to show for it. Why weren't they celebrating me as some sort of miracle boy? An image flickered across my mind. Me slipping on the fence and just letting go. Me falling to the ground with a thud, and just lying there, as they all laughed and booed. I hadn't made it to the top after all. So why did I remember it so clearly?

I rubbed at the back of my head, trying to work out what the hell was going on. Then I felt a tap on my shoulder.

I twisted around to see The Girl. She pulled her cigarette out of her mouth and flicked it into the air. It fizzed as it hit the damp grass.

"Tyler?" she asked. "Scott Tyler?"

I nodded, dumbly.

"You're under arrest."

CHAPTER THREE

A small hand pulled me to my feet, then punched me in the arm.

"What exactly do you think you were doing?" she said.

"Whaa?" I was never good around pretty girls. Especially bad when it appeared I'd done something to really piss them off.

"Shifting in public. Just to show off to your mates! Are you nuts?" She shoved my shoulder.

"Oi! That hurt."

"It's nothing compared to what the Regulators will do to you when they get here." She shook her head and tutted.

"Huh?'

"So you can come in nice and quiet with me, or wait and get bagged and tagged, up to you."

"I really don't know what you're on about. Sorry," I added, not entirely sure what I was apologising for.

She took a step back and looked me up and down, her pale forehead wrinkling. "You're a Shifter, right?"

"Er, no. Not that I know what a Shifter is."

She tilted her head and stared at me, sizing me up.

"Scott?" Hugo walked over. When he saw The Girl his eyes lit up and his eyebrows disappeared under his shaggy fringe. "Well, hello, there. Enchanted, I'm sure." He stretched out his hand. The Girl ignored it. I had to hide my grin as Hugo glanced at his empty hand and then slipped it back in his pocket. "So. What is a lovely lady like yourself doing in a nasty place like this?"

I'd never seen Hugo around a girl before, and I was glad I hadn't. He was an embarrassment.

"I'm here to steal Scott away for the evening."

To my shock, The Girl slipped her arm under mine and leaned her head against my shoulder. I didn't know what the hell was going on. All I knew was that there were little bolts of electricity shooting up my arm and across my chest.

"I… I…" was all I managed to say.

"Well, lucky old Scott," Hugo said, waggling his eyebrows. It looked as if he was having a stroke.

"I guess. Must go. Great meeting you." She grabbed my jacket and yanked me away. I goggled helplessly at Hugo. He made an obscene gesture and waved me on. Some friend he was turning out to be tonight. Didn't he realise that this girl was clearly insane?

Stumbling, I was dragged down an alleyway. It stank of tramp piss. I saw a rat skitter past.

"Nice," I said,

The Girl pushed me against the wall.

"Stop doing that!" I said, rubbing at my throbbing shoulder.

"You seriously don't know?"

"Don't know what?"

She gave me that up and down look again, as if she was disappointed by what was standing in front of her. "You're a Shifter."

"I've said already, I have no idea what you're on about. And if you've done shouting at me, I'd like to leave now."

I half turned, but she grabbed my arm, a little more gently this time.

"I've heard of rogues, but never people who just didn't know," she said, more to herself than to me.

Her eyes met mine: the green of the sea in winter. Any pretence I might have made at leaving evaporated.

"Who are you?" I asked, my voice a cracked whisper.

"Aubrey," she said. "Aubrey Jones." She stretched out her hand.

I rubbed my damp palm on my jean leg and shook her hand. "Scott. Scott Tyler."

"Yeah, I know. Your friends were chanting your name, right till you fell on your arse."

"About that… did you see me climb to the top of the pylon? Cause I'm pretty sure I fell from the top."

"Nope. But that doesn't mean you didn't."

"I think maybe I hit my head."

"Listen, Scott Tyler. There's so much you need to know. But we can't talk here." She glanced back up the alley. The crew had gathered at the opening, watching us. "Do you know anywhere safe?"

"What, we're not safe here?" I asked.

"The Regulators will have registered the Shift and I give it…" She let go of my hand to check her watch. The absence of it made me realise how warm her hand had been. "Oh, about thirty minutes before they pinpoint the exact location. Less if someone who actually knows what they're doing is on duty." She chewed on the inside of her cheek seemingly trying to weigh up her options.

"Come on. I know a place," she said.

Hugo's mum is from Peru. Or Paraguay. Some South American country. Anyway, she once said: "If you see a ship on the top of a mountain, a woman's fanny got it there." Not only was I horrified I'd just heard Hugo's rather attractive mother say "fanny" I also didn't have any idea what she'd been on about. But I do now. It means that men will do anything for a beautiful woman. Or rather for the chance to get near one. So if you're wondering why I followed Aubrey Jones farther down that dark, stinking alleyway, that's my excuse. I couldn't put a ship on top of a mountain, but I could trudge after her like an idiot. It wasn't as if I had a choice. Not really.

"The place" Aubrey knew turned out to be Copenhagen's Casino. Only it didn't look like any casino I'd ever seen. In fairness, I'd only ever seen one casino, in Bognor Regis, and that had been a temple to tat. But this place was more like a posh gentleman's club than a flashy gaming joint.

"Are we going in there?" I asked, pointing at the polished brass plaque on the white-bricked wall, which said the place had been Est. 1828.

Aubrey rolled her eyes at me, then knocked on the black door. Knock, knock, knockknocknock, knock. And waited. I heard an electronic whirring from overhead and saw a security camera jerking to focus on us. An electronic voice crackled from a speaker embedded in the wall. "Password?"

Aubrey leant close into the speaker. I could have sworn I heard her say "Swordfish": I heard the sibilant echo of the word in my mind. But the word that actually came out of her mouth was "Sturgeon." The two words rang in my head, making me feel dizzy and confused, like a weird kind of déjà vu. I shook my head to try and clear it of the eerie feeling.

Three heavy clunks and the door opened. I waved at the camera in a lame greeting, wondering what the fascination with fish was all about, and followed Aubrey over the threshold.

The hallway smelt of leather and cigar smoke. Large, faded playing cards lined the walls and the Victorian kings and queens seemed to watch me as I passed. They didn't look impressed. Aubrey pushed open the green-leather doors at the end, and the sounds of laughter and rattling dice filled the hallway.

Beyond was a domed room, filled with green card tables

and spinning roulette wheels. Men dressed in suits and women in cocktail dresses were huddled over the games, their eyes glinting with greed. Aubrey's face lit too.

I took a step forward, but my way was barred by a man so big he blocked out the light.

"Ms Jones. I wasn't expecting anyone from ARES tonight." He was dressed in a sharp tuxedo, which barely contained his muscles. His square jaw tightened, as Aubrey glanced away to watch a screaming woman scoop her winnings into a very low-cut cleavage. "As I'm sure you know, our licenses are fully up-to-date. I had an *inspection* only last week," he said, with a touch of bitterness.

"Relax, Shipley. I'm off duty," Aubrey said, patting his massive arm.

"In that case, we have a game of poker about to start. In the back." The man mountain stepped aside and gestured with a dismissive jerk of this thumb towards a bookshelf on the far side of the room. Whatever was going on here, we weren't welcome.

"Thanks, but we're here to drink. Not to play. More's the pity… But you know ARES."

"Only too well," he said, watching us walk away.

I followed Aubrey through the room, staring up at the gold-painted arches and glinting chandeliers. I hadn't felt so uncomfortable in a place since my father dragged us to a golf club he was hoping to join last year. Although at least then I was wearing an M&S suit, rather than my tatty jeans and Atomic Rooster T-shirt. Even if it was vintage.

A few of the gamblers gave us a confused look, probably wondering what a couple of kids were doing in a casino, then turned back to their games.

A croupier raised her head as we passed her table. She had long, dark hair and coffee-coloured skin that shone in the golden light. Without taking her eyes off us, she shuffled a deck of cards at high speed, her hands a blur. She dealt the cards, flicking them across the table. They seemed to switch places midair. Watching her dealing was like watching someone moving under a strobe light. Unsettling, but utterly irresistible. She winked at me.

I banged into Aubrey who had reached the bookshelf. I could see now that one section of the shelves was set back further than the others, creating a hidden space. Unless you got up close, it looked like one whole wall of books but it was three walls positioned perfectly. I swayed to the left and the right, admiring how the optical illusion had been set up. One book out of place and it wouldn't have worked. Aubrey sighed and pulled me to the right. To the rest of the room it must have looked as if we disappeared.

Hidden from the rest of the gamers, Aubrey pulled a thick, blue volume named *The Theory of Games* from another wall of books. The bookshelf slid across, revealing a room on the other side. It was smaller than the last, darker and less ornate. The card tables looked like rejects – the baize faded and torn – and the furniture was mismatched and chipped. Instead of Regency wallpaper and gilt-framed pictures, the walls were covered with shards of mirror, so you could only see tiny fragments of yourself, broken and shattered, as if Picasso had got hold of your reflection.

Games were still taking place, but instead of suits and cocktail dresses, everyone here was in jeans and trainers. Although designer jeans and limited edition trainers, by my reckoning. I felt even more out of place in here as if I'd not only stepped into another room, but another world. There was something weird about the place and the people in it. Something I couldn't put my finger on. Maybe it was just me and I was suffering from shock, but everything felt somehow fluid. As if I was looking at it all through thick glass.

On the left, three young men wearing mic headsets sat facing a bank of TV monitors. The screens showed close-up images of what was happening on the other side of the wall.

"Play the queen," I heard one say.

They paused to stare at Aubrey, looking as if they'd been caught out.

"Don't mind me," she said, heading for the bar. I shuffled after her, trying to appear as inconspicuous as possible. Not easy when you're six foot and have a picture of a huge cockerel emblazoned on your chest.

Aubrey raised two fingers to the stocky man serving drinks. He grunted and a minute later slammed two tall glasses in front of us. She gathered them up without paying.

She nodded for me to follow her towards a booth

pressed up against one wall. It had two cracked green leather sofas either side of a dark wooden table, and was already filled with a group of kids who were laughing and playing cards. Aubrey smiled at the assembled group. They finished their drinks, threw down their cards, and cleared off. She hadn't even said a word. Placing the drinks on the table, she sat down and I slid in opposite her, in small jerking movements, banging my knees on the table as I did.

She folded her hands under her chin and watched me. I tried to copy her, but my elbow slipped off the table and I jabbed myself in the leg. I leaned back in the leather seat, hoping she hadn't noticed, and reached for the pale drink in front of me. I sniffed it. It smelt like paint stripper crossed with mint.

"Aubrey," I said, coughing and putting the glass back down. "I should probably tell you, I'm only sixteen."

"So what? I'm only fifteen," she said. She laughed at my surprised face and smiled properly for the first time since we'd met. It was like a spotlight going on. "Scott, the rules that apply to normal people no longer apply to you. You've got a whole new set of rules to worry about." She took a swig of her drink. "Besides, with what I'm about to tell you, you're going to need it."

CHAPTER FOUR

The ice in her drink danced as she spun the glass in small circles. I watched the shattered light from the mirrors leave dappled trails on the pockmarked table. And waited.

Whatever she had to tell me, she didn't want to and I was happy not to hear it. In my experience, if something makes a person that uncomfortable to say it out loud, it's never good news. Like when Mum told me she was pregnant with Katie. Or Dad tried to give me The Talk.

I lifted my glass to my lips again, but still couldn't bring myself to actually drink it. Aubrey had this cute wrinkle above her nose, in between her eyebrows, which I guessed meant she was thinking. Every now and then she'd open her mouth as if about to start speaking. Then stop. And return to spinning the glass.

I reached out and stopped it. "Look, you don't have to tell me. I could just go home and we could pretend none of this…" I waved my arm around. "Whatever this is, ever happened. Because if I'm honest, I don't really want to know."

Aubrey's confused expression vanished. Her brow was

smooth once more and her eyebrow hitched upwards. My cowardice was clearly not inspiring confidence.

"You're a Shifter, Scott. A person with what I guess you could call a special power."

I snorted and leant back in the sofa. "So can I fly? Go invisible?"

"Don't be stupid." She rolled her eyes. "Shifters have the power to change reality. And by doing that, shape reality around them. We can change decisions we make, take paths we didn't take, and change our present."

She really had lost me. I stared blankly, wondering when anything she said was going to start making sense. I must have looked pretty dumb, because she shook her head and sighed. "I don't usually have to explain any of this. I'm just a Spotter. I track Shifters down and the Regulators bring them in."

"And you were tracking me?"

"No actually. I was following that kid, Lucas."

"Lucas? Seb's mental little brother? What did you want with him?"

"The guys at ARES had intel he might be a Shifter. But nope. Just another messed-up kid." She sighed.

"And who or what is ARES? Because I'm guessing we're not talking the god of war here?"

"The The Agency for the Regulation and Evaluation of Shifters. The government division set up to deal with all Shifting affairs. And they don't take too kindly to people Shifting just to show off. Which is why you're lucky I spotted you first."

"But I don't know what a Shifter is and I don't know what I did wrong," I said, desperately. "All I remember is climbing the Pylon and falling."

Aubrey took a sip of her drink. "How much do you know about quantum physics?"

I laughed.

"What?' she said. "You have a problem with quantum physics?"

"No, it's just that you're…"

"What? A girl? Is that what you're saying? You think a girl can't know about quantum physics?"

"No, of course not," I stuttered. It was exactly what I'd been thinking. I coughed. "What about quantum physics?"

"Originally no one knew what was going on with Shifters. They thought it was magic or whatever. But when they started unravelling the mysteries of quantum mechanics it all started to make sense. Schrödinger's Cat. The Double Slit Experiment."

I laughed again. "Sounds like an all-girl punk band."

Aubrey gave me her look. I stopped laughing. "Yeah, Double Slit. Go on," I said.

"You know light acts as a wave and a particle?"

I didn't. "Sure," I said, nodding.

"In the Double Slit Experiment they fire a light particle at a sheet with two slits in it. You'd expect particles to just go straight through one of the slits, right? Like a bullet being fired at a wall through a hole. But instead of behaving like a good little particle, it acts like a wave and goes through both slits at the same time. It's as if it goes left and right at exactly the same time. Unless," she said, taking another sip. "And this is where it gets really weird, unless which slit the particle travels through is being observed – then it starts to behave normally again. That's called the collapse of the wave function. It's as if the particle is aware it's being watched."

"How can something be in two places at once?" I said, lagging behind.

"It isn't in two places so much as it exists in a state of probability. A state of two potential realities. One reality where it goes through the left slit. One where it goes through the right."

"Hang on, are you talking parallel universes?" I'd watched my fair share of *Star Trek*.

"No, there is only ever one universe. One reality." She held up a long finger tipped in chipped blue nail polish, illustrating her point. "But there are infinite potential re-alities." She spread her fingers wide, as if revealing the end of a magic trick. But the only thing she'd managed to make vanish was my grasp on what the hell was going on. If I'd ever had a grip in the first place. "What quantum physics proved is what Shifters have known for millennia. That we can change the way reality behaves just by observing it."

"My head hurts."

I'd always considered myself a pretty bright guy, es-pecially when it came to science and stuff. But this was confusing the hell out of me. Which must have been clear to Aubrey.

"OK," she leant forward, trying a new approach. "The Pylon."

I nodded.

"You say you remember climbing to the top?"

"Yeah, and then the strut snapped," I said.

"Ah, that might explain it. So you were falling? And your mind was racing through all the choices you made, right?"

"Exactly. I was wishing I hadn't even bothered."

"Well, you got your wish. You undid your choice and that's when the Shift happened."

"And I ended up lying on my arse having never made it over the fence?"

"Precisely. You Shifted to another reality, making it *the* reality. And the previous reality–"

"The one where I fell," I interrupted.

"Yes. That ceased to exist as soon as you made the Shift. It collapsed."

The sounds of laughter filled the silence between us. I didn't know what was worse, the fact that it was starting to make some kind of sense or that I was now officially a freak.

I reached for the drink and took a glug. It was hideous. "OK," I said, coughing from the alcohol burning my throat. "Let's say I believe you, and I'm not saying that I do, but let's just say I did believe you that I had this power to move from one reality to another. So what?"

"So what?" She was stunned.

"Yes, I mean why would the government care what I get up to?"

"Do you really think that the government, any government, is happy with the idea of people going around and making their own realities, having choice over what they do?" She shook her head. "Government is about control. So it makes sure that it controls the Shifters. That's what the agency was set up to do. Make sure that there's no unlawful Shifting going on."

"How do they stop it?"

"They find Shifters and train us up. Watch us, regulate us, and make sure we don't go crazy. Like cheating at exams or winning the lottery. They also protect us and stop us being manipulated by the bad guys."

"Like who?"

"The terrorists. The Americans. Whoever."

"And you don't go to school? At all!"

"What? And live a normal life? ARES couldn't allow that!"

Aubrey sounded bitter, but I was really liking the sound of this. I still wasn't convinced by any of what she was saying, but the idea of somehow being able to have total control over my life sounded pretty awesome. "Show me where to sign up!"

"I'm serious, Scott. It's hard. Especially now I'm an official Spotter." She tapped the golden S on the arm of her jacket. I'd assumed it was just a fashion accessory. "Most Shifters just go through the Programme and then head out to live normal, Shift-free lives. But if you're really good you stay on and join ARES for proper." There was-n't a hint of embarrassment in referring to herself as really good. If anything, there was a sadness there. "There are perks of the job, though," she continued, sud-denly smiling. "No one gives you crap for a start."

That explained why the group at this table had cleared off. "What's a Spotter?"

"We spot Shifters. Sense their power and then hand their arse over to the Regulators for processing."

I put my drink down and looked at her as she gazed out across the room, her face now expressionless. Be-neath the makeup and without her wry smile she did look young. Too young to be making what sounded like life and death decisions. "So why didn't you hand me over?"

I notice that her pale cheeks flushed a little pink. She stared into her drink and refused to meet my eyes.

"I guess I felt sorry for you. You clearly didn't have a clue what was going on. Although I'm not sure the Reg-ulators would believe that. I've never heard of an unregistered Shifter as old as you. Someone your age, Shifting without a licence, they'll probably think you're a rogue."

"Rogue?"

"Unregistered Shifters. Those who manage to stay one step ahead of ARES. But they're normally really power-ful and really clever." She peered at me over the rim of her glass. Her expression made it clear she thought I was neither.

I swallowed. "And what do ARES do to rogues?"

"Depends. Sometimes they let them go with a warning. Other times they lock them up until entropy sets in."

Just when I thought I was getting a grip on it all, I'd lost the thread again. "What now?"

"The ability to Shift fades when you're about nineteen, twenty maybe. We call it entropy."

"Hang on." I choked on a mouthful of my drink. "You're telling me only kids can have this Shifty power?"

She nodded. "Sure. It's something to do with the shape of our brains." She tapped her temple. "The teenage brain is different to adults'. Besides, have you ever met an adult who could change their mind on anything?"

I had to agree with her on that one. I scanned the room, noticing properly for the first time that there were no adults in here apart from the grumpy barman. The oldest person had to be twenty, tops.

"Is everyone here a Shifter?" I asked.

"Most. This is a place where we can come and just relax. Play games without getting in trouble. It's officially unofficial, and if any member of ARES got caught here, we'd be in trouble. But mostly the agency turns a blind eye as it allows kids to learn skills they're not allowed to teach them."

"Like what?"

"Cheating mostly. It comes in handy, believe me. And it's not easy, what with the random luck element. So ARES charge Shipley a small licence fee, and pay him a surprise visit every now and then to make sure everything is within set limits and that he's not creaming the public too much."

"How does he do that?"

"The games are rigged. Not in here – there's no point in rigging games with Shifters – but on the other side it's all controlled. Some of the croupiers are Shifters. And see those kids with the headsets?"

I glanced over to where the three boys were watching the TV screens. "Yeah."

"They're telling the plants what to play. Only if the cards don't go their way, they Shift and tell them to play a different hand."

"But isn't that unfair?"

She laughed. "Why do you look so surprised? Do you think any casino in the world is fair? No way. The House always wins. Here, Shipley just brings in some extra skills to make sure of it."

"So Shipley is a Shifter? But I thought you said only kids could do it."

"He was a Shifter. One of ARES' best. But after entropy, he left and set this place up. It's kind of sad. I think he misses having the power."

"Hey, I'm not surprised. I mean, having total control over your life. It's so cool."

"It really isn't," Aubrey said, unconvincingly. "And it's not total control. For a start, if you come up against someone stronger, and you try and make a Shift that they don't like, you're stuck in their version of reality."

I rubbed my face, trying to take this all in. Aubrey was bombarding me with this stuff like she was explaining why two plus two equals four to a toddler. I'd never felt so stupid in my life. "So you don't always have control over your reality?" I said, trying to keep up.

"Not always. See those two?" She nodded to a guy and girl sat alone at a card table. Other kids stood around them, watching the game.

"What about them?"

"Watch."

I did. They didn't do anything. They just stared at each other like they were playing that not-blinking game Katie and I used to play. "They're not doing anything."

"They're trying to force their Shift. They're pretty equally matched. But the more powerful of them will see their version become reality."

I stared longer and I don't know if it was the drink kicking in, or if I really needed to get my eyes tested, but I thought I saw ripples coming out from each of them, as if someone had dropped a stone in a pond. Where the ripples met, they repelled each other, bouncing back and creating more ripples. I sensed rather than saw the cards fall and it was over. The boy jumped up and punched the air in triumph.

"You might think you're all master-of-your-own-destiny and whatever," Aubrey said. "But really, you're caught up in a huge game of Top Trumps. The stronger Shifter, the person with more focus, more willpower, will always win. As long as your choices don't affect another

Shifter's plans, then you'll be fine. But if you go up against them and try and create a reality that's out of step with theirs. Well..." Aubrey shrugged and didn't bother finishing.

"So, let me get this straight," I said. "There's this weird quantum power that only some people have. Only some kids to be exact. Although some are more powerful at it than others. And there's a secret government unit that controls it all and if I'm not careful I'll be banged up quicker than I can say Scrotum's cat."

"Schrödinger's cat. But yes, that about sums it up."

I reached for the drink and downed it.

CHAPTER FIVE

———

Two more drinks arrived out of nowhere. Aubrey ignored hers and scanned the room. I guess she was giving me time to let it all sink in. And I needed it. Within five minutes, I'd been told I had the power to change reality and, whether I believed it or not, it was probably going to get me thrown in jail. Normally, in comic books and films and what have you, when people are told they're special they always say they somehow knew – that they had a sense they were destined for something big. Well not me. I'd always believed I was perfectly normal, destined for nothing more exciting than your bog standard A-Levels, mid-league university, followed by dull desk job. And it wasn't that I minded being normal. It was comforting. Safe. I sipped at my drink feeling depressed.

"Damn," Aubrey said, her eyes widening. She clenched the side of the table so hard her knuckles went white.

"What?"

"They're here."

I looked around trying to see who "they" were and why they were upsetting her so much. My heart pounded. Had the mysterious ARES tracked me down?

A group of young men wound their way through the tables, pausing to check out the games. I caught the buzz of excitement their presence was causing.

"Are they with ARES too?" I asked, starting to wonder if everyone at ARES was impossibly cool. These guys looked as if they'd just stepped off the pages of one of those fashion magazines that are so trendy they don't even bother with a name; all expensive leather jackets and artfully torn jeans.

"No way. They hate ARES. They call themselves the SLF."

"Are they a band or something?"

"More like a gang. Although they like to think of themselves as a resistance group. SLF stands for Shifter Liberation Front. The prats. They spout all this anti-ARES propaganda, about how Shifters should be free, to do what they want to do, yadda yadda yadda." Aubrey hadn't taken her eyes off the leading member. He had draped a leather-covered arm over the shoulder of a girl with bright pink hair. She giggled and stumbled after him. He led the girl and rest of his gang over to a huddle of sofas on the other side of the room.

"Who's he?"

"Zac. Their self-appointed leader." Aubrey watched them stride past with an expression that I really hoped was hatred given how good-looking they all were.

Especially Zac. He made Seb Cartwright look like a trainspotter.

"And they're all Shifters?"

"Only Zac and the ape-looking guy with him, I think. The other three are wannabes. You get them a lot."

"Wannabes?"

"Kids who find out about Shifting from siblings or hunt down rumours on the net. They seem to think if they hang around with us they'll be given the power too. Like vampires or something. Idiots. Once they find out you have to keep them sweet so they don't tell. Although, who would believe them if they did?" Aubrey didn't take her eyes of Zac as she spoke. I gave up trying to think of something to say to distract her and finished my second drink. I'd stopped being able to taste it, which probably wasn't a good sign.

The girl with the pink hair started nibbling at Zac's throat. He stopped her, leant over and started whispering in her ear. Aubrey flexed in her seat, as if trying to stop herself from moving.

While still whispering in the girl's ear, Zac reached out a hand and one of the other boys passed over a thing like a skeletal hand made from plastic. Wires trailed from each of the fingers into a small black cube. Zac placed it on the seat between him and the girl. He brushed her fringe away and fitted the thing over her head so the three points touched the centre of her forehead and either temple.

I wasn't sure if it was Aubrey's reaction, or something in the girl's nervous expression, but I felt very uncomfortable. "Is he supposed to be doing that?"

"No."

"Shouldn't you call ARES?" I asked.

Aubrey didn't answer.

Zac reached inside his jacket and pulled out a syringe. The girl rolled up her sleeve and presented him with her pale arm. I couldn't believe this was going on in full view of everyone. I tried to get the barman's attention, wondering when someone was going to stop them.

Aubrey jumped out of her seat so fast she knocked her drink over, spilling it all over my lap. It was freezing.

"Come on," she said.

I brushed the cubes of ice away and stood up. The room span and my knees felt as if they were made of jelly. I couldn't get my legs to work. "I can't feel my lips," I said.

Aubrey rolled her eyes and yanked me out from behind the table. She shoved me in the direction of the sofas and somehow my feet agreed to move.

"So we're stopping them then?" I asked, slurring slightly.

"Yes."

"But there are five of them."

Aubrey ignored me and headed for the SLF. The gorilla guy stood up to block her path. He laid a hand on Aubrey's shoulder and the world flipped.

They moved in a series of half-finished movements, as if different images had been layered on top of each other. It was like watching two films playing on the same screen at once and it made me feel a little sick. In one layer, Aubrey grabbed the ape's hand and twisted his arm around his back. In the other he dodged her grab and wrapped his hand around her neck. A new layer appeared as Aubrey's leg flew up and her boot connected with his face. He spat blood.

Then everything righted itself and the ape's hand was hovering over Aubrey's shoulder. He hadn't even touched her.

That was the first time I saw Shifters fighting. And it's not something I will ever forget. Both versions of what had just happened struggled to find a place in my muddled brain. Neither seemed to make any sense.

The big guy stepped aside and Aubrey approached Zac. The girl with the pink hair had a strange smile on her face and her eyes were rolling in her head.

"Unplug her," Aubrey said.

"Aubrey, it's good to see you," Zac said and he sounded genuine. His sharp features went soft and he leant forward as if trying to distance himself from the girl drooling next to him.

"Unplug her."

"You're looking especially fine, Brey. Although blue never was your colour." He shook his head. "I can't believe you're still with them. I always thought you'd be the first to go."

"Did you hear what I said?"

Zac glanced at the girl. "She's in deep. Unplug her now and I won't be responsible for the fallout."

"ARES will be here in five minutes."

Zac twitched and then gathered himself. "The stims aren't against the rules. But as far as I remember a Blue-coat being seen in a place like this was."

"You let me worry about that. You'll be busy worrying about spending the next seven years in prison. By the time they let you out, entropy will have set in."

"Entropy? Come off it, Aubrey. You of all people know what I think about entropy," he said and smiled, his perfect white teeth flashing. There was something about that smile. Something knowing.

Aubrey tilted her head, considering him. Then snapped back to centre. "You've got five minutes," she said, holding up five fingers.

"Come on, Aubrey," Zac said. "You should give it a go. Are you telling me there's no choice you were too frightened to make? Nothing you wished you'd tried, but didn't want to get caught? No guy you wished you'd…?" He raised a suggestive eyebrow.

Aubrey's eyes tightened. If that had been me under her stare I'd have wanted to crawl away. But Zac met her head on. "It's not real," she said. Which wasn't exactly the same thing as saying no.

"It's as real as it gets."

"So is that some kind of virtual reality thing then?" I said, pointing at the wires entwining with the girl's hair.

"Nothing virtual about it, my friend," Zac said, not taking his eyes off Aubrey. "It's reality I'm offering here. Pure and simple. Consequence-free."

"What you're offering is a lie," Aubrey said. "You

might think the stimulators work in a closed environment, but there are always consequences. You just don't know them yet."

"Looks like your friend would like to give it a go. Looks like he's so excited he's pissed himself."

I peered down at the wet stain on my crotch from where Aubrey had knocked her drink onto my lap. The group laughed and Zac looked slightly ashamed of himself, as if it had been a low shot.

"Four minutes," Aubrey said, folding her thumb away.

Zac unfurled himself from the couch. He was almost as tall as me, but had bulk to go with his height. He and Aubrey stared at each other, their eyes locked. It was like watching that couple playing cards, as if they were trying to psych each other out. For a full minute no one flinched. Then Zac stepped back and rubbed at his jaw as if he'd been slapped.

"Do we understand each other?" Aubrey said.

Zac smiled that perfect smile again. "All you had to do was ask, Brey. You know I can't resist you."

Aubrey walked away and I staggered after her.

"If you change your mind, you know where to find me," Zac called out after us. "Oh, no wait. You don't. ARES don't seem to be able to track me down, do they? I'm always one step ahead, Aubrey. One step ahead." Zac's cronies laughed on cue.

We headed back to our booth. Girls coaxed me to join their games. It was almost tempting. If I hadn't known

I'd zero chance of winning.

A high ringing noise sounded, drilling into my head.

"That's annoying," I said, covering my ears.

Aubrey stared around like a meerkat that's spotted danger. She wasn't alone. As one, the kids started to scatter, knocking over the cards tables, heading for every exit.

"Come on!" Aubrey shouted.

"What's going on?" I asked as she herded me through panicked people and towards the emergency exit.

"It's ARES," Aubrey answered finally. "I guess it's time for one of their surprise visits."

CHAPTER SIX

She pushed me towards an open exit and I stumbled out into the night. The door slammed behind us. The stench of overflowing wheelie bins hit my nose and my stomach lurched. But before I even had time to complain, Aubrey grabbed me by the hand and started to run.

We darted down a series of back streets. Each time we came to a choice of a left or right, Aubrey stopped and closed her eyes for a moment. Then we'd be moving again. It must have been the drink, but it felt as if the walls of the alleys and streets she dragged me through kept changing. One second we'd be running down an alley covered in band posters. The next it was a passageway between blocks of council flats. And with each junction she'd stop. I'd just have time to catch my breath before she was off again. Never letting go of my hand.

I gave up trying to work out where we were and just focused on not falling over. We ran and ran, and the streets blurred into each other. We'd been going for about ten minutes and my lungs were starting to burn.

"Stop," I gasped and pulled my hand free of hers to hold my side. Aubrey skidded to a halt.

She walked back to me slowly. "I think we've lost them, anyway."

"I thought you said you'd called ARES?" I said, gasping for air. "Why are we running away from them?"

"Because agency members aren't supposed to go to Copenhagen's. Because I couldn't let them find you. Besides, Zac was right, the Regulators would never have caught him. He'd just have Shifted."

"But all that facing off, 'do we understand each other' stuff. I thought you were the more powerful Shifter?"

"No. He was just messing with me, the egotistical tosser." Aubrey scanned the street, a little confused.

"Where are we?" I asked, squinting up at the towering buildings around us.

"I'm not sure. I Shifted so many times back there, I've sort of lost track."

"You were Shifting?"

"I kept changing which direction I chose. Undoing whether we went right or left. It's pretty simple really, when you know how. Didn't you sense it?"

"I thought it was the drink. So that's why you kept stopping?"

"Yes. You can't just run wildly. You have to make conscious decisions about where you're going. Decisions you can undo."

"And won't these Regulators have registered the Shifts?" I said, straightening up.

"Probably, but in the chaos it'd be hard to pin it down to one Shifter. Come on, I think it's this way."

We wandered down side streets as Aubrey tried to get her bearings. The mix of adrenaline and alcohol flooding through my system was making me feel giddy. I was walking the streets of London with a beautiful girl and I was thinking that anything was possible. Apart from going home, it turned out.

It took me a while to place the repetitive bleeping coming from my inside pocket. At first I thought it might be another alarm. I finally remembered it was my phone and answered the call.

"Scott, where the hell are you?"

"Hugo! My man. You wouldn't believe me even if I told you."

"I've been trying to get hold of you for hours. These men turned up at the Rec. Official looking, like something straight out of *Men in Black*, you know?"

That started to sober me up. I looked at Aubrey and mouthed the word "ARES".

"They started asking questions about whether anything unusual had been going on, and Lucas, the idiot, told them about you trying to climb the Pylon and they started asking all kinds of questions about you and what you were like and how they could find you, and Lucas, the absolute moron, gave them your address. And then they left. It was really weird."

"S'OK, Hugo. It will be fine. I'll catch you tomorrow." I hung up as Hugo started to mumble about aliens.

"Looks like they've tracked me down after all," I said to Aubrey.

"Well, it was going to happen, I guess. I'll take you in tomorrow and we'll try and explain. In the meantime, you can crash at mine," Aubrey said. "My place isn't too far from here."

Shock and confusion chased themselves around my foggy head. Settling on smug satisfaction, I grinned.

"Don't even think it," Aubrey said, glaring at me.

"No, of course not, I mean, I never even thought," I lied badly. "I'd better call my parents."

I fumbled in my pocket for my phone and tried to bring the glowing screen into focus.

The phone rang about fifteen times before it was finally answered.

"Hello?" I heard a tired Katie from the other end.

"Katie? What are you doing up?"

"Well, there was this annoying ringing noise," she said sarcastically. "And given that Dad's snoring in front of the TV and Mum's out in the shed, someone had to shut it up. What do you want, Scott?"

"Oh, right, well, I'm sort of not coming home."

"Are you drunk?" she whispered, and I could hear a muffle as she covered the phone with her hand.

"No! Well, I might be a teeny weenie bit tipsy. But that's not important. Katie, I need you to cover for me."

"What do you want me to say?"

"I don't know. You're good at making things up. Just make it believable."

"I'll tell them you and Hugo have finally come out and you've run away to get married then?"

"Ha bloody ha."

"I say you're staying over at Hugo's. Playing your dumb monster games, will that do?"

"I love you Katie."

"Yeah, yeah. You owe me, big time. Oh, and you might want to come up with something better to explain why two men from the government came looking for you earlier," she said and hung up before I could ask any more.

I leant the cold screen of the phone against my head. I was going to be in so much trouble. But I could worry about that tomorrow.

Aubrey was patting a painted sculpture of an elephant, which seemed pretty random in the middle of the street. But given the evening I'd had, I was lucky it wasn't a dancing, talking elephant.

"All good?" she said.

"Um, yeah. All good," I said.

We walked down a street of kebab shops and minicab places. This was what my mother would call, "not the nice part of town". The old tramps growling at us as we walked past and the young men standing on street corners, their hooded jumpers pulled up and hands thrust deep into their pockets, told me that much. One of the hoodies hissed something at me, but Aubrey pulled me on.

"Here we are," she said stopping in front of a row of concrete flats. A badly-carved sign below the roof said Palace Row. There wasn't much palatial about it. The windows in the bottom flat had all been boarded up and the walls were covered in graffiti. "FUCK OF," read one particularly misanthropic, not to mention grammatically-challenged, tag.

"Nice," I said.

Aubrey fished out her keys from the pocket of her jacket. A small toy kitten hung from the chain. She slotted the key into the lock and jiggled. "There's a knack," she said as the door opened onto the communal hallway. The floor was lined with broken black and white tiles, and a black gloss spiral staircase disappeared into the roof. Bicycles were propped up along the banisters the whole way.

"I'm at the top."

My already wobbly legs barely held my weight by the time we got to the fifth floor. Her front door was painted a bright red and had brass numbers on it that I guessed were meant to say 4d but actually said 4p. She threw open the door, kicked some shoes and a pile of letters out of the way, and threw her keys on the hall table.

"Are you going to stand there all night?" she asked, without turning around.

I mumbled an apology and stepped over the threshold. The dark hallway was covered in old sci-fi movie posters. *Creature of the Black Lagoon. Attack of the 50 Foot Woman. The Wolfman.* They stared at me, as if asking what did I think I was doing here.

I followed Aubrey into what turned out to be the living room. She flicked a switch on the floor and the room lit up. Strings of fairy lights were nailed to the wall and wrapped around pot plants.

"The electricity was cut off a few months ago. So I'm running these lights from the phone jack," she said, pointing at the tangle of wires coming from the socket. "Neat, huh?"

It looked like a fairy's cave. "I like it," I said.

"I still have gas though. So you want a coffee?"

I remembered jokes at school about a girl asking you in "for coffee" and answered automatically. "Does coffee mean what I think it means?" I said, my eyebrows waggling. I wanted to bite my own tongue off.

"Only if you think coffee means a punch in the face."

"Sorry, no. I mean yes. A coffee would be great. Just white, thanks." I kept forgetting that Aubrey was just fifteen and I was acting like a serious creep.

She left and I smacked myself in the forehead a few times. The last smack actually hurt, which was a good thing. I collapsed onto a tatty red sofa, and the springs groaned. When Aubrey returned a few minutes later, she was carrying two steaming mugs. I reached for the coffee like a man in the desert and sipped it gratefully.

Aubrey sat on the floor in front of me, cross-legged. She'd taken off her boots, and a painted toenail poked out of a hole in her striped tights. I looked around the room. There were two tall bookshelves that groaned under the weight of piles of books, but, I registered, no TV.

"So," I said eventually. "Do you think ARES caught those Freedom for Shifting guys?"

"The Shifting Liberation Front? Probably not. They've

managed to avoid getting caught this long."

"How?"

"Zac's pretty smart."

"You guys know each other well then?" I said, rubbing my finger around the edge of my cup and surprised at the heat of jealousy bubbling away in my stomach.

"We went through training together and were…" She paused, trying to find the right word. "Friends. For a while anyway. Funny how things change. When we first met I was always the one getting into trouble and he was the one bailing me out. We were inseparable for the first three years of the Programme. He called us the Alphabet Squad. A to Z? Get it? He always liked his stupid names. Anyway, I started training to be a Spotter and he started training to be a Mapper. They're the guys who specialise in predicting consequences. He's still one of the best around. So good, in fact he hardly, ever needs to Shift."

"Why wouldn't he want to Shift?"

Aubrey took a deep breath. "Oh, he has this big conspiracy theory about entropy."

"That's when the Shifting power goes away, right?"

"Yeah. Well Zac thinks that it's not brought about by age but by the amount of times you use it. And that all the training at ARES is designed to make us burn through our power."

"And is he right?"

"No! He's just stupid. Entropy is what it is. It's a reaction to growing up and you just have to deal. But Zac refused. He went on and on about it and I started to get really bored of the whole thing. Then one day he broke into some files at HQ to try to find evidence to back up his theories. He got caught."

"And ARES have been after him ever since?"

"I guess. Although they don't have anything firm on him. Just theories. So far all the SLF have done is graffiti some buildings and make some internet videos. Nothing that warrants actually arresting them."

"But what about that simulator thing he used on the girl? That can't be legal, can it?"

"A stimulator," Aubrey corrected. "It sends currents to the part of the brain that controls Shifting and, along with a drug, makes you experience other possible realities. They're used in Mapping training. The headsets are supposed to let the users try out different Shifts and see the consequences without them actually affecting anything. Zac stole one from ARES and made a few modifications to it."

"And you've tried it?" I asked, resting my mug on my knee.

"Once," Aubrey said, staring down at her feet. "When we were still friends. But never again. When you Shift normally, you don't hold on to the memories of the old reality. They fade away. But with the stims... they stay with you."

A truck rumbled by outside, making the room shake and the fairy lights flicker. I felt as if I might never be on stable ground again.

"I've been thinking." She put her mug down and pulled

up her knees, hugging them with both arms. "Maybe I don't need to take you in tomorrow. Maybe I can tell the Regulators that the Shift was mine and there's been a big mix up."

"Would they believe you?"

"Probably not. You're so old that they'll be sure to think you're a rogue. But it's worth a shot."

"What if…" I hesitated. "What if I want to go in? I mean the bagging and tagging doesn't sound too great, but the training and all that does."

"Oh, and hardly ever seeing your family again? How great would that be?"

"Are you kidding me? That would be awesome! I hate my family."

"Shut up. You're lucky. It's rare a Shifter gets any time with their family. Usually we're taken away from home when we're just kids for training."

"Seriously, I think my parents would be happy to see the back of me."

"I used to think that," she said, looking out the window. "I was such a difficult kid, you know? Dad left when I was only four and Mum tried her hardest but it wasn't easy, just the two of us. She became really… sad. That's when the Shifting started. Mum would walk around like a zombie all day hardly speaking and I'd keep trying new ways to piss her off just to get a reaction. I'd keep Shifting till I found something that would make her really snap. 'Seeking negative attention,' the shrinks said." She laughed, only I could tell there wasn't anything funny about it.

"When I was about seven I pushed it as far as I could. I threw a crystal vase she got for her wedding out of the top window right onto the car. She dragged me to a psychiatrist and that's when the agency found me. When I left with them, I really thought Mum would be happier without me." She rested her chin on her knees. "I was wrong."

"What happened?"

"She killed herself three years ago."

"Oh, um, Aubrey…"

She let out a little snort of laughter. Only nothing was funny. "You should see your face," she said. "That's why I've never told anyone."

I hated situations like this. Where people trusted me enough to tell me about their lives and I just mumbled. Katie would know what to say, I thought. She always said the right thing at times like this, which was often exactly the very thing that no one else was willing to say. Katie was brave like that. I wasn't.

Instead of saying anything, I slurped at my coffee.

"I can't help but wonder," Aubrey said, as if I wasn't even there. "If I'd stayed, could I have stopped it?"

"So why don't you–"

"Change it? Don't you think I've tried?" She stood up and paced back and forth. "I can't. No matter how hard I try, I can't find a way back. And you know what that means? What that really means, about me?" She hit herself in the chest with a clenched fist. "You can only make Shifts that you want to make. Shifts that you believe are in your 'best interests'." She spat the last two words. "Something to do with the brain's stupid survival mechanism. So the fact I can't make that Shift means I don't want to. Which means I'm a selfish, spoilt cow who would rather have a happy childhood than a Mum."

For a minute I didn't know what to do. Eventually I stood up and walked over to her. I placed a shaking hand on her tiny shoulder and patted it. "Aubrey, it wasn't your fault. You told me, you can't affect other people's decisions."

She looked up at me, her green-grey eyes hazy with tears and I remembered just how young she really was. "But if I was there, I could have stopped her. Or checked on her, or something. But I can't make myself do it. I just can't make myself…" She dropped her head and turned away.

"How is this anything to do with you? You were just a kid. You're still just a kid."

"But I should at least try, shouldn't I? Now that I can control my power, I should try to change it. But I know if I change my decision to go with ARES then… then I'd be stuck. My whole childhood I'd be stuck there. With her." She closed her eyes and dropped her head. When she opened them again a minute later any sign of sadness was gone.

She sat back on the floor, legs crossed, and when she met my eyes again there was a look of stubborn resolution. Whatever emotional jack-in-the-box Aubrey had just let out, was firmly back under its lid.

I sat back down on the sofa my head spinning more than

ever. "I'm sorry it was so hard for you Aubrey, but I'm sixteen. I'm ready to leave home and get my own place."

"I had to put up with living in dorms for years before they finally let me move out. Do you want that? Stuck with a bunch of kids all day?"

I thought about leaving Katie. Then decided she could look after herself. She was the strong one after all. "Better than stuck with my parents."

Aubrey wasn't convinced. "That was your first Shift? The Pylon?"

"As far as I know, yeah."

"Then it might be a one-off thing. You might not ever really develop the power now. And as long as you don't Shift again you can just stay off ARES' radar."

I started to protest. But Aubrey cut me off. "Just forget about it, Scott. Just pretend tonight never happened and go back to your normal life."

"But having that control. Being able to undo any decision–"

"It's not any decision. You can't suddenly change what grade you got in exams. Or make someone fall in love with you." She halted as she spoke, as if she was revealing too much, and tugged at the hole in her tights.

"Well, I, for one, think it's pretty amazing."

"It's not. Believe me. The problem is the consequences. You can't calculate them. At least I can't. The Mappers can. They can sense the ripples that each decision will cause and take the path that's almost guaranteed to lead to the reality they want. Me, I'm looking forward to entropy. And then I can just relax and focus on doing one thing at a time. Without having to balance it all up. It's exhausting." She stretched out her legs, as if shaking off a long day. "I'd like to be normal."

I studied Aubrey. Her green piercing eyes and dyed hair. Those perfect lips and arched brows. There was no way that Aubrey Jones would ever be considered normal.

She yawned. "I'm going to bed. You can sleep on the sofa. We'll talk about it more in the morning." She stood up and threw a blanket at me. "Night, Scott." She flicked off the lights, throwing the room into darkness.

I lay down on the lumpy sofa my legs hanging over the armrest. My head was still spinning and it didn't help if I closed my eyes. That second drink had been a really bad idea. To take my mind off the returning feeling that something was trying to make its way out of my stomach, I started to think about the other bad choices I'd made in my life.

I'd had my fair share of screw-ups in my sixteen years. Making a total prat of myself in the school play. Smashing the headmaster's window. Jane Nagle. But my biggest regret was giving up kick boxing. I'd been doing it for a year and really enjoying it. Then Katie started coming along and while I was still struggling to get to grips with it all, she took to it like a natural. As always.

It was fun at first, the two of us hanging out together. But when she knocked me out with a flawless round-house I decided I'd had enough. Annoyed at her and myself, I stopped going. Dad gave me a long talk about how I had to stick at things and how I didn't want to be a loser my whole life. It had almost worked. Almost. But I'd still quit.

I wriggled, trying to get comfortable on the couch and thought about what would have happened if I actually listened to my Dad. I'd probably be a black-belt by now. I drifted off dreaming of being a kung fu ninja.

I woke up when my head hit the concrete.

CHAPTER SEVEN

It took a while for the pieces to fall into place. I'd fallen asleep on Aubrey's lumpy couch and ended up... where? I sat up slowly and took in my surroundings. I was lying on the freezing ground, next to a bench, in a park somewhere. Mist hung close to the ground and a shiver passed through my body. My head pounded and I held it in my shaking hands, trying to stop it from exploding. I swore loudly and promised myself that I would never, ever, drink again.

I risked letting go of my head and pulled myself off the ground and onto the bench. My ribs ached and my hands were covered in cuts and bruises. I stared at my fingers through blurry eyes and shook my head. What the hell was going on?

The bench stank of sick so I stood up and sent an empty bottle of vodka skidding across the path. I walked away, staring at the bottle and wondering how it got there. The foul smell followed me. I inspected my clothes and saw a vomit stain down my jumper. A jumper I had not been wearing last night. A jumper I didn't even own.

A jogger panted past, her breath sending out clouds in the cold morning. She tutted as she had to interrupt her stride to jog around me.

"I'm sorry," I tried to say. But all I managed was a dry rasp.

Something must have happened after I fell asleep last night. Maybe Aubrey kicked me out. And for some reason I'd drunk even more. But why? My aching brain was coming up with nothing. I remembered going out with Hugo. Meeting Aubrey. Then back to hers. She'd told me something, something really important. But the harder I tried to remember it, the less of a grasp I had on it. It was like trying to remember a dream after waking up. I had flashes of images, but nothing was making any kind of sense.

I hit my head with the heel of my hand and it hurt like hell. I rubbed at my face and felt the damp track of tears. I was crying and I couldn't stop. Great sobs racked my chest and I fell to my knees.

"Try!" I shouted to myself. "Try to remember." A memory burst behind my eyes.

Truck lights flashing. And someone screaming.

I ran my hand through my hair, trying to make sense of the image. Where I had expected to feel my long, curled fringe, my hand ran across nothing but stubble. I was getting really scared now. All I wanted was to get home and maybe everything would be all right. But an alien presence in my soul whispered that nothing would ever be OK again.

I scraped myself off the concrete and looked around. A worn-down playground caught my eye. The familiar sight struck me with a staggering sense of relief. I was on the common, not that far from home. I used to come here all the time with my parents and Katie. As soon as I thought about my sister my lungs contracted as if someone had tightened a belt around my chest.

I started running.

After ten minutes something else struck me as weird. I'd been running at full speed for almost a mile and it didn't feel as if my heart would burst. Normally, I could barely manage to run for a few minutes before I had to stop. Now it felt as if I could keep going forever. Maybe it was the fear driving me on.

Five minutes later, I reached my road and stopped. My house was up ahead. Something awful waited for me behind that blue door. Aubrey had told me it might not be safe for me to come home. That was something I could glean from the mess that was my memory. Not safe. But I couldn't remember why.

I took a deep breath and was hit by the stink from my clothes again. Whatever had happened, Mum wouldn't be too happy with my state. I pulled off the jumper and threw it into a nearby bin. The white T-shirt underneath was mostly clean.

I walked towards the door. The gravel crunched under

my feet. I patted my pockets for my key, but they were empty.

I knocked.

Nothing.

I checked my watch. It was only 6.30 and Mum and Dad were probably still in bed.

I knocked again.

Eventually I heard the sound of shuffling from behind the door.

As soon as I saw Dad's face my heart stopped and I had that flash again. *The lights of a truck and the sound of screaming.* Dad's eyes were bloodshot and his skin was the colour of day-old porridge.

"Scott," he said. His voice ached with sadness.

A wail sounded from the top of the stairs and a woman raced down the steps and charged towards me. It took me a few seconds to realise it was my mother. Her usually perfect hair was a wild mess and she was wearing a tracksuit that looked as if she'd been wearing it for days. There were four red marks down the side of her right cheek. Nail marks.

She paused for a moment and then launched herself at me. She flailed her arms and instinctively I blocked her punches before giving in and letting her rain the blows on my chest and shoulders. They kept coming.

Dad pulled her away, wrapping her in his arms. "Hush. Hush now," he said rocking her. She melted to the floor, still screaming. Beneath her animal howls I made out one word. "Katie."

Dad looked at me, his eyes unfocused. "Scott, I think you should go."

"But Dad," I begged, "I don't know what's happening. Please." I broke down and started sobbing too. All I knew was that my heart was breaking and I didn't know why.

"Someone explain. Anyone. Dad. Mum. Katie!"

"Don't you dare!" my Mum screamed. She dragged herself to standing. "Don't you dare say her name. You murderer!"

She shoved me and caught one of my aching ribs. It felt like a bomb going off in my chest. Dad pulled her away and pushed her gently back down the hallway.

Murderer? What did she mean? Then a memory so fresh, so raw, erupted in my head.

I'm on my moped. It's raining. Katie is behind me on the pillion. She's annoying me by tickling me. I keep slapping her hand away. And she keeps poking me in the ribs. We're slapping hands like playing one potato, two potato, like we used to when she was little. And we're laughing. Like we haven't laughed in ages. Then I hear the screeching hiss of brakes. I look up. A truck's headlights flash across my damp visor. I'm blinded. Katie is screaming. I try to steer the bike away. But I know it won't do any good. We're skidding under the truck and I hear the sound of metal crunching. Then everything goes black.

"Dad," I gasped.

He shook his head and, ever so gently, so it didn't even make a sound, he closed the door.

CHAPTER EIGHT

The memory was real, that much I knew. But it didn't make sense. How could I have been riding a moped? I didn't even know how to. And how could Katie be dead?

I started thumping my fists on the closed door, screaming for my parents. But they didn't come. I stopped banging when I saw streaks of red against the blue. My fists were bleeding.

I slid down against the door and sat on the rough welcome mat. I wanted to stay here, maybe just die on my own doorstep. But I couldn't give up until I understood what was going on.

Katie had been dead for nearly two weeks. The doctors had told Mum and Dad she'd died instantly. But I knew better. I'd heard her screaming while I tried to get her out of the crumpled mess of the moped. Then she'd gone quiet. And I'd lain on the wet concrete holding her cold hand. I refused to let go when the ambulance men arrived.

I hit my head against the door behind me. Katie couldn't be dead. She just couldn't be. Because while I remembered seeing her tiny body being taken away on a stretcher, I also remembered sitting and having dinner together only yesterday. She'd been sad and I, like a coward, hadn't wanted to talk about it. So I went out and Katie had covered for me. We'd spoken on the phone only hours ago and she promised to lie so I could go back to a girl's house. A girl who had told me I was special.

Aubrey.

Aubrey would know what was going on. I had to find her. Only problem was I couldn't remember where she lived. There had been a sculpture of some kind. I scrunched up my eyes, willing the image to become clearer. A statue of an elephant. Near an Underground station. I stood up, rubbed the tears from my eyes, and started running.

The row of rundown buildings was the most welcome sight I'd ever seen. I jogged past the doors, trying to pick out which flat was Aubrey's. I saw a graffiti-covered wall and could have hugged the little ASBO who'd told the world to "Fuck of".

My finger hovered over the line of buzzers. The scribbled names had faded under the plastic shields, but one name jumped out at me. I pushed the buzzer marked Jones and waited. I didn't even know if she would be home.

"Hello?" a voice crackled through the intercom.

Hearing her voice was like walking into a warm room. "Aubrey. Aubrey thank God! It's me, Scott."

"Who?" Aubrey said.

"Scott. Please let me in. I don't know what the hell is going on."

"I don't know who you are. Push off will you?"

I knew I had just seconds to prove that she knew me. Seconds before she hung up the intercom and walked away. I felt like a man grabbing at a fraying rope. In an instant it would snap and I would fall into the abyss. I needed something to make her understand. Some kind of password.

From somewhere in the depths of my dissolving mind a word appeared.

"Swordfish!" I shouted into the grey box on the wall.

There was a pause. Then a buzz and clunk of the lock opening. I pushed at the door and walked in. The black rail of the stairwell was oddly solid, as if it was the first real thing I'd touched all day.

When I made it to the fifth floor, Aubrey was waiting in her open doorway, wearing a silk kimono that came to just above her knee. Even amid the fog of my tears I was struck by how pretty she was.

"Who are you?" she said as I reached the top step. Her eyes narrowed in suspicion. "Did the SLF send you?"

SLF. The name resonated. "No. I'm Scott. We met last night."

"We really didn't."

"We did," I snapped. "We met at the Rec. And you told me something about me being special. And then I woke up this morning on a park bench and my whole life is falling apart. My sister is dead. My little sister." I slammed the wall in frustration.

Aubrey flinched. Then tilted her head and considered me. "I told you, you were special?"

I nodded. "Yes, but I can't remember. I can't remember anything. I can only remember you."

"Did I tell you…" she paused and looked down the stairway behind me. "Did I tell you that you were a Shifter?"

It was like an alarm going off in my head. The buzzing bells and flashing alarm of a pinball machine. "Shifter! Yes," I said.

"You'd better come in. Sounds as if you're having a reality attack."

I followed her into the hallway. Nothing had changed since the last time I had been there. The tangle of fairy lights still twinkled in the living room. The same monster movie posters snarled down at me. After what I'd been through, it felt like a kind of sanctuary.

The only difference was in Aubrey. She was being distant, as if she really didn't know who I was. She stood, her arms folded across her chest, considering me through narrow eyes.

"You stink," she said finally. "Shower's in there. But be quick. The longer you leave it, the more you'll lose your grip on the old reality."

I didn't fully understand her. Parts of it made some vague sense. But the idea of a shower sounded like the best idea I'd ever heard.

Her bathroom was small and painted purple, with a surprisingly large roll-top bath in the centre of the room and a *Psycho*-style shower over the tub. I peeled off my clothes, turned on the large taps and stepped in. It took a while for the water to heat up and the icy rain made me yelp. After a minute, it was steaming. I rubbed at my face, my chest and aching ribs. I looked down at my body and almost slipped over in shock. I didn't recognise myself. My skin was covered in greenish bruises, but that wasn't what was making my head spin. It was what I saw under my skin that was so unfamiliar. Muscles. Real defined muscles, rippling down my stomach. The last time I'd checked I had a small, pale pot belly. I had been almost proud of it. But now, I had a six-pack.

"Hurry up!" Aubrey shouted from the other side of the door. "I've left some clothes in the hallway. They were here when I moved in, but I think they'll fit."

I quickly scrubbed myself with a bar of soap I found, switched off the taps, then pulled a white towel off a rail and wrapped it around my waist, before carefully opening the door an inch. I pressed an eye to the gap and peered out. I wasn't happy with the idea of Aubrey seeing me half naked. Although, a new feeling flickered across my mind. Pride. Aubrey seeing this new, ripped body, wouldn't be so awful. The idea passed quickly and I opened the door and gathered up the pile of clothes.

When I emerged, wearing a slightly too-tight T-shirt and cut off tracksuit bottoms, I was still steaming from the shower.

I found Aubrey in the living room. She pointed to a mug of coffee on a side table: the same mug she'd given me last night. As I wrapped my hands around it, I wanted to cry.

"So…" Aubrey said. "Tell me what happened."

I tried as best as I could to explain. Even as the words came out I knew how insane I sounded. I only had fragments of memories and they were being pushed out of my head by images of a new life I didn't recognise. The two memories were fighting to take hold of me and there was only one I was willing to accept. The one where I hadn't killed my little sister.

"What was the last thing you remember before waking up on the common?" Aubrey asked.

"I was thinking about the choices I made in my life. The ones I'd regretted. And I was thinking about…" I stopped. The thoughts were just out of reach, like when you're trying to remember someone's name and it won't come to you. You know it, but it's hiding from you in a dark part of your brain. "I was thinking about something I wanted to do." It came to me. "Kick boxing!" I shouted. "I was thinking about how I regretted giving up kick boxing."

"So that's when you made the Shift. You Shifted to a reality where you hadn't given up kick boxing. And everything else rippled out from there."

"So I know kick boxing?"

"I don't know. Do you?"

I closed my eyes and thought about it. Yes, I did. In

fact, I knew a lot about it. Memories, at least that's what I thought they were, unlocked themselves. Me and Katie going to classes. Me getting my brown belt before her. I opened my eyes and tried to follow the threads. In one reality I'd quit. But in this new reality, I'd woken up in a world where I hadn't. And that had somehow got Katie killed.

I remembered now. I'd been taking Katie to class one night. Dad was away on a work conference and Mum was at one of her book club things. Mum had told Katie and I to stay at home, but I had a competition coming up and really wanted to go. And Katie refused to stay at home alone. So we hopped on my moped and rode off into the rain.

"I have to undo it," I said, my nails digging into my palms.

"You can't," Aubrey said gently. "You can't undo a Shift."

"But my sister. It can't be…" I couldn't speak any further.

I buried my head in my hands. I didn't know what was happening to me and with every second I was losing more and more of the old life. The life with Katie. I couldn't even remember how I'd met Aubrey. All I knew was that she was my anchor in the storm I'd found myself.

I felt her rest her arm on my shoulder. "We can try," she said softly. "Find another way. Where were you, when you made the Shift?"

I looked at her, my eyes clouded by tears. "I was here," I said, pointing at the sofa we were sitting on.

"Here?" Aubrey said. "Here?" She jumped off the sofa.

I nodded, even more confused.

"Then you have to get out. They'll be here any minute."

"But you said you'd help me," I said, sounding annoyingly pathetic.

"I will. But I can't help you if you're locked up." She dragged me to my feet and pushed me towards the door.

"Maybe I should be locked up. At least I couldn't hurt anyone again."

"Don't be an idiot."

We'd made it as far as the hallway. "I don't have anywhere to go."

She paused in her shoving and considered me for a second. "Just hide out. I'll find you."

But it was too late. Someone knocked at the door.

CHAPTER NINE

I saw outlines of bodies through the foggy glass of the front door. Aubrey and I looked at each other. "Is there another way out?" I whispered.

She shook her head.

"Ms Jones," a cold male voice shouted from the other side of the door. "This is ARES. Please open up."

Aubrey looked from me to the door. Her shoulders sagged, like a little girl waiting for her punishment. I didn't recognise her. Right then, I was really afraid of the men on the other side of that door. If they could do this to Aubrey Jones, who was the most confident girl I'd ever met, then what hope did I have?

"It's OK," I said, trying to reassure myself as much as her. They banged on the door again and she flinched. I hated seeing her like this. "I'm coming," I shouted.

I squeezed Aubrey's shoulder, pushed past her, and opened the door. I had a glimpse of a man in a grey uniform and behind him a line of men in black combat gear. Then a bag was thrown over my head, I was pulled through the door, and pushed to the floor.

They were shouting at me to get down, which seemed kind of redundant seeing as my face was already pressed into the cracked tiles. How much more down could I get? My hands were yanked behind my back and bound together with something metal. It cut into my wrists and vibrated gently; my skin prickled with what felt like an electric current.

"Don't move. Don't Shift," the men were shouting. I just lay there, wishing they'd stop shouting. It was hurting my head.

"Who is this man?" I heard the cold voice ask.

"I don't know," Aubrey responded. "He forced his way into my apartment. I assumed he was a rogue and I was about to call you." She sounded convincing enough. She even had a hint of disgust in her voice when referring to me as a rogue. I prayed they believed her. I'd pulled all this trouble down on her head and the best I could hope for is that they would take me away and leave Aubrey alone.

"We'll take care of it from here, Ms Jones. One of the Regulators will be back later to take a statement."

"Yeah, sure, whatever I can do to help." Her voice was dripping with sarcasm. But the man didn't seem to register it.

His voice softened slightly. "I'm just glad you're OK."

"You really didn't need to come out, you know? I could have handled this myself, Dick." I heard the man cough. "Sorry. Richard," Aubrey said. The man coughed again. "Commandant Morgan," Aubrey finished and for some reason I imagined her pulling off a mocking salute.

Whoever this guy was, I already hated him. Hated that Aubrey was having to kowtow to him. Or maybe she wasn't. Maybe she was flirting with him. Just what I needed along with all the mad mix of emotions that were flooding through me right now: jealousy.

"We'll be in touch soon," the voice I now knew as Morgan said.

I heard the door close and I was alone with the men from ARES. They frogmarched me down the stairs and out onto the street.

In the light, I could make out hazy images through the weave of the cloth: men and women gathering outside their houses to watch me being dragged away, small children laughing and pointing and, across the street, the silhouette of a huge man resting on a small wall. Even through the hood I could sense his dark eyes trained on me. He raised a podgy hand and waved. It sent a shiver down my spine.

I heard the clunk of metal doors being opened beside me and I was thrown roughly forward, banging my head on something hard.

I didn't even try to get to my feet. I just curled up into a ball on the cold metal floor. I heard footsteps of men getting in around me and the hum of an engine start up. As the vehicle pulled away I slid forward on the floor.

I tried to gather my thoughts. I was in a van, most likely, being taken to ARES HQ. As for what was going to happen to me once I got there, I didn't know. I had ideas all right. Horrible, nausea-inducing ideas, fuelled from watching too many spy movies. I pulled my knees up closer to my chest and hoped the men in the van couldn't hear my sobs.

After what felt like hours, but was probably only about thirty minutes, the van rumbled to a halt. The door clunked open and I was dragged forward and hefted to my feet. The heavy hand on my shoulder guided me up some steps and across a slippery, I guessed, marble floor and into a lift. He let go of me for a moment and I heard the beep of a button being pressed. After a moment, the drifting in my stomach told me we were moving up. A second beep and he pushed me forward. I had the sense I was walking down a narrow corridor, as I kept banging into the walls. The man leading me wasn't doing a great job. Or maybe it was his exact intention that I was roughed up a bit before they started on me. Something electronic beeped and I heard a door opening. A final push forward and the bag was whipped off my head.

I scrunched up my eyes against the sudden light and directed my face away from the glaring overhead bulbs. The room came into focus. It was about ten feet by ten feet, white walls on three sides and a mirror on the fourth wall. A table stood in the middle, with a metal chair on either side. Unless I did have an overactive imagination, like Mum always said, it was an interrogation room.

"Take a seat," said the cold voice from behind me.

I turned around to face the man I assumed was Morgan and was a little taken aback. He wasn't much older than I was. Twenty maybe. With neat, brown hair and a ratty, pointed face. He wore a grey, uniform jacket, with five golden stripes on the arm and a metal badge that read ARES pinned to the collar.

"Take a seat," he repeated, gesturing to one of the chairs.

I kicked it away from the table and sat down, which wasn't easy with my hands still tied behind my back.

Morgan's chair screeched across the floor as he dragged it opposite me. He spun it around so the back was facing the table and sat astride it. Only he couldn't get his leg through the gap between the armrest and back. After a few seconds of struggling to pull his leg free, he turned it the right way and sat down.

He smoothed back his slick hair, which had been ruffled in his fight with the chair, and steepled his fingers under his chin

"So, shall we start with you telling me your name?" His voice was icy, as if he was preparing himself to break some hardened criminal. Well, I was about to spoil his fun. I was going to spill my guts.

I started with my name and then told him everything. Everything I could remember, that is. I told him about Hugo and the Pylon, about wanting to do kick boxing. Finally I told him about the moped and how I'd got my sister killed. I kept Aubrey out of it as much as possible and invented some guy who'd given me Aubrey's address telling me she might be able to help. When I was finished, there were tears flowing down my face, and Morgan seemed disappointed.

"So you didn't know you were a Shifter?"

"Not until last night, I didn't have a clue. I still don't know what's going on. It's as if I've got memories in my head that don't fit any more. And the more I try to make sense of them, the less I understand."

"Oh, Scott. Silly, silly Scott," he said, leaning back in his chair. "You are having what we call a reality attack. It's a sort of psychosis when you find yourself in a new and disturbing reality, because you didn't carefully plot out the consequences of your Shift." He shook his head and sighed dramatically. "It's a rookie mistake, really."

I ignored the fact he was talking to me like a six year-old. "You've got to help me. I don't know how to control any of this."

"It's unusual that your Shifting capabilities are only emerging now," he said, squinting at me so hard I could hardly see his eyes. "Normally they present themselves at a much younger age. In fact, I don't think I've ever heard of a Shifter coming to light at such a late age. Most Shifters begin their training at eight, ten at the latest. I'm not sure there is anything we can do for you. Apart from processing."

Processing. He meant torture, I was sure of it.

"Why don't you let me see about that, Commandant?"

Another man had entered the room, so quietly I hadn't even heard the door open. I turned my head to face him. He wore a grey uniform like Morgan's, but it appeared faded with age. The jacket was slightly too tight for him and there were five darker lines on his arm, the shadows of where golden stripes might once have been. He had slightly greying hair, large black eyes, and his dark skin was lined with deep wrinkles.

Morgan shot to his feet and started to protest about how a Shifter had to lead any interrogation. The man ignored him, his kind eyes fixed on me.

"My name is Mr Abbott, I head up the Regulators." His voice was deep and soft. "It's good to meet you, Mr Tyler."

"I'd shake your hand, but, you know…" I shrugged, indicating my bound hands.

"Hmm, yes. I think we can do without the cuffs, don't you?"

Morgan hesitated. "But he might Shift." He sounded like a kid being told it was past his bedtime.

Abbott's expression didn't change. "Oh, I don't think Mr Tyler is going to give us any trouble."

Morgan shuffled behind me. My cuffs snapped open and my hands were free. I rubbed at my wrists, thinking I would never take my hands for granted again.

"Why don't you let me take over? I'm sure you have much more important things to be doing," Abbott said taking Morgan's seat in front of me. "Sir," he added, smiling.

Morgan scowled. "Yes, you are right. I do have some pressing matters that require my attention. I expect a full report at the end of the day, Mr Abbott." He put unnecessary stress on the word "Mr" and then slammed the door behind him.

"Commandant Morgan is very thorough," Abbott said, "but slightly overeager. He sees master criminals everywhere."

"I'm just a normal kid," I said.

"But you are anything but normal, Mr Tyler. You are, as I am sure you are coming to realise, very special."

"But I don't want to be special. I just want everything to go back to how it was. I just want my sister…" My voice trailed off.

"Ah, yes… your sister." He laid a brown folder on the table and opened it. "You said your last Shift led to her death?"

"Yes, but I didn't mean to."

"Of course you didn't. Let us see what we can do to put that right."

A wave of hope and gratitude passed through me. "Can you? Can you help?"

"That's what we do here, Scott." I noticed the switch to my first name. "We help people and we will help you. After all, we have to take some responsibility. We should have spotted you earlier." He turned over pages in the file. I caught glimpses of what I thought were my school reports, my birth certificate, even what looked like my library card. "We have systems in place to spot the signs and the signs were definitely there with you. Getting into fights. An inability to forge close friendships." He didn't sound as if he was judging me. Just saying it as it was.

He closed the file and looked up. "The truth is, Scott, that Commandant Morgan was wrong. There are cases when a Shifter's ability only emerges at a later stage. And when it does happen, that Shifter invariably goes on to be very powerful."

"I really don't think that's going to be the case with me," I said with a small laugh. "I'm pretty useless at almost everything."

"We'll see." He gazed at me, a half smile playing about his dark lips. "The thing that interests us about you, Scott is your ability to hold on to your past reality. It's rather unusual. Most Shifters can hold onto the old reality for a few minutes, half an hour if it's a particularly traumatic event. But it's been," he checked his watch, "nearly two hours since you made your Shift. It's impressive."

"Friends always told me I was no good at letting go of stuff."

"Well, that could work to your advantage, Scott. It's likely you'll need specialist training. But first, we have the problem of your sister to clear up. I'd like to ask you something, Scott."

"What? Anything."

"If I help you, help you put things back in order as much as is possible, will you come back to ARES, under your own volition, and join the Programme?"

"I don't understand. I'm here already."

"Ah, but if I help you make this Shift then you might not be here. I don't know what the consequences will be. If your sister doesn't die, you will have no need to go running to Ms Jones's house for help, and we may never track you down. As I am sure you've come to realise, this is the problem with Shifting. You never know where the ripples will take you. Even here, where we have the finest minds and some of the most advanced technology, most of which I don't even begin to understand, we struggle to map it out." He paused. "You need us, Scott. And we want to help you."

I didn't even have to think. If it would get my sister back, I'd sign over my life. "Yes, I'll join."

"Good. Now, you said your sister died in a crash when you were both on your moped. Yet, you also said in your alternate reality you didn't have one."

"Not that I can remember, no."

"Well, that could be the key. You made a decision somewhere to get this moped. If you can find that point, you can Shift it. But there had to be a real choice."

I squeezed the bridge of my nose between my fingers and tried. "It was so I could get to the competitions," I said, as the pieces slotted into place. "Mum didn't want me to get one. She was convinced I'd kill myself." I laughed bitterly at the irony. "She and Dad argued over it. He wanted to let me have the moped. He'd wanted one when he was a kid." It was all coming back now. "But his Mum hadn't let him. So I think he wanted to make up for it with me. He'd shouted that it was just another example of how Mum tried to control everyone. That she was stifling us all. In the end, he won."

I dropped my hand from my face. Suddenly, I remembered the exact moment Mum gave in and Dad had turned to me and smiled. I'd never seen him look prouder. That moment hovered like a seesaw between two points, perfectly balanced. I focused on that moment. Mentally willing myself to listen to Mum. To ignore the desire to please my father.

I felt a flipping sensation in my chest, as if my internal organs had decided to rearrange themselves. My head pounded and I saw a flash of light. I looked up as Abbott's smiling face started to flicker. Then everything went black.

When I dared to open my eyes I was lying on a tatty red couch, a purple throw pulled up to my chin. The room glowed in the pale morning light breaking through Aubrey's curtains and traffic hummed on the road outside. I checked my watch. 8.15am – a full hour since I'd been dragged off to ARES. But in this new reality, I was still in Aubrey's living room. I probed my memories. They were a mess. A flash of car crashes mixed in with the feeling of freewheeling down a long hill on a bicycle. There were no memories of mopeds.

I kicked off the blanket and checked my body. The muscles were still there, but the bruises were gone. I sprang off the couch.

"Aubrey!" I shouted. "Aubrey!"

"What?" came a muffled reply from the room I assumed

was her bedroom. I skidded down the hallway and threw open the door.

"Get out!" She pulled her duvet up over her shoulders.

"You know me?"

"Yes, you idiot. Stop shouting and get out of my room. My head hurts."

Mine felt spectacularly clear. "How did we meet?"

"You were lying on your back, having singularly failed to climb a pylon."

"Yes!" I punched the air. It had worked. Things were back to how they had been. I launched myself on to Aubrey's bed, threw my arms around her and hugged her.

She pushed me away. "Scott, what's going on?"

"I Shifted. I think. And everything went to hell. But then…"

"You what?" She didn't appear happy.

"I Shifted."

"Here?" She threw her duvet away. She was only wearing a singlet and shorts. "You absolute moron. You have to get out. If you've been Shifting, ARES will be here any minute."

"I, er…" I didn't know why she was so upset. I'd just brought my sister back to life and I didn't care what ARES would do to me. Besides, they had been the ones to help me. They'd been a little rough in getting there, sure, and given the choice it would be better if I didn't have to be dragged out of Aubrey's flat with a bag over my head. Then I realised, I did have the choice. If I left now, I could save myself the embarrassment and Aubrey the guilt of handing me over.

"Calm down. It's OK. I'll leave."

Aubrey twitched her button nose. It was all I could do to stop myself from kissing it. She reached down to the opposite side of her bed and retrieved a notebook with a pen hanging from it. She scribbled down a number, tore the page out, and handed it to me.

"Call me. Leave it a couple of days, till things have calmed down. Then we'll talk. Till then, try not to make any more Shifts."

I pushed her number into the back pocket of my jeans. "Thank you," I said. "You have no idea."

She waved me away and lay back down on her pillow. "Just close the door on your way out."

I left her sleeping and raced out of her front door, down the staircase and out onto the street. Where I ran straight into the arms of someone who wanted to kill me.

CHAPTER TEN

At first I thought it must have been a member of ARES who'd caught me after all. Running into him was like running into a soft rubber wall. To say he was fat was an understatement. He was enormous. Gargantuan. He was just a few all-you-can-eat buffets away from ending up on one of those freak documentaries where the guy ends up being winched out of his house by a crane or where they get dragged into hospital to have their TV remote surgically removed from a layer of flab. I was surprised he was able to stand under his own weight without a small, motorised vehicle to carry his stomach for him.

I bounced off him, muttered a hasty apology and tried to sidestep him. But there was too much of him to sidestep.

"Excuse me," I said, staring at him. His eyes glinted like black buttons in a sagging sofa.

He didn't move. "Excuse me," I tried again.

He grinned, revealing a row of black, stained teeth,

inside a mouth so red it was like looking into a raw wound. His breath stank and I had to turn my face away to avoid being sick all over him. "If you would just let me past…" I said, trying not to breathe in.

Instead of moving out of the way, he took a step forward, pinning me to the shut door with his wobbling stomachs. He licked his lips with an ulcerous purple tongue.

Heart pounding, I hesitantly pressed my hands against his shoulders and pushed. My palms started to disappear inside the folds of flesh and I pulled them back with a squeak of terror.

He still hadn't said a word. "I don't know what you want," I stuttered. I knew exactly what he wanted. He wanted to eat me. Clearly, there wasn't enough food left on the earth for this guy and he'd moved on to human flesh. If I'd known how right I was at that moment, I think I would have fainted in fear.

"A fresh Shifter." He breathed in, as if he were inhaling a delicious aroma. "I do love it when they're fresh. So much sweeter." He licked his lips again and I felt my stomach curdle.

"How… how do you know?" I gagged.

"Oh, you silly boy. I can smell you." He sniffed my face like a dog.

"Please, please," I begged. "I don't know who you are. But I'd really like it if you let me go."

He laughed, a snorting, wet laugh. "You should be thanking me. I've put ARES off your trail so I can have you all to myself. So, tell me this. Are you going to try and Shift your way out of this… tight… squeeze?" He wriggled his flesh tighter against me, pushing the air out of my lungs. My head went dizzy and white lights danced in front of my eyes. Any second now I was going to pass out.

I thought of Aubrey upstairs, safe under her duvet. Weird, wonderful, Aubrey. I'd only just met her, the girl of my dreams, and now I was going to die. Squashed to death by Jabba's big brother. And I didn't even know what I'd done to deserve this.

Shift! A desperate, instinct driven part of my brain cried out. But nothing happened. My head was spinning and I barely had a grip on this reality, let alone a good enough picture of another one I could Shift to. I was stuck.

Blindly, I felt along the wall for the row of buzzers and started pressing random buttons, hoping someone, any-one, would open the door and free me from this blubber creature. He caught my hand in his sausage-like fingers and licked from the base of my palm to the tip of my fin-gers. The stench of his breath combined with the pressure on my stomach was enough. I heaved, and a projectile of last night's drinks hit him straight in the face.

He staggered away, pawing at his eyes, trying to rub the contents of my stomach away. I didn't wait to apol-ogise. I ran. Even halfway down the road I still heard him screaming, like a toddler who'd just had his toy taken away from him.

I only stopped after making it a few roads away. If I'd been thinking logically, I'd have realised there wasn't much chance of a guy as fat as him catching up with me. But after what I'd been through in the past twelve hours, I'd sort of given up on logic.

I slowed to a jog and finally, breathless and shaking, started walking. This day was getting weirder by the second. It was only as I started walking normally that I realised I was walking with a limp. I stopped and pulled up the jean on my left leg and winced at an angry red scar that ran from my ankle to my knee. It was pocked on either side with the marks of stitches. It wasn't a scar I remembered. Clearly, whatever reality I'd found myself in now still wasn't perfect – fat, murderous men included. But I was safe now. And it didn't matter what had happened to my leg because my sister was alive. The thought of seeing her face wiped the image of the fat man from my head. I had to get home to see her.

I hesitated for a moment before our blue front door. Inside I heard the clanking and muffled shouts of breakfast in the Tyler household. I dug my key out of my pocket, opened the door and raced down the hallway and into the kitchen. There they were. My mother, father and little baby sister. In two leaping steps I scooped her up into a hug.

"Geroofme!" Katie said, her face pressed up against my chest. I let her go. "Oh. My. God, Scott. You are such a freak. I should call Childline." She rubbed at her shoulder and scowled at me. No one could scowl like Katie.

I ruffled her mousey hair, just for good measure. She mimed stabbing me in the thigh with a fork. Everything was back to normal then.

Mum watched me a little oddly, while Dad peered over his newspaper. "So," Mum said. "What exactly did you get up to last night?"

"Huh?" I said, a big grin on my face, although I was starting to lose hold on the precise reason I was so happy to see everyone. Mum raised a suspicious eyebrow. "I was at Hugo's," I said. "We hung out. Played games, you know?" I took a seat at the kitchen table and started pouring myself a bowl of cereal.

"Sure... games," Dad said.

I looked from Mum to Dad, trying to work out what they were on about. Mum reached into her dressing gown pocket and pulled out a black rectangle of cardboard. She handed it to me. Punched out of the black were four letters. ARES.

A tingling was working its way up the back of my thighs and heading for my neck. I had completely forgotten that ARES had paid my parents a visit.

"Oh, yeah," I said. "Them."

"Yes, them. They said they wanted to talk to you about a special government programme. What exactly have you been up to, Scott?"

"Nothing. Really. It's something to do with college. A recruitment thing," I said, turning the card over and over. I forced my mouth into a smile. "Seriously. Nothing to worry about, Mum."

"Hmm, OK," Mum said, fixing herself another cup of coffee from the fancy machine she'd bought when she was thinking about opening an art-gallery-cum-café thing last year. I didn't know if she believed me. "They said they'd be back."

"So could you tell them to come at a more reasonable hour next time?" Dad said, shaking his paper out and yawning. "They made me miss *The Cube*."

I mumbled something about being sure to tell them, and scooped a spoonful of muesli into my mouth. I was ravenous and realised that in this new version of events Mum had served up a measly salad last night, instead of the meatballs I'd eaten in the other reality. I was still hung over but, I realised, not bad as before. In the club with Aubrey, I'd stuck to beer. The subtle differences between this reality and the other jostled against each other, falling quickly into place.

I put down my spoon and pushed the empty bowl away. "I'm going to have a shower."

"Good," Katie shouted as I left the kitchen. "Because you stink."

I bounded up the stairs, closed the door of my bedroom behind me, and threw myself onto my bed. My quicksand brain registered slight differences in the room. A movie poster I didn't remember pinning up, although it was for a film I had seen about thirty times. A pile of comic books in a different position than I'd had them before. And a brown kick-boxing belt slung over the back of my chair. I ran it through my hand, remembering now that I hadn't been to training in weeks. Not since I'd come off my bicycle and mangled up my leg. I rubbed at the scar under my jeans. It had been a nasty accident. I'd been on my way to practice when I skidded on a puddle and went sliding towards a moving truck. They'd said I was lucky I'd only hurt my leg. Only I knew just how lucky. The ghost memory of the moped crash made me shiver.

I sat up and moved a model robot to where I thought it should have been. But then that felt weird too, so I moved it back. I didn't know if the changes were because someone had been in my room, or if I'd been the one to arrange it like this. A paranoia itched at my temples. How could you be certain of anything in a world you could change with a thought? And what scared me most of all was that I had no control over any of it. I hadn't even meant to Shift last night, and it had almost destroyed my life.

I needed help. Training. And I only knew of one place for that. I stroked the card I still held in my hand, feeling the embossed number printed under the name.

CHAPTER ELEVEN

"You what?" Aubrey said, glaring at me.

It was Sunday morning and we were sat in a greasy spoon. Aubrey was tucking into a full English breakfast and I'd ordered toast and a cup of tea.

I didn't meet her eyes. "I rang ARES. I'm going in tomorrow."

Aubrey threw down her knife and fork. "What?"

"I said I–"

"I heard you. Who did you speak to?"

"I was put through to a guy called Morgan–"

Aubrey groaned and threw her head back. "Morgan is such a dick. I bet he gave you his power and responsibility line."

"Yeah, and he said he was glad I'd called as it would save us all the embarrassment of having to come and arrest me, and that my mother seemed like a very nice woman."

"But you could have said it was a mix-up. All they had was that Lucas kid giving them your name. They had no real way of connecting you with the Shift. You should have just played dumb, Scott. You of all people would have been good at that."

"You mean they didn't know that I'd Shifted?"

"No! The sensors at ARES only register when and where a Shift has been made. They can't actually sense who made it or what it was."

I hadn't known that. I'd just blurted everything out about the Pylon and my sister and begged Morgan for his help. I'd stuck to the story about how some mysterious guy had told me I was a Shifter and kept Aubrey out of it. Morgan had tutted and sighed and patronised the hell out of me going on about how lucky I was that it was him handling my case.

"Oh, well, they know now. But Morgan said that he'd pull his connections and try and get me on the training programme. That has to be good, doesn't it?"

"I don't know which one of you is worse! Him with all his self-important bull or you for buying it! It's standard procedure to get all Shifters on the Programme, Scott. He wouldn't need to pull anything. Not that he could if he tried."

I took a bite out of my toast, only now realising just how naive I'd been.

"I can't believe you. I had it all planned," Aubrey said, waving her fork around. "Well, don't expect me to vouch for you." She stabbed her fork into an unfortunate sausage. I knew how it felt.

"I'm sorry Aubrey. But I need help. I need to

understand what's happening to me."

"I'll teach you!"

I met her eyes. "And who taught you?"

She shook her head as if she didn't understand what I was saying.

I tried again. "Who taught you to control Shifting?"

She twisted her mouth over to the left, chewing the inside of her cheek. "OK, yes, ARES taught me. But…"

I reached out my hand to cover hers. "I'm sorry. But I just can't do it alone. You have no idea what I went through after meeting you. What I did. What I did to my family." I hit the table with the clenched fist of my spare hand and the ketchup bottle fell over. "I can't let something like that happen again."

"But it's not too late. I've been thinking about this. If I can get my hands on a pair of the cuffs from the Regulators, they will stop you Shifting. OK, you'll look a bit weird wearing them for the next few years. But it means you can just go on living your normal life."

"But I don't want to be normal. I want to be like you."

She pulled her hand away from under mine and folded her arms across her chest. "All right then. See if I care. Oh, and just you wait till you start training." She stood up and grabbed her coat from the back of the chair. She leaned over to stare at me, her face only an inch from mine and I smelt vanilla. "It will break you." She straightened up and walked away.

"So, do you want to do lunch on Monday then?' I asked, ever the optimist.

She opened and closed her hand in a jerky wave. The café door jingled as she left. I picked up her abandoned fork and stabbed a sausage off her plate. Well, if she wasn't going to eat it, I thought. It tasted of sawdust.

Explaining it all to my parents wasn't much easier.

"It's a fast-track programme for IT skills?" Mum said as I sat them down to explain why I wasn't going back to school in September.

"That's the idea. They train you up and there's a guaranteed job at the end of it. If you make the grade that is." I remembered Morgan's whiney voice being quite clear about that on the phone.

"And it won't cost us anything?" Dad asked for the third time.

"Nope," I said. "Not a penny."

"I don't know Scott, what about your A-Levels? And university? I always wanted to see you in one of those black hats."

"Do you have any idea how much university costs these days?" Dad said, turning to Mum. "This ARES place makes sense. Good training. A good job at the end of it. We have to face it, Gloria, he's not the sharpest kid. We should take this opportunity while we have it."

"Gee, thanks, Dad," I said.

"Oh, you know what I mean, Scott," he snapped. "You're very good with science and computers and stuff but you're not really cut out for the real world are you?"

"Takes after you in that regard," Mum mumbled into her tea.

"So can I go?" I asked quickly before they started rowing again.

"I'm not sure. I'm not very keen on these academy schools. What's to say they won't shut down in a year's time and then where will you be?"

"It's been around since 1840!" I said, remembering the spiel Morgan had given me and getting a little frustrated. "I think it's going to be around for at least another year."

"But East London is such a long way to go," Mum said. "And I don't want you cycling again, not after the accident."

"Then let him get the moped, for god's sake!" Dad said.

That was the last thing I wanted. "It's OK," I said quickly. "I'll get the Tube. Look, how about I give it a go for summer and if it doesn't work out, I'll go back to school and do my A-Levels like planned?"

"Hmm, I suppose. But I'm not too keen on you only doing IT. What about your creative side, Scott? Everyone needs a balance in their lives. Maybe you can take night classes in art? Or macramé?"

"Oh, you and your creative nonsense!"

I snuck away and they didn't even notice.

Mum had been right about one thing, though. East London was a long way to go. It took me an hour and a half – one train and two tubes – to finally arrive at Old Street. The station was bustling with people who all seemed to be sporting angular haircuts, thick-rimmed glasses and their grannies' cardigans. As I emerged onto street level, it only got worse. It was like the whole of East London was populated by art students. These people were, literally, too cool for school. I felt overdressed in my grey M&S suit and shining loafers and loosened my tie a notch.

I'd gone over the route from the station to ARES HQ in my head again and again. Now that I was standing in front of the massive roundabout crawling with traffic, I didn't know which way to turn. I spotted the old fire station to my right and headed that way.

ARES HQ, it turned out, was a converted hospital. Or at least, that's what I assumed 'St Anthony's Medical Facility and Research Centre' had once been. It was an old Art Deco building, with smooth white walls and geometric carvings. Stone angels with two heads towered over the entrance. Although they had been made slightly less impressive by the speech bubbles somebody had drawn coming out of their mouths. One bubble read: "We don't stop playing because we grow old. We grow old because we stop playing." And the other read, "I'm a big fairy." The vandal must have gone to a lot of effort, scaling the sheer wall just to leave his mark. A red-faced man in blue overalls scrubbed at the wall from the top of a ladder.

I walked up the few steps that led to the glass double doors. My heart was thudding in my chest. The way Aubrey had been going on, I was willingly handing myself over to the Gestapo here. But then, she was in there somewhere, and that knowledge gave me some hope. I pushed the door and walked in.

Inside, everything was carved in brilliant white marble. A staircase curved up and around the entrance hall. Straining my neck to look up, I saw more double-headed angels, each with their arms crossed in front of their chests. A kid wearing a blue military jacket ran past on the level above. The sound of his squeaking trainers echoed around the stairs.

"Can I help you?" A man in shabby security guard clothes sat behind a desk. He had his feet up on the table and, from the hooting I heard spilling out of his small TV, he was watching the Jeremy Kyle show.

"I've been told to report to Admissions," I said, walking up to the desk.

"Sign in," he grunted, sliding over a leather-bound book. I scribbled down my name, the date and time. Then pushed it back.

"Fourth floor," the man said, not taking his eyes off the screen. Two women were rolling around on the floor, trying to tear each other's hair out.

"Excuse me, how do I...?"

The man gave me the briefest of glances and nodded behind me before returning to the catfight. I turned around and saw the large silver doors of the lift.

"Thanks," I said. "For nothing," I added as I walked away.

I pushed the metal arrow that pointed up and stood back. The lift hummed into life, groaning as it made its way slowly downward. It pinged and the doors eased open. I stepped in.

I pressed the button marked four and waited. Nothing happened. I pressed the button again. Still nothing. I pushed the button again and again.

"Excuse me," I shouted at the security guard. "It's not working."

He harrumphed and sighed, hefted his feet off the desk and dragged himself from behind the counter. His shirt was hanging out of his trousers and I saw a glimpse of his hairy belly button.

"Can't you read?" he said as he arrived at the lift. He leant in, pointing at an empty space on the wall. "Oh." He looked on the floor at a sheet of A4 paper that lay in one corner. I bent over to pick it up. It read:

All visitors wanting the fourth floor should go to the fifth and walk down a flight or to the third and walk up a flight of stairs. The management apologises for the inconvenience.

The security guard was already waddling back to his desk. I pressed the number 3 and the doors finally closed.

After getting stuck in the stairwell, and having to ask a cleaner to let me in through the keypad-protected doors, I finally made it to the fourth floor. The scene waiting for me was a little less awe-inspiring than the reception. As secret government facilities went, this one was a little disappointing. I had been expecting something... well, something more. I had been expecting chrome and glass and ultramodern angles like you saw on spy dramas on

TV. I would have happily settled for green leather and wooden panelling like in James Bond films. But this was just like one of the sixth form colleges I'd gone to see last year. It was more local city council, than elite secret power. A temporary sign, stuck to the wall opposite the stairway with Blu-Tack, told me that Reception was to my left.

I walked down a corridor of flimsy doors. From behind one I heard high-pitched children's voices answering questions from an unseen teacher and I wondered why I'd ever been afraid.

I arrived at the reception desk, where a pretty girl was talking into a phone headset. I approached the desk and she held up a hand, telling me to wait. Her call finished, she smiled at me a little quizzically.

"Hello, can I help you?"

"I'm Scott. Scott Tyler. Here to see Commandant Morgan."

The woman consulted her computer screen and nodded.

"Yes. You are the Commandant's 10.15am appointment. You're a little early." She jerked a taloned thumb at the large digital clock behind her head. It read 9.56am.

"Yes, I know. I'm sorry. I didn't want to be late."

"Take a seat."

She directed me to a grey couch with a wave of her open palm, answered another call by pressing her headset, and promptly forgot about me.

I sat on the sofa and waited. My stomach was twitching with nerves and I was pretty sure I was going to be sick. The plant next to me looked pretty hardy and I decided that its pot would have to do when the time came for me to throw up.

The clock ticked over to 9.58am.

I reached for the scattering of glossy magazines laid out on the glass table and plucked one at random. It was called Government Industry Weekly and its pages were filled with articles about policies and budget cuts. I closed the magazine and placed it carefully back on the pile.

"Ah, Mr Tyler." The voice from behind me made me jump. I scrambled out of the low couch and turned to face Commandant Morgan.

The first thing I noticed was his teeth. They were so white they were almost blue. The last time I saw him, he hadn't been smiling. But this time, he was grinning so widely I saw almost every tooth in his mouth. The second thing I noticed was his uniform. Grey and so sharp I was surprised he didn't cut himself on it. He reached out a hand and I saw a flash of purple from the lining around his cuff. I stretched out my shaking hand and tried to remember everything they'd taught us in business studies about a firm handshake. I was pretty sure my handshake was about as firm as a dead fish.

"I'm Commandant Morgan, head of the Shifting Division." Morgan squeezed my hand and shook it in three great jerks. Now that we were standing so close, I realised I was taller than him by a few inches. He patted my shoulder, and I don't know if I was imagining it, but I thought he was arching up slightly on the toes of his shining brown brogues to even out our height difference. "Well, at last we meet, Scott. It's OK if I call you Scott isn't it?"

I mumbled that of course it was OK he called me Scott.

"Great. That's great, Scott. Ha! Great Scott." He laughed too loudly at his own joke and then finally let go of my hand. "Follow me." He crossed his legs and spun around in a dramatic turn, ending with both hands making gun gestures.

It was weird, meeting him for the second time. Although this was clearly the first time for him. This multiple reality thing was hard to get my head around. Now that everything had been put right with Katie, I was back in an alternative reality where ARES hadn't come and dragged me out of Aubrey's flat. As far as Morgan knew, I was just a kid who'd tried to climb a pylon and had discovered I was a Shifter. Nevertheless, I kept flinching, expecting Morgan to start shouting at me again or cuff me to a chair.

He led me away from reception and down a long, dark corridor. It smelt of new carpet.

"The Agency for the Regulation and Evaluation of Shifters comprises two main divisions," Morgan began. "The Shifters and the Regulators. Shifters are broken down into three separate divisions; Spotters, Mappers and Fixers. While the Regulators includes Enforcement, Analysis, IT and what have you." He waved his hand as he spoke, as if dismissing these Non-Shifting departments. "And of course beneath all of that is the Programme." He turned and grinned at me. "Where you shall begin your training and we shall see what you are made of, Mr Tyler."

We turned a corner into another corridor, with peeling grey wallpaper and portraits of stern-looking men glaring down at us.

"ARES was established in 1840 by Queen Victoria after an assassination attempt was thwarted by a Shifter," Morgan said, continuing his induction. "A Shifter named Jack Locke pushed the shooter out of the way and saved the day. Back then, most Shifters were wild children, living off their wits. Circuses and traveling magic shows were filled with them. A far cry from the focused and disciplined youngsters who pass through our doors today, isn't that right, Scott?"

I laughed, thinking he was joking, then swallowed it in a quick cough when he pursed his lips at me.

"Yes," I said, quickly. "I guess."

Morgan turned on his heels and continued his lecture. "When Queen Victoria learned of the presence of Shifters, she set about finding a way to harness their talent. One of her closest advisors revealed himself as an ex-Shifter and was appointed to create and oversee ARES."

We stopped in front of one of the portraits: a man with a huge handlebar moustache and small squinting eyes. His cheeks were red and his expression made him look severely constipated. The name under the portrait read Lord Cuthbert Morgan-Fairfax.

"He was my great, great, great..." Morgan paused and counted on his fingers. "...great, great uncle. And we Morgans have been in the service of ARES ever since." I looked back down the line of portraits. Each man did bear a resemblance to the man before him – they each had small, dark eyes and a distinct lack of chins. The last painting in the row showed a man with dark, slicked-down hair and too-big teeth. "My father," Morgan said pointing at the picture, "Sir Richard Morgan, is the current head of ARES and oversees both divisions."

"So your dad's also your boss?" I asked, trying to read the expression on Morgan junior's face. Was it awe or fear? Or both?

"Well, yes. Although he's not especially hands-on. He delegates most of the more important decisions to me, naturally. Lets me get on with the business of actually running things down here." He brushed an invisible speck of dust off his shoulder, then examined his fingernails. I guessed he was waiting for me to say something.

"Er, I guess he must really trust you."

"I wouldn't call it trust, Scott. Not really. You see trust implies hope. My father doesn't need to trust when he knows I am the man for the job. Now, where was I?" Morgan glanced back to the picture of his stern father and then walked on. "Lord Morgan-Fairfax's aims were to help Shifters to become valuable members of society who could protect the British Empire. Since then the purpose of ARES has remained broadly the same. While the empire itself has waned we have remained constant.

For over one hundred and seventy years, ARES has trained Shifters and regulated them. And to what end, I hear you ask?"

I hadn't said a thing.

"*Ad verum via*. That's our motto. It means 'towards the true way', or the best possible way. And that is what each and every individual here at ARES strives to do. Work towards creating the best possible reality."

We must have circled around as we were now walking down the same corridor I'd passed on my way in. A group of children piled out of one of the doors and raced away. Morgan waved and pointed at a few as they passed. The kids nodded and grinned to his face. But I was able to catch the expressions they made to his back. They weren't very polite.

"We have eighteen cadets in training here," Morgan said. "Plus thirty-six Shifting Class Officers. It's the highest concentration of Shifters in Europe," he added, smiling at me. I tried to appear impressed. "And then we have the Regulators, the lay team supporting us, made up of ex-Shifters and other, specially-chosen, military personnel, headed up by Mr Abbott."

"And is Mr Abbot here?" I asked, hoping that I would see him again.

"He's attending to other business." Morgan stopped outside a door. "Please," he said, guiding me in with a wave of his hand. "Step into my humble abode." I walked in and he closed the door behind me.

This was a little more like it. Morgan's office had a

large window with views across East London. I could just see the tip of St Paul's spire in the distance; the dome hidden by grey concrete blocks. He gestured at a spindly chair that stood in front of a large walnut desk and took his seat in an expensive-looking leather chair. He brought both his hands together as though in prayer and raised them to his lips. I sat down.

Morgan wasn't that much older than me. But he was clearly loving the power of his job.

"So, Scott. Scotty, can I call you Scotty? Good." I opened my mouth to speak, but he continued. "Now, let's see what we have on you, Scotty." He adjusted a wafer-thin computer screen positioned on his desk and waved his hand in front of it. The screen lit up showing a picture of me dressed in my school uniform, glaring miserably into the camera. A second wave and the screen was filled with writing.

"So you say the first time you Shifted was three days ago? And in a public place too." Morgan shook his head and sighed. With each casual wave of his hand a new page of my file appeared on the computer. I tried to apologise but he cut me off with a raised hand. "Yes, I have a Shift registered on that night that tallies up with your story." He said *story* like he still wasn't totally convinced I wasn't making this all up. "And you agreed to turn yourself in to ARES in return for training?"

"Yes, I guess."

"There's no guessing, Scotty. It's all here." He tapped the screen his finger making a *dink dink* noise.

"Everything that goes on at ARES is all right here." He pushed the computer out of the way and turned around in his chair to face the window. The back of the leather seat had a large tear down one side.

"The question now is…" He spun back around, dramatically and leant over his desk, both hands pressed firmly on its top. "What do we do with you?"

The threat in that question made my head start prickling with sweat.

Morgan laughed. "Ha, don't look so worried, Scotty. You've done the right thing. Had you decided to go it alone, well… things might not have been so pleasant. We might not have been able to have this nice little chat." He stood up and walked around to perch one butt cheek on his desk. He knocked over a pen pot, which sort of ruined the effect. He ignored it and stared at me.

"So, Scotty. What do you want from ARES?"

"I want to learn. Learn how to control Shifting."

"Yes, yes, very good. We can do that. Of course we can do that. But first. A *petite faveur*, that's a small favour. From you." He smiled, but the smile didn't reach his eyes. "Who told you about Shifting?"

"I, er…" I couldn't tell them about Aubrey. I had no idea what kind of trouble she would get in if they knew she hadn't handed me over as she was supposed to. "I met this guy," I lied, not meeting his eyes. "I was out with my friends and I, well I Shifted–"

"And this was Friday night, correct?" Morgan interrupted.

"Yes, like I said."

"Just checking. Do go on. You were having fun with your little friends."

I didn't like the way he said the word "little". It was like he was saying "defenceless". Or "delicious".

I pressed on. "Yes, and after I Shifted, this guy stopped me and explained what had happened. And then when I went home, a card was waiting for me. So I rang you." I rushed through the last bit, hoping he wouldn't scrutinize my story too closely.

"And this guy?" Morgan said, inspecting the ceiling. "What did he look like?"

I hunted around for an image and I remembered Zac. I didn't care if he got into trouble. I described him, as vaguely as possible.

Morgan squinted at me. His eyes little slits. Perhaps he recognised the description or perhaps he didn't believe a word of it. He stood up and walked slowly back to his seat and rattled off an amendment to my file on his keyboard.

"Tell, me Scott. What would it mean to you if I were to say the letters… SLF?" he glared at me, as if trying to read a reaction on my face, as if trying to catch me out.

I kept my face as still as possible. "Um, are they a band?"

"How about The Shifters Liberation Front? Does that ring any bells? Ding-a-ling?"

I pursed my lips together and shook my head. "Nope. Sorry."

"Hmm, we'll look into that," he said. "But in the meantime, we have you." He stretched out his palms.

"Mr Scott Tyler who wants to learn how to control his powers. I am very glad to say that you have come to the right place. In fact," he slapped both hands together, "you have come to the only place." He laughed again.

"So you will help me?" I thought about what had happened and a shudder rippled through me.

"Of course we will Scotty. That's what we do here at ARES. Help people. Of course, you're signing up a little later than most of our..." he paused, finding the right word. "Recruits. And I doubt you'll ever become anything special. But it's never too late to learn, is it now? So." He sprang up out of his chair, sending it rocking towards the window. "There's no time like the present. Let's get you signed up and we can begin training."

"Today?" I said. I was starting to feel like everything was out of control.

"Well, we can't have you running around, Shifting willy-nilly, now can we?"

What was with this guy? He was only a teenager but spoke like he was thirty years older. It was safe to say I didn't like Morgan. Not even a tiny bit. He was smug, patronising and, well, quite a large git. But no worse than a lot of my teachers.

I stood up and he gave me that "manly" slap on the shoulder again, harder this time, and led me out of the room.

CHAPTER TWELVE

He guided me back down the corridor to a door marked *101*.

"Room 101?" I laughed, nervously. "So will you make me betray everyone I ever loved in there or something?"

Morgan stopped and took a pass card out from his inside pocket. His brow wrinkled in confusion.

"*1984*? Big Brother?" I suggested.

"I never watch reality TV," he said, turning his back and swiping the card through an electronic reader. Locks clunked and the door opened, revealing a large white room. The floorboards squeaked slightly under our weight as we walked inside. The room was occupied by five small children – three boys and two girls – and one enormous man. The man slowly turned to face me and I wanted to run out the door, down in the lift, back on to the street and never come back again. He was easily six foot six tall and almost as wide. He wore a cut off T-shirt, which barely contained his bulging muscles. But it wasn't really his bulk that scared me. It was his face. It looked as if it had been made from two people's heads, badly cut-and-shut together. A large scar ran from his left temple to his right jaw and another ran just under his hairline. He had one blue eye and one milky white eye. Both of them were fixed on me.

"I have another cadet for you," Morgan said, clearly relishing in my terror. "Sergeant Cain, this is Mr Scott Tyler. Mr Tyler, Sergeant Cain.'

Sergeant Cain took a few steps towards me, his strides booming like the steps of a T-Rex.

He looked me up and down. "He's a little old, isn't he?"

Morgan considered me too. "Perhaps. It might be he's only good for admin. But worth running up your flag-pole and seeing if he flies."

Cain turned his glare on Morgan, who shrank under its force. "Do what with my flagpole now?" Cain said.

"I, I mean, subject him to your training," Morgan muttered, handing my file over.

Cain snatched it out of Morgan's hand. "So why didn't you say so, Dick?"

The man reached out a spade-like hand and rested it on my shoulder, all without taking his eyes off the quaking Morgan. I had to bite my lips to hide my grin. Sergeant Cain might be the most terrifying man I'd ever seen in my life, but I was growing to like him.

"I'll take care of Mr Tyler. Now why don't you run off and go push some paper." Cain waved Morgan away with my file and steered me towards the group.

I twisted around in Cain's grip to watch Morgan. His eyes were scrunched into tight little creases and his fists were clenched. He span on his heels and slammed the metal door behind him.

We reached the row of kids and Cain gave me a firm shove. I staggered into place beside them. I looked down the line. Not one of the kids looked over twelve years old. They were all dressed in the same loose, black trousers that Cain wore, only in miniature and each of them wore a black T-shirt with the word "fresher" printed on the back. Although someone had crossed out the "er" in white pen and added the word "meat". Fresh Meat. Clearly, Cain had a sick sense of humour.

Cain was flicking through my papers. His eyes lit up as he read something. "Brown belt in kick boxing, hmm?" He slapped the file against his thigh. "Well, seems like you have arrived in perfect time, Mr Tyler. I was just about to give a little demonstration on martial arts. Perhaps you would like to assist?"

"I'm not really dressed for fighting," I said, indicating my suit.

"Is that so?" Cain said. "And if an assailant was to jump you on the street, would you stop him and say…" He took on a high-pitched voice and pressed his hands together as if begging. "Please don't attack me, Mr Mugger, not until I've changed out of my suit." He raised a thick eyebrow.

"I suppose not."

"I suppose not. Now if you would step forward and assume the position."

I jerked off my tie, undid the top button of my shirt and kicked off my shoes. Then stepped forward and moved into ready stance; my feet shoulder-width apart, my right fist out front and my left close to my chest.

"CP, will you do the honours?" Cain pointed at one of the little girls who stepped forwards. She was a tiny thing, with long brown hair and a fringe that covered her eyes.

"Oh, come on. I can't fight her," I said.

"I suspect you are quite right," Cain said, and nodded at the girl to continue. She stood in front of me, her body upright and her hands hanging loose by her side.

"Begin," Cain barked.

Neither of us moved. I shook my head. It was ridiculous that I should fight this girl. Sure, Katie and I had gone a couple of rounds against each other. But that was different; she was my sister. Besides, Katie had the meanest roundhouse I'd ever been unfortunate enough to come up against, whereas this kid looked like she wouldn't hurt a fly.

I decided to play along and started to circle around her. I made a few play jabs in her direction, but she didn't even twitch. I thought that perhaps if I went for a throw, I could end this silly game without hurting her too much.

The punch came from nowhere. One second I was reaching out to her shoulder, the next she was standing on my left and had punched me square in the ribs. I staggered back trying to calm my ragged breathing. The girl was back standing in front of me. She flicked a dark curl out of her eye.

All right then missy, I thought, *you want to play?*

I threw out a left jab. One instant she was in front of me, my fist heading for her chest, the next she was running up my bent thigh and raining blows down on my head. I pushed her away. She flipped over and landed perfectly on her feet.

My blood was pumping now. I punched left, right, swung a snap kick, a roundhouse, running through a simple series of moves. But with each strike I threw out, the girl had moved. Sometimes just enough for me to miss, other times she was suddenly standing behind me. My head was spinning and my ears ringing. How was she doing this? I started to get that strange dizzy feeling again, like when watching the croupier at the casino, or when Aubrey and I had been running through the streets. As if reality wasn't fixed anymore.

I tried a jump kick and the girl caught my leg in both her hands and pushed. I landed flat on my back.

I heard a clapping and sat up to see Cain slapping his huge hands against each other. "Well done, CP. Perfect work."

Cain leant over and offered me his hand. I took it and he jerked me to my feet then slapped me on the back so hard I nearly went crashing to the floor again.

"Don't be too hard on yourself, Scott. Fighting a

Shifter is not like normal fighting. And that is because?"
he asked the group.

"Shifters don't react. They anticipate," the kids
chanted in unison.

"Exactly," Cain said, grinning at his pupils. "In one reality, you did beat little Miss Finn here." The girl bowed
and returned to her place in the line. "But with every
wrong move she made, she undid it. So that she was always exactly where she needed to be to win. Do you
understand?"

I nodded and returned to the line. I didn't really understand, but I wasn't about to admit that in front of all
these kids.

"Now let's see what happens when two trained
Shifters fight." Cain pointed at two of the boys who
took their place. They stood in front of each other, looking relaxed and poised.

"Begin!"

It was that strobe light effect again. Their moves were
jerky and impossibly fast. I tried to focus through the
ringing in my head and stop thinking about the fact that
whatever was happening before me was impossible. The
two kids were leaping about throwing out fists and feet,
but for every strike one of them went to make, the other
would suddenly not be there or have the perfect block.
It was as if they were able to anticipate each other's exact
move, a constant redoing, until they made just the right
choice. Ripples of light pulsated out from around them,
swirling off into the walls and beyond.

The fight went on for about three minutes and I saw the kids were getting tired. Their faces showed the strain of the focus. The smaller boy was starting to get a little sloppy and his Shifts not so certain. I heard a yelp and a thud and it was the bigger boy who was lying on the floor, holding his nose.

"All it takes is the tiniest break in concentration and you've lost the advantage." Cain helped the losing boy to his feet and checked to see if he was OK. Apparently he was, and satisfied, Cain patted the boy on the head.

"But can't they just Shift again?" I asked. "I mean, couldn't he just Shift now and make sure he wins?"

"Shifting takes a lot of energy. And ultimately, it's the more powerful Shifter who will win. They will take it to the place where there is no possibility of their opponent winning. In any reality. OK, everyone. Now pair off and go through your routines."

CP and the other girl and the two boys who'd just fought peeled off and started sparring.

"Care to have another go, Scott?" Cain gestured towards the remaining boy. "Jake here will go gentle on you, won't you Jake?"

"Sure," the boy said with a crooked grin. He had sandy hair, coffee-coloured skin and eyes that glinted in the overhead lights. He led me by my arm away from the rest of the group.

"Don't worry about it," he said as we walked away. "I so got my butt handed to me when I first tried it. And at least you're a good fighter. You made some really sick moves there."

"Not sick enough," I said.

"But it's because you're only thinking on one level. As soon as you start to see across the possibilities, you'll be fine."

"How old are you?" I asked, depressed that even a kid as young as he was had a better grip on it all than I did.

"I'm eleven. Been here since I was eight."

"Oh, great."

"Come on. Try and hit me. I promise I won't hit you back."

It took me a while, but I did manage to hit Jake. Shifting intentionally was a strange, almost drunken feeling. As if your limbs are just a few nanoseconds ahead of your brain. The best way I can describe it is like physical deja vu. You know where you're meant to be because you've been there before. You just sort of let go and let your feelings guide you.

As I got a little more control over Shifting, Jake started hitting me back. He was good too, even though I knew he was going easy on me. Once I got the grip of strikes he showed me how to dodge by Shifting. The key to it all, I worked out, was to think about all the possible ways I could hit him and how he might hit back, or all the possible places I could move to dodge his blows, and hold them all in my head, just enough to be able to take another path. Then I focused on the alternate reality and jolted it into existence. It was exhausting and after half an hour I was panting for breath.

Cain came over to watch our last few exchanges, which ended with me getting Jake in a headlock. I had a sneaking feeling Jake had let me win, but I was too grateful to protest.

"You learn fast, Scott. Might be a future for you beyond Admin after all." He grinned and then turned to address the group. "OK everyone, good work. Quick break and then I want you all outside room 104 at 11.30 ready for the poles." The group groaned.

"What are the poles?" I asked Jake.

"Oh, you are gonna love them," he said.

And I knew I really wasn't.

CHAPTER THIRTEEN

"The poles" turned out to be a terrifying assault course in a large gymnasium. There were about fifty poles in total, each the diameter of a small tree, sticking straight up out of the floor as if someone had taken a chainsaw to a forest and taken the tops off leaving only the trunks. The poles themselves were between six and ten feet high and they wobbled slightly. The floor was covered in blue crash mats, the kind we had in PE at school. The kind that were supposed to stop it from hurting if you fell, but never really did.

I already knew what we had to do. I'd seen enough kung fu movies in my time to recognise a set up like this one.

"So we have to run across them?" I asked Jake.

He nodded.

"Sounds easy enough."

He shook his head. "They move," he said by way of explanation.

I heard a loud clunking noise and the poles started

groaning as they moved, like a huge engine, going up and down like pistons.

OK, so this made it slightly more difficult.

"Are we ready to dance, people?" Sergeant Cain's voice boomed. He strode forward and gazed up at the sliding poles, a grin of pure malevolence on his twisted face. He loved this, I could tell, pushing little kids to their limits. He was like every PE teacher I'd ever had.

He studied the group, his mismatched eyes glinting. "Who's first?"

The kids inspected their feet, no one wanting to be picked for this latest challenge. I followed their example and tried my hardest to make myself look invisible, not easy given I was about two feet taller than any of them. Cain's gaze hovered on me for a moment and then passed on. I guessed he decided to go easy on me. Either that or he was leaving my humiliation for later.

"Max, you're up." He gestured to the poles with his thumb.

Max was a tall, gangly kid with brown hair and freckles. His pale skin went even whiter as he stepped forward and looked up. He swallowed hard and threw his arms around the nearest and shortest pole, then started shimming his way up it. He reached the top and pulled himself up, planting both feet on its surface. It jerked slightly and he wobbled, waving his arms about trying to regain his balance.

I looked across at the course he had to take. I couldn't see any pattern to the movement of the poles; sometimes they were slow and steady, other times they jerked up or down fast enough that if you happened to find yourself standing on one at the time, you would need to be a limpet not to fall off.

As one, we all peered up to watch Max. He had that same expression on his face I'd seen on Aubrey's – a sort of unfocused stare, as if he was looking through the poles rather than at them. He stretched out one leg, his bare toes wriggling as he prepared himself to make the first leap. He jumped and landed on a pole to the left. It hissed upwards just as he landed, bucking him a clear ten feet into the air. We all shuffled around trying to get a better view of him. I couldn't see his face any more, just his twiggy legs stretching out for the next step. He leapt onto the pole that had been right under his feet but was now suddenly three feet lower. He went hurtling to the floor, banging against the poles as he spiralled downwards. He hit the crash mat with a heavy thud. There was a collective sucking in of breath and wincing.

"Come on. My daughter could do better than that and she's six!" Cain helped Max up and patted him on his back as he got unsteadily to his feet.

"Next!" Cain shouted.

CP stepped forward, whether to either get it over and done with, or because she had something to prove, I didn't know. I didn't really care. If she was mad enough to give it a go, more power to her. She worked her way up the pole and took her place at the top with more grace than Max had displayed. She stretched her arms out, like a gymnast on the bar and jumped. She didn't hang about. Before we knew what was happening, she'd already made it to the top of the third pole. It juddered, and I was sure it would shake her off, but she crouched down and stayed on top. She glanced to her left and her right, and I guessed she was carefully considering her options so she could Shift to another path if she needed. She sidestepped to her left, or at least I was sure I saw her going to the left and then I saw that strange twitch again and suddenly she was clinging on to the pole on the right. She pulled herself up, her small arms straining with the effort.

"Nice work, CP," Cain shouted up. "Keep focused now."

She straightened up and took a few steadying breaths. She closed her eyes.

"Use the Force, Luke," Jake shouted and the group tittered.

"Shut up, Jake," CP said scowling down at us. She had a faint accent that I couldn't quite place.

"Yes, shut up," Cain said. "And you're up next, Jake."

Jake groaned.

Disruption over, we all turned back to CP. The pole she was on started twisting, and I was reminded of a jewellery box my sister had, with a fairy ballerina spinning around on a coiled spring. CP was such a tiny thing, with huge blue eyes fixed in total concentration. She stepped forward. But the pole she was reaching for wasn't there.

She fell through the air, her arms flailing, and landed right in Cain's arms. I was sure he'd been on the other side of the mat when she fell. But he must have anticipated her fall and been in the right spot to catch her. Judging by her muffled curses she wasn't happy with her attempt. Cain put her down and coughed. "Come on then, Jake. Let's see how funny it is when you're up there."

I gave Jake a weak thumbs-up of encouragement. He jerked his head in thanks and took his place at the bottom of the first pole. I could see his knees quaking beneath his baggy trousers. He looked as if he might be sick.

He dragged himself up the pole, eyes clenched shut the whole way. When he made it to the top, he steadied himself, pointed his arms out like a gymnast and leapt.

Like CP, he went for the fast approach, hopping onto the first and then second pole in a matter of seconds. I had to look away as the slices in reality were making my head spin. Like watching a 3D film without glasses. Jake was a pretty good Shifter, I'd gathered that much from our fight. I wonder if I'd ever have even half the control he had. But even his skills weren't enough. He screamed as a pole he'd just landed on hurtled upward like a bucking bull and sent him flying into the air.

"Ha!" CP said, in triumph as Jake landed on the mat. Her smile slowly vanished. Jake wasn't moving. He laid on the floor his eyes closed and his leg bent at a weird angle. CP was the first to run to him. I watched as she bent over his tiny body. Oh, god, please. Don't let him be hurt, I thought.

"Got ya!" Jake shouted.

"You eejit!" CP said, kicking him in the side. But just like me, I knew she was relieved. Jake crawled to his feet rubbing at his backside.

"OK, thank you for your performance there, Jake. That's five poles to beat," Cain said. "Scott, your turn."

My stomach turned to ice as I approached the first pole. I wrapped my arms around it like the others had done and stood there hugging it, my face pressed against the rough wood. I hooked one leg around the pole and then didn't know what to do next. I didn't even know how to climb it properly, let alone how to stay alive once I got to the top. The pole made things even harder by jerking into the sky and suddenly I was clinging onto it, three feet off the floor. No going back now. I started to shuffle my way to the top.

My fingertips reached for the flat surface and I pulled myself up. I'd done a few balancing exercises in kick boxing, but nothing like this. Now I was gazing across the stubby forest of poles, the floor was farther away than I'd imagined. The safety of the raised platform on the other side might as well have been a mile away. I thought about just leaping off the pole and getting it over with. But as I looked down and saw five little faces turned up to watch me, my pride kicked in. I didn't want to shame myself, not in front of a bunch of kids. Jake gave me a thumbs-up and I returned it.

The poles hissed up and down. The first one was only a couple of feet away and only a little higher than the pole I was standing on. But the question was, would it still be there when I tried to step on it. I tried to plot a route across to the platform but every time I worked one out, the poles would change position and it would be impossible.

I then remembered what the whole thing reminded me of. It was like a computer game I used to play, where you had to make it across a crumbling pile of columns before they turned to dust. In the game there had been one clear route that would take you across the chasm. But it took about six goes before you learned the path. And I didn't have the option to 'play again?' here. Or did I? Perhaps that was exactly the way to think about Shifting: it was like getting another go on a computer game. You accepted that you were probably going to fail on your first, even second or third go, but with each attempt, you got a little closer to finishing the level.

I decided to not even bother trying to work out which way to go on my first attempt and took a step forward.

My foot landed on the pole perfectly. I'd been lucky. With my next step, I missed it on the first attempt, but Shifted just in time to make it on the second. I jumped forward, focusing not on where I was going as much as holding all the possible places I could be. Before I knew it I was six poles in. A murmur came up from the kids below. Leap, and I was seven poles. Leap, Shift, and it was eight. On pole nine I almost lost focus and it took two Shifts before I was clinging on with my fingertips.

The gasps from below fired me on. I took one, big leap, and was standing on the platform. Safe.

I turned around and looked across the poles. They had stopped moving, as if I had them under my command. I was buzzing with adrenaline and the joy of success. At that moment, I felt as if I could achieve anything. I wanted to go again, only I wanted the poles to be higher. Why not throw some fire jets in for me to dodge while you're at it?

The kids all erupted in cheers and Jake was cheering loudest of all. I raised my hand and waved, drinking in their applause.

Cain was watching me, his shattered face fixed in an expression I couldn't quite read. But I thought it might just have been approval.

CHAPTER FOURTEEN

Jake walked me to the canteen when the lunch bell rang.

"That was awesome!" he said, punching the air with his little fists. "You were like, bam, bam, bam and then whooo! Done." He sighed, out of breath after his overly-enthusiastic recreation of my path across the poles.

"Beginner's luck," I said, trying to keep my swelling head in check.

"Na-ah," Jake said. "You totally nailed it."

"I did, didn't I?" I said giving into the bravado. I was enjoying having someone to show off to. It reminded me of when Katie was little and I was still her hero. Before she grew up enough to realise what a loser I was. I wrapped my arm around Jake's neck and knuckled his hair.

I heard the clatter of plates and the hum of conversation before we reached the large double doors that led to the canteen. Jake pushed the doors open and the chatter grew even louder.

The rest of the cadets were in line already. CP was at the front, piling her tray up with food.

"Jeez," Jake rolled his eyes. "CP has to be first at everything."

"Why is she called 'CP'?"

"They're her initials, though I don't know what they stand for. She doesn't talk much. Max said he knows, but he tried to tell once and she knocked out his last milk tooth." I watched him watching her and recognised the expression.

"You fancy her," I said, nudging him as we fell into place at the back of the queue.

"Wha'? No way. Urgh. Like urgh, urgh." He protested a little too much.

"Come on, she's cute. And she's totally kickass."

"Yeah, she's a pretty good fighter," he said, dragging the top of his trainer across the parquet flooring. "Guess she's had a lot of practice."

We shuffled a few people closer to the food serving. "What do you mean?"

"When she first arrived all she did was fight. People made fun of her and her family and she fought."

"What's funny about her family?"

"She's a gypsy."

"Oh. Well, that's nothing to be ashamed of."

"I never said it was," he said a little too defensively. "And besides you get loads of Shifters from gypsy families and stuff. It kind of goes with the territory."

I remembered my induction from Morgan. "Oh, yeah. Rogues."

Jake looked up at me his dark eyes still for a moment.

Then he just shrugged.

We'd arrived at the end of the queue and a burly woman with frizzy hair escaping out of a small white hat smiled at me. "What will it be, love?"

I scanned the silver trays of food and was surprised to find it all looked pretty decent. Better than anything I'd get at home, that's for sure. "The lasagne please."

She scooped the meaty pasta onto my plate, added a flourish of salad and turned to Jake.

"Just chips for you, petal?"

Jake grinned as she piled his plate high with chips.

I followed him over to the table where the rest of the kids from class were eating, including CP who was sitting at the end on her own. Jake headed for the end away from her, but I wasn't going to let him get away with it that easily.

"Is it OK if we join you?" I said, squeezing my legs over the plastic bench attached to the table.

CP looked from me to Jake and then nodded, her long fringe falling into her face.

"You were pretty great back in class. Jake was telling me you're the best in the year."

I heard Jake cough next to me, choking on a chip. I patted him on the back and poured him a plastic cup of water from the jug on the table. CP watched him and smiled a little, her small mouth curling up at the corner.

"Thanks," she said softly, the dropped "th" giving away her accent.

"Are you Irish?" I asked, playing as if I didn't know

anything.

"I'm from a lot of places."

"Yeah, a lot of places that don't want her back," Max said from the middle of the table. Some of the kids laughed, but most just carried on with their food.

"Shut it, Max," said Jake. "Or she'll knock the rest of your teeth out."

CP's smile grew bigger.

I waited, hoping that these two might pick up the conversation on their own. But they were both too busy picking at their food.

"So your family moved around a lot?" I asked.

"Yeah, a bit."

"Mine too,"' said Jake. "I went to eight schools before I was eight."

"That must have been tough. My parents never made me go to school."

"I guess. The lions made up for it though."

"The lions?" CP and I said at the same time.

Jake laughed his loud bark. "My family owned a circus. So we had lions and elephants and couple of zebra but…" He leant forward conspiratorially. "They were really just donkeys painted black and white."

CP laughed so much, her water came out of her nose.

"My sister was a trapeze artist. The best ever. Man, you should have seen her fly through the air, she never fell. Well, even if she did, she'd Shift."

"Your sister is a Shifter too?" asked CP, leaning forward and watching Jake intently now.

"Sure. It runs in families. Wasn't anyone else in your family a Shifter?"

"My grandma, or so my cousin told me. Only I never met her. But go on."

"Well, I was supposed to join the act, 'The Flying Baileys' they were called. But you saw me on the poles. I get dizzy when I stand on a chair. Anyway, before Mum and Dad could work out what to do with me, ARES came along. Mum and Dad didn't want me to join. But my sister persuaded them it was the best thing. So she stuck around and they carried on with the rest of the circus. And here I am! Ta da!"

"That sounds cool," CP said. "I've never been to a circus. We went to lots of horse fairs, but they're probably not the same."

"Next time my folks are in town I'll take you. I'll give you the whole backstage tour!"

"I'd like that," CP said, beaming now.

I leant back, smiling at my handiwork. Call me Mr Matchmaker.

"What about your family, Scott? Any Shifters?" Jake said.

"Me? Ha, no way. Nope, we're your regular, boring family. The most exciting thing that happened to me before all of this was when we went on a camping trip to Wales and the caravan got washed away."

"That happened to one of our caravans," CP said. "Only it wasn't washed away, it was blown over in a hurricane."

She started telling the story of some great storm. Only I wasn't listening. I'd just seen someone enter the canteen.

Aubrey was dressed in her sharp, blue military jacket. The orange hoodie she had worn beneath it on Friday night was gone, and instead she was wearing a crisp white shirt and matching blue trousers.

"Sorry, guys. I have to go." I crawled out from under the table and headed over to her. She was walking head down, as if she didn't want to make eye contact with anyone, white headphone wires trailing out from her ears. She almost walked into me before she looked up. Her mouth dropped open in shock, and then shut with a loud snap. Her eyes checked the room, as if she was nervous we were being watched. I glanced about. Everyone was tucking into their lunch, busy catching up on the day's gossip.

I pointed to my ears. Aubrey's forehead wrinkled in confusion and then she caught on. She pulled the earphones out and I heard the tinny beats of the track still playing.

"Kings of Leon?" I asked, recognising the song.

She nodded. And then got down to business. "You're here then?"

"Yep, I'm a card-carrying member of the Fresh Meat brigade. Literally!" I pulled out my ID card as proof, although regretted it as soon as she yanked it out of my hand.

"Nice photo," she said, examining it.

"Yeah, well I don't photograph well."

"I don't know. They've caught your stupid grin

perfectly." She handed my card back with a smile. "I honestly thought they'd lock you up."

"Apparently I'm special," I said, giving her my stupid grin.

"Special? That's one word for it." She raised an arched eyebrow and looked me up and down. "So you're sure about this, about joining ARES. Because it's not too late you know. You can always Shift."

"No. I'm enjoying it. And I know it was hard for you, what with your Mum's suicide and all."

Aubrey gasped and she swallowed hard. "Her... how did you know about that?'

"You told me."

She stepped in close to me and lowered her voice. "Have you been spying on me?"

"No, I swear you told me. When we went back to your flat and you made me coffee and you told me about–"

"I never told anyone about that. Anyone." She stared up at me, her eyes hopping from one of mine to the other, as if they didn't match.

I bit my lip and tried to remember. Aubrey was right. She hadn't told me about her mother's suicide, only that she'd died. In this reality anyway. But in the other one, before all the mess with my sister and ARES dragging me in, she had. It was another left-over fragment. Another jigsaw piece that belonged to another puzzle.

"Aubrey, I–"

"Goodbye, Scott." She brushed past me and headed for the counter.

"Hang on," I said catching up with her. "I'm sorry. I thought… I thought we were friends." Of course, I'd been hoping for a little bit more than just friends. But it would do as a start.

"Look, you're Fresh Meat." She indicated the black T-shirt I'd changed into and then tapped the two golden stripes on her arm. "And I'm an officer. And the two don't mix. It's just the way it goes. See you around."

I watched her walk towards the queue but she must have lost her appetite. She peeled off and headed for the doors, walking so fast her heels clacked on the floor.

"Do you know that girl?" Jake asked as I returned to the table.

"In another life," I said, watching her leave.

"Do you want a chip?" Jake waved a soggy specimen in my direction.

I shook my head. I wasn't hungry any more either.

I sat beside Jake and the rest of the kids anyway. Fresh Meat together, after all. They babbled about training and quickly moved on to TV programmes. I only vaguely followed what they were talking about. A bell rang, and everyone started packing up.

"What's next?" I asked Max who was shoving his last spoonfuls of pudding into his mouth. As he tried to swallow I thought about what essential skills I would need to become an officer. More fighting? Interrogation techniques? Tracking?

"History," he said, after gulping down the sponge.

"History?"

CHAPTER FIFTEEN

The classroom was your perfectly normal classroom. Although the chairs were too small for me and the table kept buckarooing every time I tried to move my legs underneath it. I gave up and sat with my knees to the side. The rest of the class dug out notebooks and chatted excitedly. Not something I'd experienced in a classroom before. The only time there had been any excitement in any of my classes was when someone set someone else on fire.

The door opened and a tall black man walked in. All the kids in the class suddenly descended into silence. He turned and nodded at the group. His dark eyes met mine for a fraction of a second and then passed by, clearly finding nothing remarkable about a kid five years too old sitting in his class.

"Afternoon, class."

"Afternoon, Mr Abbott," the kids chanted in reply.

I was relieved to see him. Although the memory of our last meeting was starting to fade, I remembered bits of it. Him being kind to me mostly. I was sort of getting used to the mismatched fragments of memories in my head. I knew if I tried too hard to hold on to them, I'd just end up losing a grip on whatever reality I was in now. So I let the thought slide away and focused on what he was saying.

"Once Shifters have come to terms with their powers, one of the first questions that occurs to many of them is 'Can we change history? Can we stop atrocity x or tragedy y from happening? Why' – and many of you may have asked yourself this already – 'if we can change our reality do we allow terrible things to happen?'"

There were a few eager nods in the class. Personally, I hadn't begun to think of my ability as able to affect anything bigger than my own pathetic life. I'd not stopped in the whirlwind to consider how I could use my ability to Shift to help others beyond saving my sister. I felt a pang of guilt at my selfishness.

"Well, stop worrying about it, because you can't," Abbott said. "Because, as you all know, the First Law of Shifting is…?"

"Shifters can only change their own reality," the class sang. I looked around the room, trying to see if they were all reading this rule off something. But there was nothing on the walls except baffling diagrams and historic timelines. I recognised a picture of Lord Cuthbert Morgan-Fairfax standing next to Queen Victoria.

"Which, of course," Abbott continued, "means a

Shifter can only undo his or her own decisions, and therefore can only affect events within their own lifetime."

The kids all scribbled in their notepads. I thought I should probably at least look as if I was following what he was saying, and picked up my pen.

"But what about world-changing events that are in your lifetimes, can you affect them?" He looked around the class, hoping for an answer.

"Only if you have made a genuine choice? One that has a direct impact on the event?" Max suggested.

"Ah, the problematic second law of Shifting. 'Only true choices can be undone.' Good answer, Max, but no. Not even then." Abbott turned to face the board and started writing in a blue pen. We waited while the squeaking letters appeared on the white surface. I copied it into my notebook.

Some events cut through all realities.

I looked at the words on the page and back at Abbott. I was starting to wish I was back up on the poles again.

"There are some events that are so tragic, so scarring, that they cut through all realities. They become a fixed, immovable point and all realities bend around them. They are no longer one of many possible realities, such as the minor things we deal with each and every day. They are bigger than any one of us."

"Like what?" Jake asked.

"Well, for most of you this will be before your time, but the one event that obsessed my generation of Shifters happened on 11th of September, 2001."

I'd only been four at the time but I'd been told about when the two planes crashed into the Twin Towers in New York.

"Is it because of the amount of people who died? Is that what causes the scar?" CP asked.

"Good question," Abbott said, pointing at her with his pen. "That may be part of it. But there have been other events where more people died and Shifters have been able to alter those. There is a reported case of a leak in a nuclear plant in Russia, where a Shifter of only six years of age was able to save over five thousand lives by calling in a fake fire alarm. But the events we are discussing today, which we call singularities, appear to be moments in time that send shock waves through every culture. When all the eyes of the world observe an event, as it did on 9/11, the collective consciousness of the human race resists the act of a Shift."

"So there's no way we can Shift singularities?" CP asked before I had a chance.

"Not once they have become global events, no. But sometimes a Shifter finds themselves in a position to act before an event has time to cross over into a singularity. I take you back to the Russian Shifter and the nuclear plant. He was only able to save those people because he'd been playing around making fake calls all day with his friends. And one of the numbers had been the plant. In the first incidence he decided not to call that number. So it was a simple decision to change. But rarely do we find ourselves gifted with these easy choices." He looked down at his desk and sighed. I wondered about when he was a Shifter and how many times he'd tried to change an event and failed.

Abbott looked up. The cloud of his memories had passed. "So, can anyone else think of an event that might be considered a singularity?"

Slowly, the class called out names of some of the most horrific events in human history. One by one they filled the white board, from World War I to the tsunami in Japan. I was starting to get really depressed. What was the point in having a cool power if you couldn't help anyone? Abbott seemed to read my mind.

He slowly capped his pen and put it down. "What I want you all to know now is that this board would have many, many more tragedies on it if it weren't for people like you. Throughout the ages, children able to Shift have quietly saved thousands if not millions of lives, without it ever leaving so much as a scratch on history. And why? Because the events they changed ceased to exist as soon as they changed them. There have been wars stopped by children changing their mind about begging their parents to stay at home. People saved from earthquakes, because a child decided to speak up when her dog ran away in the night."

I felt a swell of hope in my chest. "So we can help?"

"Of course you can. But it is why you must be aware of what is happening around you at all times, so you can predict the consequences and act fast. Speed is what makes the difference between a tragic event and a singularity. Those of you who have parents in positions of power, you must watch them and keep them on track."

The eyes in the room looked to Max. Now that I thought of it, his surname did sound familiar. The name of some politician or other.

"Even those of you who think the adults around you are useless good-for-nothings, they may have a part to play. I know it's a struggle that you have to keep your powers secret and that as children you don't get taken as seriously as you deserve. But that is the Shifters' burden. It is a great shame that the ability to Shift leaves just as we are gaining our voice in society or that the world is not ready to know how important you really are." He smiled out at the group, a sadness in his eyes. "But don't let the ignorance of adults stop you. You can make them listen. You can make them change."

We sat there in silence, taking in what he'd said. When the bell rang a minute later, marking the end of the lesson, no one moved. They were all staring at Abbott just as I was. In awe.

"OK, off you go now. I want an essay on the theory of singularities delivered by next week."

Slowly, we stood to go. As I reached the doorway, I nodded for Jake to carry on and turned back to Mr Abbott who was tidying up his things.

"Can I help you, Scott?" he said without looking up.

"You mentioned the rules, sir. The Rules of Shifting. It's just, everyone seems to know them…"

"Weren't you given our little blue book when you arrived?"

"I haven't been given anything."

"Hmm," Abbott said, straightening up. "All cadets should be issued with a copy. I will have a word with Commandant Morgan. But in the meantime..." He reached into his inside pocket and pulled out a small book, bound in blue leather. "You can have mine."

I took the book and looked down at the cracked leather cover. *The Universal Laws of Shifting, by Oswald Price* was written in embossed silver paint. It looked really old and really expensive. "I can't take this, Mr Abbott."

"Don't worry. I know the rules by heart. Besides, they no longer apply to me."

I opened the small book and turned the frail pages. There was so much I had to learn.

I closed it and slipped it in my pocket. "Thanks, Mr Abbott."

He considered me for a moment, his eyes wrinkling at the edges. "Walk with me, Scott."

We left the classroom and entered the corridor. It was bursting with kids getting to their next class. I realised that I should probably be one of them, but I had no idea what my next class was.

"How are you finding your first day?" Abbot asked.

"Good. I mean, I'm totally out of my depth, but really good."

"But you'll find your feet soon enough. If it makes

you feel any better, I was only a couple of years younger than you when I first entered ARES. And I've done all right." He patted my shoulder with his large hand. "You know, quite often when a Shifter's ability emerges later in life, they go on to be quite powerful."

"Yeah, you told me that when we first met. I still don't quite believe it, sir."

"When we *first* met?"

I got the feeling it was probably best not to mention how I remembered stuff they didn't. "No I mean, when I first arrived, Commandant Morgan said something similar." I coughed and looked at my shoes.

Abbott nodded, and I knew he didn't believe me for a second. "Well it's true. It won't be easy for you though. So much to learn in such a short space of time. But hopefully we can ensure you've made the most of your ability before…"

"Before entropy kicks in?"

"Yes, and then you can decide whether to go back out into the world and live a normal life, or stay here with us at ARES, and prepare the next generation of Shifters."

"Is it even possible to live a normal life after all of this? I mean, having experienced all of this and not being able to tell anyone."

"Some people do struggle, it's true. It can be hard to form relationships with people when you've been used to, well, having your own way. But the skills you learn here will prepare you for that. You'll learn how to measure your consequences and think before you act.

Not many normal people ever learn that. But don't you worry, Scott. You'll be fine. Especially with our help.

"Which reminds me, you'd better hurry, I fear I've kept you from Commandant Morgan's class on Integration and I'm sure he won't be too happy. Room 52," he added seeing the panicked look on my face. "Mr Bailey here will show you I am sure."

I turned to see Jake leaning up against a row of lockers behind us. He waved a little sheepishly.

"Jake, shouldn't you be in class?" I asked.

"I thought you might need a hand finding the room."

"Off you go now. If Commandant Morgan asks, tell him I sent the two of you on an errand."

"Thanks, sir."

He nodded and waved us off.

"Abbott's cool hey?" Jake said, as we started running.

"Very cool," I answered, feeling the weight of the little book in my pocket.

"They say he was the most powerful Shifter, like, ever."

I remembered what Mr Abbott had said about being only a couple of years younger than me when he'd started training. Suddenly being the big kid in class didn't worry me quite as much.

CHAPTER SIXTEEN

I'll save you the montage scene but over the next couple of months I was trained. And better than that, I was getting good. Especially at the fighting; not even CP could beat me now. I'd even caught Cain off his guard once. Although I knew that had this been out in the real world, he would have beat me to a pulp, Shifter or not.

We'd had more mind-blowing lessons with Abbott about Shifters throughout the ages, including a couple of very famous names, although we were all sworn to secrecy. But let's just say a couple of charming US presidents were mentioned.

We learned about the science behind Shifting from a tiny little woman called Professor Wheeler, including a recreation of the Double Slit experiment Aubrey had told me about when we first met, with lasers and everything. I still didn't understand it, but Prof Wheeler reassured me that if anyone thought they understood quantum physics, they really didn't.

Morgan's Integration lessons were less inspiring. They

were supposed to be preparing us for life after ARES; giving us the skills we needed to slip back into society if we "weren't cut out to join one of the non-Shifting units". But really they were like going to see the worst careers adviser ever. He ran aptitude tests on us all and not one of us seemed to have "the right stuff". Whatever the right stuff was supposed to be. According to the test, Jake was destined to become a social worker. And I could look forward to a bright future as an accountant. CP had stormed out when she'd been told she make a great secretary.

When he wasn't making us all feel like morons, he'd go on about all the important people he'd met, dropping ridiculous hints about how he'd helped them out by Shifting. None of us believed his stories. But given no one in the outside world was supposed to know about Shifting, there was no way we could bring him up on it. Instead, we played along and took to running a bet before each class on the amount of times he would say "My father".

I was even getting used to being a commuter. Unlike the other kids who lived in a dorm at ARES, it had been decided that I could stay with my parents, because I was so much older than the rest of them.

So I would come home, tired, battered and bruised at the end of the day, with another fabricated story about what I'd learnt, and Mum would fuss over me. She'd cook me dinner and let me watch whatever I wanted to on TV. She'd never been the most maternal mother, but she seemed to be making up for it by looking after her "working son". Even Dad started showing more interest. He'd gone so far as bragging about me being chosen for an elite programme.

"University degrees are worthless these days," I'd overheard him saying to a colleague whose son had just got into Oxford. "Ever since every tinpot poly could call itself a university. No, my son has a proper chance now. A guaranteed job at the end of it. And we don't have to pay a penny."

Katie hadn't changed. She still called me a loser and made fun of me having to work through the summer holiday. But I got the sense she missed me a little.

I didn't even mind the early starts. I took a weird pleasure cramming myself onto the Tube and watching my fellow commuters. Lawyers, accountants, bankers, all plugged into their phones, creating bubbles to protect themselves from the insanity of travelling fifty feet underground. I wondered about their dreams. Had they grown up wanting to be businessmen? Or did they still secretly dream of being firemen or astronauts? They seemed so ordinary to me now. So dull. Deluding themselves that they were in control of their lives. If only they knew.

I was on my way home one Thursday. The sun lay low in the sky, but it was still bright and I had the music on my iPhone turned up loud. I was walking in time with my private soundtrack and I felt good.

A bleeping interrupted my music and I pulled out my phone. Hugo was calling.

"Hugo!"

"Scottster! The man of mystery himself. I have been trying to get hold of you for weeks!"

He was right. I'd been pretty slack at returning his texts and calls as I was so wrapped up in life at ARES.

"I'm sorry, man. Things have been pretty frantic."

"Why weren't you back at St Francis's this week? Did you fail everything? Is that why you're ashamed to show your face?"

My GCSEs. I'd almost been surprised when my results had arrived in the post a couple of weeks back, as I'd totally forgotten about them. It wasn't like they really mattered to me any more. "No, I passed everything."

"Then what the hell, Scott?"

"Well the programme I told you about, it's all going really well and so this is it. No more school for me."

"You lucky sod. How can I get on it?"

"Er, I think it's fully subscribed now."

"Oh, don't give me that. You just don't want me cramping your style, you dog you. Tell me, are there girls there? Are they hot?"

I thought about Aubrey. I'd only seen glimpses of her in the past few weeks, looking busy and important. I guess she'd been right. Fresh Meat and officers didn't mix. "There are a few. But I'm too busy to think about that kind of stuff."

"Oh, Scott, when will you learn? A man is never too busy for any of that kind of stuff. Look, there's a back-to-school party at Seb's this weekend. You have to come.

No, I won't accept any of your lame excuses, I want to hear all about the programme."

"Sure. Why not?"

"You promise?"

"I promise."

I slipped my phone back in my pocket and crossed the road.

As I reached the steps leading down to the Tube I saw a glint of copper light: a penny lying on the pavement. Now, I wouldn't say I'm superstitious but I do like the old "See a penny pick it up" thing. There's something nice about picking up a coin and slipping it into your pocket, as if you've bought yourself a day's protection. But as I thought about slowing down to pick it up, I was struck by the idea that I was beyond such silly notions now. I didn't need a penny to protect me. I had the power to protect myself. I walked on, an extra spring in my step.

I dodged the crowds, made it through the gates without breaking my stride and glided down the elevator. A pretty girl was coming up on the other side and we smiled at each other. She had blonde hair and a tiny button nose that reminded me of Aubrey. I was so busy watching the girl that I stumbled a bit as the escalator spat me out onto the tiled floor. A musician was playing an accordion so loudly that his wheezing chords penetrated my wall of music. I turned the volume up.

The Tube was waiting as I turned the corner on to the platform and I dived through the closing doors of the last carriage, just in time. I grinned, feeling like Indiana

Jones. The Tube stopped almost as soon as it started, and sat in the dark tunnel. People started to look up at the speakers, so I turned my music off to hear what the driver was saying.

"I apologise for this folks, but there's another Tube in front of us that doesn't seem to know where the accelerator is. I'm sure those of you who use this line regularly are used to all of this. So just sit tight and we'll be moving shortly. In the meantime, why not make friends with the person sat next to you?" The assembled commuters chuckled to themselves, careful not to be too amused. None of us would break the rule of no speaking. But it was nice that the driver had a sense of humour.

One man didn't seem amused at all. He was sitting on one of the fold-down seats near the door, hugging a briefcase. He had a badly fitting toupee, which slid further down his forehead as sweat started dripping off him. He began rocking back and forth in his seat and muttering to himself. The girl next to him shuffled away, trying to get as far away as possible without actually giving up her seat. His muttering became louder.

"I'm in control here. I'm in control here."

I guessed it was some self-help mantra he'd learned to deal with panic attacks. I was almost feeling sorry for the guy, and then he stood up. He was broad and had the look of a once-muscular man who'd let himself go.

"I'm in control here," he shouted at the passengers. "Look at you. You're like sheep. Baa Baa. Sheepy people." Everyone became very interested in their shoes or the copy of *Metro* they'd been sitting on. No one wanted to look at the mad man.

His eyes bulged as he stared down the carriage and his face started to spasm. "You should all bow to me, I am your master. You miserable worms. Do you know what I have done, so that you can sit here, clutching your papers?"

"Shut up," somebody from behind me said.

The man whipped his head around and stared right at me. He opened his mouth to speak and then stopped. His eyes glazed and a thin trickle of blood started running out of his right nostril. He coughed and his mouth was red with blood. He looked at me, all the madness gone from his eyes, and mouthed one word. "Help."

Then his head exploded.

It was like a flower appeared above his right eye, a bright red carnation made from flesh. He staggered on his feet slightly and caught hold of one of the yellow bars overhead, leaving behind a red handprint. Blood was pouring down his face and the people on the carriage started screaming and running away from him. I stepped forward, knowing I could do nothing for him. His eyes were cold and his limbs heavy in my arms. He was dead.

I let him fall to the ground and looked around at the panicking crowd. "Someone pull the emergency cord," I shouted.

No one was listening to me, so I got to my feet and pushed a dumb-looking businessman away from the emergency alarm. I punched the glass, surprised at how easily it broke, and pressed the button.

I felt the explosion before I heard it. It threw me off my feet and sent me hurtling backwards. My arms and legs flailed, as if I was trying to swim in the air, or grab hold of something to stop myself from falling. There were bodies flying everywhere and I remember seeing the dumb businessman looking surprised as he smashed through the window. I had a sense of heat. Incredible heat. Flames engulfed me and I felt them tearing at my clothes and my skin. I hit a pole with a bone-shattering thud, the back of my skull crunching against the yellow paint. Everything went white and I felt a cold liquid dribbling down my cheeks.

I had an image of a single penny lying on a grey pavement. In my mind I reached out to the penny, my fingertips inches away from it.

The insides of my stomach flipped and I was falling backward. I hit the tiled floor of the platform. All the air was smashed out of my lungs and I heard a sharp ringing in my ears. Shattered glass rained down around me, biting at my skin. I managed to look up and saw a fireball in the tunnel up ahead and the crumpled remains of a Tube train. Anyone who had been on it would have been a goner.

I felt something sharp cutting into my hand. I unclenched my fist and saw a single penny lying in my palm. And then blackness.

CHAPTER SEVENTEEN

I woke up blinking at strip lights overhead. Dull pain radiated through my body, mostly in my head. I saw people moving around in the corner of my eye. I tried to turn my head to follow but it wouldn't move.

"Excuse me?" I said, tentatively, never one to want to make a fuss. But not being able to move seemed pretty damn fuss-worthy.

A fuzzy shape came into view and slowly sharpened into the face of a smiling nurse. She mouthed words.

"I can't hear you," I said and realised I couldn't even hear myself.

I guess I must have been shouting as she put her finger to her lips and mimed turning a volume knob down.

My ears were still ringing – a constant screeching noise that was boring into my head. "Why can't I move?" I said, hoping it was quieter.

The nurse patted my shoulder and mouthed a word at me. "Explosion."

She took my hand and led it up to my neck. My fingers

met with a foam ring of material around my neck. The nurse smiled again. "The doctors say you'll be fine." She held out a curled thumb and first finger; the universal symbol for OK.

She reached behind my head and fiddled with a mass of tubes. I felt a floating sensation starting in my toes and flowing up my legs. The nurse's face started to wobble and I was asleep.

"You have a visitor," the nurse said.

I'd been in the hospital for four days. My hearing had returned, the neck brace was off and I was bored out of my skull. The careful administrations of Nurse Myers weren't enough to distract me from the tedium of being stuck in a bed all day.

I hadn't had any visitors yet. I'd not been allowed to tell my parents about the injury and they'd been fed some story about me being on a placement in Leeds. Why Leeds I have no idea. I wasn't too happy about it. When you're lying in bed, with your head half crushed and your ribs aching, a boy really needs his mother. But given how Mum had reacted when I fell off my bike and needed the stitches – which was to say, she freaked – if she found out about me being blown up it would probably mean the end of my career at ARES. Whatever their reasons, it meant I was now bored out of my skull. So the thought of a visitor was quite exciting.

Abbott appeared from behind the white curtain surrounding my bed. "How are you doing, Scott?" He sounded concerned, but also as if he was trying to hold back a lot of anger.

"I'm good, thanks, Mr Abbott. Getting a bit bored if I'm honest. And no one will tell me what happened."

He stepped closer to the bed and checked we were alone. "It was a suicide bomber."

I was stunned. I'd been a victim of a genuine terrorist attack. "I... How do you know?"

"These are the pictures from the CCTV camera on the Tube." Abbott handed me a grainy picture of a man, dressed in a suit, hugging a briefcase. It was the same man I'd seen. "His name was Charles Warner and we believe he has connections with the SLF."

"What makes you think that?" I said.

"This," Abbott said and passed over a second photo. It showed Warner sat at a café next to a young man wearing a leather jacket and mirrored aviator glasses. I gasped as I recognised Zac, the leader of the SLF.

"Ah, so you know Isaac Black?" Abbott said.

"I, er, I met him once."

"Then you will know he is a very dangerous young man. We believe that Black recruited Warner to assist the SLF in this attack. According to reports from his work-place, Warner has been having trouble of late. He left the army a few years ago and did not adjust to civilian life. So perhaps, the SLF used this to their advantage."

I stared at the photo of Warner, at his bad toupee and wide, scared eyes. He didn't look anything like the mem-bers of the SLF I'd seen in the club. Maybe they were somehow forcing him into it. But that didn't explain why he was already dead before the explosion went off.

"What do you think they want?" I asked, not taking my eyes off the picture.

"The SLF believe that Shifting should be unregulated. Uncontrolled. What they singularly fail to grasp is the responsibility that comes with the ability they have been blessed with. Shifters have the ability to craft a better society for everyone. Not just themselves. But then as Shifters are only children, it can be hard for them to realise that."

"Warner can't have been a Shifter. He's too old."

"No. But he used to be one, once. It can be hard for people to adjust to entropy." Abbott rubbed unconsciously at the arm of his jacket, where his Commandant stripes had once been. Then quickly smiled, that kind smile of his. "At least you weren't too badly hurt. I hate to think what would have happened if you'd been on that train."

I decided not to tell him about the penny that was now lying under my pillow – the penny that had caused me to miss the train by a matter of seconds. If I hadn't Shifted my decision about stopping to pick it up I'd be dead. "Did anyone survive?' I asked.

"No one who was on the carriage with the bomber. Seventy-two killed in total."

I felt a pang of guilt. "Is there something, anything, I can do? A Shift I can make?"

"You're not a time traveller, Scott. You can't go back with a message, or return to stop the bomber. You can only change your own choice. And as you had no part in what happened... I'm sorry, but there is nothing you can do."

"Well, I hope the SLF are proud of themselves now," I said.

Abbott sighed. "If only they would come to us and we could sit down and try to understand what they want. Instead they strike without warning and then disappear like–"

"Like cowards," I said.

Abbott smiled, almost proudly, like a teacher whose pupil has grasped a tricky subject quickly. "All terrorists are cowards, Scott. Bullies who hide behind principles to justify the violence."

I'd had my fair share of bullies at school. Whatever this group stood for, I was going to stand against them.

As well as angry, I felt pretty scared. Finding out I was a Shifter had given me a sense of confidence. I thought I was unbeatable. Unstoppable. And then I got blown up. But that's the way life works, right? Just when you think you're in control, just when you think you're the master of your own destiny, fate comes along and reminds you that you are her bitch.

"I had better let you get some rest," he turned to leave. "Oh, I meant to tell you. You've graduated from the freshers. We've been really impressed with you, Scott. So we're recruiting you. You are now one of the Bluecoats."

He reached inside his jacket and pulled out a slim envelope. The letter inside was printed on heavy-duty cream paper and bore the ARES stamp at the top and Abbott's signature at the bottom.

We hereby promote Scott Tyler to the post of Fixer, 1st Class, ARES – Shifting Division.

"A Fixer, first class?"

I must have looked really confused. Because it was the first time I'd heard him laugh. "It's just the first rung as an officer in ARES, on a basic starting wage."

I scanned the letter again and saw the figure that was to be my wage. It wasn't much, but I wouldn't have to buy crappy, vintage T-shirts any more, that was for sure.

"I'll explain everything when you're better. There are some people who want to see you." Abbott stepped aside as the freshers piled through the curtains and jumped up on my bed. Max, Jake, Molly and Ben. Cain appeared behind them. He nodded to Mr Abbott who smiled and walked away.

"They said you'd lost a leg," Jake said, prodding my thigh. "Will you get a cyber one now?"

"Afraid my leg is still very much attached."

"Shame," said Jake.

"When will you be coming back to training?" Max asked.

"He won't be coming back, kids," said Cain. "Mr Tyler here has graduated."

"What?" Jake said. "But he only just started."

"It seems the powers that be have bigger plans for Scott than spending his days being beaten up by us."

The kids laughed.

"Hey, where's CP?" I asked, noticing that she wasn't

there.

The group went silent and looked at their feet. Then Jake spoke up. "She's gone to Australia. Her parents just took her out of the programme and we never even got a chance to say goodbye."

"Her parents? But I didn't think she saw them?"

"Well, it seems like they've finally decided to settle down," Cain said.

"But she was really good," I said.

"It happens." Cain's jaw clenched for a second. "Besides, she'll continue her training down under. She'll be kick-boxing kangaroos in no time, isn't that right?"

The freshers tried to laugh, but it was obvious they missed their friend. Especially Jake.

"Right, come on you lot. You can see he hasn't been hurt. Just the odd scar and that adds character," Cain said rubbing at his face. "The girls dig it," he added, winking. "Isn't that right, Ms Jones?"

I hadn't seen Aubrey standing behind them. It was the first time I'd seen her close up in weeks. She'd changed her hair. It was even shorter now, with a shaggy fringe covering her eyes. They twinkled out at me from behind the straw-coloured locks. My instinct was to flash her a smile, but I resisted it. I was angry with her. She'd been the one who'd thrown me off like an old kebab. I wanted to make this as uncomfortable as possible for her. Only problem was, I was so happy to see her. My treacherous heart leaped at the waft of vanilla.

"Hey," Aubrey said.

"Hey," I said with less enthusiasm than I felt.

"OK, come on then," Cain said. "Back to training. The poles are waiting." The group groaned and then piled out. Jake stopped to mime frenzied kissing from behind Aubrey's back. I raised my middle finger at him and he skipped off, giggling.

Aubrey looked around the cubicle, her eyes settling on the book on my bedside table. She picked it up. "Is it good?" she asked, turning the book over and looking at the back cover.

"Not really," I said. "It was all the nurse could find."

"When do you get to go home?"

"Tomorrow I think."

"Ah, OK. If it was any longer I could, you know, bring you some stuff."

I'd never wanted to have a broken leg so much in my life. Or something that would keep me stuck in this bed just a little longer.

"Well, maybe I should ask the SLF to have another go."

"So it really was them?"

"Abbott thinks so."

"I never thought that they were capable of something like this. I should have called the Regulators that night in the club and then none of this would have happened." The book started to shake in her hands.

"It's not your fault," I said.

She returned the book to the table. "I'm really glad, you know, glad you're OK. And I know I was a bit of a dick before. It's just that…" Her voice trailed off.

"No, it was my fault. About your Mum, I swear you told me Aubrey. Only not in this reality."

"I know. Well, I mean I don't actually know. But I realised the only way you could have found out about it is if I'd told you. It's so just weird, Scott. You being able to hold on to old realities as long as you can. I've never met a Shifter who could do that. I've heard of them, but... Anyway, I hear you're doing well at training."

"I guess. It's the first time I've felt as if I was actually good at something."

"Like getting blown up you mean?"

"Yeah, seems I'm pretty good at that."

We laughed and she perched on the side of my bed.

"You were lucky," she said.

"Not really."

"What do you mean?" she asked.

I waved her closer. "I Shifted. Otherwise I wouldn't be here. I'd be a big smoky, gooey mess on the train lines."

Her eyebrows gathered, doing that cute thing to her nose. "Hmm, no wonder they're fast-tracking you."

"You heard then?"

"The guys were talking. A Fixer, hey? Who'd have thought it?"

"I don't even know what a Fixer is."

"They're supposed to be able to stop other Shifters from changing reality. They're the powerful ones."

"Sounds like there's been a massive mistake. I still don't know what I'm doing!"

She laughed. "I guess you'll need someone to show

you the ropes then."

"I guess. But I'll probably be teamed up with someone really annoying."

"Someone you want to strangle after about ten minutes of being with them."

"Someone totally headstrong and impossible, most likely."

She smiled and brushed her fringe out of her eye. "Best of luck with that." She picked at a thread in the duvet cover.

My phone buzzed on the sideboard breaking the moment. I glanced angrily at the screen.

> **YOU, SCOTT TYLER, SUCK. PARTY WAS AWESOME. I GOT OFF WITH A GIRL. BUT YOU WILL NEVER KNOW THE DETAILS. SO THERE. H.**

The fact Hugo was punctuating correctly was a sign of just how annoyed he must be. I turned the phone off. I could deal with him later.

"I'd better go," Aubrey said standing up. "You need your sleep because right now, you look like shit."

"Gee thanks," I said.

"Anytime."

She stood to go. "Aubrey?" I said. She turned. "It's good to see you."

"I get the feeling we're going to be seeing a lot of each other."

CHAPTER EIGHTEEN

———

"Morning, boss," I said, as I approached Aubrey's desk. I placed a cardboard cup of coffee in front of her.

"What's this?" she said, staring at it.

"A coffee."

She looked up at me and laughed. "We're not in an American cop drama, you know?"

"I know, I just thought…"

"It's sweet, thanks. And I need it today." She sipped at the coffee. "How did you know I take two sugars?"

"Lucky guess." I decided not to tell her I'd asked around and instead prodded the file she was reading. "What's that?"

"Today's assignment."

She slid the folder over to me. I opened it hopefully. It was only my second week in the Shifting division and I was hoping to get stuck into something exciting. I'd been given my licence, the sharp blue jacket – which earned the Shifter division its nickname – and pretty much told to get on with it. Although I still didn't have much of a clue of what "it" was. I glanced around the floor. About twenty other kids aged from twelve to sixteen lolled around their desks, chatting, laughing, and every now and then checking their computers. It was like looking at a really cool office populated with children.

I'd been told that not every Shifter stayed on with ARES after graduating training. Some just went off to live normal lives, although they had to have all their Shifts approved by ARES, which was, according to Aubrey, "a right pain in the arse". But most stayed on and then joined the Regulators as soon as entropy set in. It was all so new to me I didn't have a clue what I was going to do next.

I looked back to the file at a grainy image of a young boy on a swing. He was holding two fingers up to the camera and had his tongue sticking out. "He looks a charmer. Is he a Shifter?"

"Perhaps. The signs are there."

I read the file of the kid called Tommy Brookes. Six years old and he'd already been to three schools because of his "unmanageable behaviour". The medical report diagnosed him with ADHD, which was one of the classic signs. Tommy was now at a special needs school in South London.

"Road trip?" I said.

"Nope. The kid's being dragged in to us by his Mum. She's been told we're some fancy military medical facility that can help manage his condition. Which I guess is true. He'll be here at 10am."

"Oh, right." I shuffled in my seat. "And what exactly

do I do?"

"You," Aubrey said standing up and hitting me on the chest with a pad of paper, "take notes."

The room was almost identical to the one I had been interrogated in. Same buzzing lights and large mirror. Now that I was on the other side of the experience I had a satisfying sense of control and confidence. I swaggered into the room, dragged out the seat and sat down. Aubrey casually smacked me on the head with her files as she took her seat next to me. She leant in and whispered, "Take it easy, he's only six."

I looked at Tommy Brookes. He was a tiny little thing, half-hidden by the desk, wearing a black sweatshirt and faded jeans. He was banging his heels against the legs of his chair, over and over. His mother was standing, pressed into the corner, wringing her hands around an old hankie.

"You're just children," she said. "Where's the charming young man, Mr Morgan?"

"Commandant Morgan is busy," said Aubrey. "So he sent us to have a chat with Tommy about what it's like here."

"Oh, right. Like teacher's aides?" Mrs Brookes asked.

"Precisely nothing like that," Aubrey said brightly. The woman registered Aubrey's tone, but not her words, and nodded. Aubrey turned to the kid. "Hey there, Tommy," she said. Tommy let his jaw hang open and stared at her.

"Tommy, say hello to the nice girl," Mrs Brookes said.

"Shut up. Shut up!" Tommy shouted at his mum. She squeaked in response and held her hankie to her face.

"Oh, Tommy doesn't have to say hello," Aubrey said. "In fact, Tommy doesn't have to do anything he doesn't want to. And isn't that exactly the problem?"

Aubrey lowered her head so her eyes were level with Tommy's. His only reaction was that the banging of his heels got louder. I really didn't like the boy. I scribbled down "Annoying brat" on my notepad.

Aubrey clapped her hands together. "Right, do you fancy playing a little game, Tommy?"

There were three white plastic cups on the table; one still had some water left in it, and another had Mrs Brookes' red lipstick on the side. Aubrey emptied the first and wiped the lipstick off the second, then turned all three upside down on the table. She reached over and tore out the first page in my notebook, giving me a meaningful glance after reading my note, and scrunched the paper into a small ball. She put the ball under the first cup.

"Have you seen this game before?" she asked Tommy. "You have to watch the cups and then guess where the ball is. OK?"

He shut his mouth and shuffled forward on his chair a little, which I guess meant he was interested. Aubrey moved the three cups around and around in little figures of eight. Then she stopped and waited.

Tommy reached out a stubby finger and tapped the middle cup. It's where I thought the ball was too. Only when Aubrey lifted the cup, the ball wasn't there. She lifted up the cup on the left, revealing the crumpled paper. She must have Shifted, only I hadn't registered it.

"Try again," she said, replacing the cup.

Again she moved the cups around. Tommy's dark eyes watched them intently. When Aubrey stopped, he reached out his hand and tapped the end cup. Aubrey picked it up. Empty.

They played the game twice more and each time Tommy failed to spot the ball. By the last attempt he was getting angry. The cup he'd chosen came up empty again and he grabbed it and threw it at the wall. "Dumb game. You're dumb, you're all dumb."

"Thank you, Mrs Brookes. I think we're done here."

"Wait. What? I mean you haven't had your chat. You are going to take him, aren't you?" She stood behind her son's chair.

"I'm afraid not," Aubrey said.

The woman went stiff and started shaking. Her knuckles turned white as they gripped the back of her son's chair. She raised her hand and slapped Tommy around the back of the head. Aubrey flinched.

"What did I tell you about behaving?" the woman roared. "You've embarrassed me in front of these people!" She dragged a bawling Tommy off his chair and pushed him out the door. Her shouting and his wailing echoed down the corridor.

"So, he's not a Shifter then?" I asked, ready to scribble a note on my pad.

"Precisely what I was about to ask." A voice came from

a speaker in the room. The mirror rippled and turned to glass, revealing Morgan. He'd been watching everything.

Aubrey raised an eyebrow. I knew that look. That was her "you total idiot" look. I'd been on the receiving end of it a fair few times.

"Well, he didn't even try and change his choices when picking the cup."

"And you were Shifting where you put the ball, right?" I asked.

"Nope. I just palmed the ball and popped it under the cup when picking it up." She demonstrated how she'd hidden the ball under her thumb. "Why bother Shifting when you can just use magic!" She waved her hands and the crumpled paper had vanished. She reached forward and seemed to produce it from my ear. Then she threw it at my forehead.

"So is he a Shifter or not?' Morgan said, sounding impatient.

"Definitely not. He's just a mundane," she said.

I wrote "Not Shifter" on my pad and circled it.

"Thank you for your assistance, Ms Jones, Mr Tyler." I looked up. I hadn't done a thing. "I have another assignment for you if you wouldn't mind waiting."

The glass flicked back to mirror and Aubrey rolled her eyes. "Joy," she said, quietly.

Morgan joined us in the room and handed a file over to Aubrey. She opened it and read the name off the top.

"Mr Heritage?" she said, her forehead wrinkling. I guessed she knew him.

"Yes," Morgan said, rocking back and forth on his

feet. "Mr Abbott tells me he's been having a few diffi-
culties and asked me to check on him."

"So why don't you check on him then?" Aubrey
asked, handing the file back to Morgan. He pushed it
back at her with a single finger.

"Because I'm delegating to you, Ms Jones. I think I've
made everything clear in the notes. I'd like the report on
my desk by the end of the day." He softened slightly
under Aubrey's glare. "If you please," he added. He
turned to go then stopped. "Oh, I forgot to say, congrat-
ulations on making Bluecoat Mr Tyler." He spun around
and mimed shooting me with a gun while his face
spasmed in a wink. "I knew when I first met you that
you would do well. And you couldn't have a better part-
ner than Aubrey here." He patted her on her arm.
Aubrey looked down at his hand as if it were something
unpleasant crawling on her jacked. He snatched it away,
coughed, and shuffled out.

"What an asshat," I said.

Aubrey didn't answer. She was examining the file.

"So this Henry Heritage,' I said reading his name upside down. "Is he some master criminal or something?"

"He's one of our top analysts," Aubrey said. "He's
worked for ARES for years. He was a member of the
Regulators until he left to join the army's Intelligence
Corp after getting shot at or something. And then he
came back to ARES after leaving the army. He spe-
cialises in spotting trends in the market. Predicting
financial climates and all that stuff."

I looked at the headshot photo clipped to the file. The man had bright ginger hair, a flat nose that looked as if it had been broken at least once, a small scar on his temple and a thick muscular neck. "So what are we supposed to do with him?"

Aubrey was engrossed in the file. "Weird," she said after a moment.

"What is?"

"He's been making claims that he can Shift," she said.

"And can he?" I said, not looking up from the round, bland face.

"Of course not. He's old. But I guess that's why Abbott's sending me."

"Because you can sense if someone can Shift?"

"Exactly. I'm a Spotter. It's what we do." She pulled the headshot photo away and revealed a second picture. The set up was eerily similar to the photo Abbott had shown me a few days ago. Heritage, sat at a café, talking to a young man in a leather jacket.

"Zac!" I said.

"Yep," Aubrey agreed.

I grabbed the files off her and started to read them properly. "What would the SLF want with a financial analyst?"

"I guess that's one of the questions we ask him."

"Hang on," I said, reading further down. "It says here he was screaming about being in control." 'I'm the one in control, you're all my puppets,'" I read. "That's odd."

"Well, yeah. He's clearly a few pencils short of a case."

"Not that." I looked suspiciously at the two-way mirror. Then leaned in closer to Aubrey. "The guy on the Tube. The one they say was the bomber. He started freaking out like that too and then his head blew up."

"It what?" Aubrey said, loudly.

I hushed her. "About a minute before the big bomb went off, this guy flipped out and then... pop!" I mimed the top of my head exploding.

"Why didn't you tell anyone?"

"I don't know. It was all kind of hazy. And I didn't want anyone to know about me Shifting without a licence. Someone told me that could get me in serious trouble."

"Shifting to save your life is allowed, you idiot." She punched me absentmindedly, pulling the files out of my hands.

"Oh. I probably should tell Abbott then."

Aubrey hesitated. "Let's go and see Heritage first."

CHAPTER NINETEEN

We left ARES HQ and stepped onto the street, instantly having to dodge a guy cycling a BMX on the pavement. Aubrey waved down a passing black cab and we crawled in.

"Shire Road, Maida Vale," she said, giving Heritage's address. The cabby grunted and pulled away. I sat on one of the fold down seats, while Aubrey sat in the middle of the back row.

"So, this is cool. Us off on fieldwork. It's like being spies," I said, a little too enthusiastically.

"Fieldwork blows," said Aubrey looking out of the window.

"Well, it's better than training. So far no one's shouted at me or tried to knock me out."

She smiled. "It's early yet."

I laughed. "Actually I think I'll miss the kids. And Cain. And CP, now she's off in Australia."

"Australia?" Aubrey said, her eyebrows knitting in concern. "One of the freshers has gone 'Down Under'?"

She put bunny ears around the words "down" and "under".

"Yeah, why?"

"It's just… I'm really sorry, Scott, but that means she's dead."

"What? No. They said her parents had taken her out of school and she'd emigrated."

"It's sort of code for when a kid dies. I'm sorry, but it happens sometimes. Sometimes the brain just can't take the power."

I stared out the window at the drizzling rain. I felt empty and numb. I didn't quite believe it, I didn't want to. "Cain said she would be boxing kangaroos," I said, sadness catching at my throat.

"He said you might just be the best he's ever trained, did you know that? Cain I mean. I probably shouldn't have told you, you'll get all cocky now."

"I won't. I promise," I lied, and I'm ashamed to admit it but it made me feel a little bit better. I tugged at my new jacket and stroked the single gold stripe on the arm. The collar was digging into my chin and the little metal ARES scratched at my neck, but I already loved it. I was a Bluecoat now. A Fixer. There were only two other Fixers at ARES. Morgan was one and I'd not had a chance to meet the other one yet as she was on assignment somewhere in Africa.

I reached inside my jacket and pulled out a small black wallet. I flipped it open. It held a licence that declared me, Scott Tyler, to be a Shifter First Class. I hadn't been able to stop grinning when they took the photo, so my picture on the licence made me look like a complete idiot. As usual. Opposite my name and photo, ARES' motto was stamped into the leather: *Ad verum via*. Towards the true way.

"I guess it doesn't always have to turn out…" Aubrey paused.

"Badly?" I finished, slipping the wallet back into my jacket pocket.

She gave the tiniest of nods. As she gazed out of the window I snuck a chance to really look at her face. It was small and heart-shaped and she had tiny, almost translucent ears that merged into a soft jaw. It was the face of a young girl, younger even than her fifteen years. It was her eyes that threw you. They looked as if they'd seen too much.

"Aubrey," I said, my voice cracking and dry. "If you hate ARES so much, why don't you leave? You can, can't you, after finishing training and getting your licence? That's what Jake told me."

She used the heel of her hand to wipe away some of the steam on the window. It was fogging up and it was hard to see where we were going.

"I…" she started. "It's all I know."

The cab jerked to a halt. "I can't go any further than this, love. They've dug up all the roads," the cabbie barked through the intercom.

Aubrey snapped out of her daze. "No problem," she said. "We can walk from here."

She passed him some notes and waited while he performed the usual cabbie slow hunt for loose change. It was raining heavily when we emerged from the cab. I squinted and wrapped my jacket around me tighter, but it didn't seem to bother Aubrey one bit. She turned her face to the sky and let the drops fall on her face.

"Is it far?" I asked, not so keen to be drenched.

"No, just down there," she said pointing down a tree-lined road filled with large, posh houses. "But do we have to rush? It's so good to be away from that building."

I shoved my increasingly cold hands into my pockets and shrugged, like, sure I didn't mind getting cold and wet, we could just stay out here all day. She smiled and linked her arm through mine. "Come on then."

Walking arm in arm with Aubrey was kind of awkward and I had to change my pace to match her small strides. But it also felt really good. Did this mean that she liked me? I mean, I knew she liked me, but did she *like* me like me? I was so busy thinking about keeping my bicep flexed under her curled hand that I didn't see the puddle. My trainer was soaked as I pulled it out. Aubrey laughed, slid her arm away and ran off through the rain.

I looked down at my feet and thought about Shifting. I had considered wearing my boots this morning.

"What are you waiting for?" Aubrey shouted. "We're here." I squelched over and joined her in front of number 47. "OK, here's how we're going to play it. I ask all the questions and you keep your mouth shut."

"Fine by me," I said. "I have no idea what to say to a nutter."

Aubrey reached up and banged the knocker. The door swung back on its own. We looked at each other.

"Mr Heritage?" Aubrey called as she pushed the door open and stepped in. No reply.

We walked down the hallway, past neat little picture frames holding photos of stern-looking men and women. I wondered if they were relatives of his.

"Mr Heritage?" Aubrey tried again. Still nothing.

We peered into the living room on the left. It was empty apart from a small sofa, draped with a crocheted head cover, a small TV set and a nest of coffee tables. I heard a mewing from the other end of the house. Aubrey and I pushed on further, peering into the rooms as we passed. I was starting to get a horrible feeling about this.

I tripped on a rucked rug and banged into a bookshelf in the seemingly never-ending hall. Aubrey threw me a look of annoyance.

A white cat came hurtling out of nowhere and launched itself at Aubrey's head. It tangled its claws in her blonde mop and tried to scratch at her face. I was too shocked to do anything, and just stood there, my mouth wide open. Aubrey managed to pull the hissing beast off her head and threw it away. It span in mid-air and landed on its feet, hissed once more and padded off.

"What the…" I said, my heart thudding.

Aubrey leant against the wall opposite me, taking

deep breaths. Then her face contorted in disgust. "Can you smell that?" she said.

I sniffed at the air and the stench hit me. It smelt like sewage and rotting food. We looked at each other, pretty certain we knew what we were going to find in the kitchen.

Henry Heritage's body was lying splayed across the white tiles of his kitchen floor. His legs and arms were stretched out at weird unnatural angles. Pots and pans lay beside him, as if he'd put up a fight and pulled his kitchen down on top of him. But it hadn't done him any good. He was dead. The fact that he was missing the top of his head was a pretty clear sign of that. There were small tufts of red hair left either side of his ears and then nothing but a bloody mess.

Judging by the smell and the ragged bite marks all over his body, it looked like he'd been dead for a few days. He had an expression of abject terror frozen on his pale face. Whoever said that death was peaceful had never seen a body like this one.

A tabby cat appeared from under the counter and delicately walked across Heritage's chest, causing a hiss of air to escape his decaying lungs. The cat jumped off the body and proceeded to nibble at its owner's brain. Aubrey grabbed a nearby mug and threw it at the cat. It missed and shattered next to the corpse. The cat looked up, completely unfazed, licked its lips and sauntered away.

Which was when I threw up.

CHAPTER TWENTY

ARES' forensic specialist arrived about twenty minutes later. He was a short man, with small, round glasses and a long nose. Aubrey and I were sitting on the doorstep, huddled against each other, as he stepped out of his small van.

"Dr Kepple," he announced flashing a badge at us. "Apologies for the late arrival. There were road works. Where is the deceased?"

"In the kitchen." Aubrey gestured down the hall with a jerk of her thumb.

Kepple stepped over us and strode down the hallway. I twisted around to watch him as he disappeared into the kitchen.

Aubrey was holding a cigarette up in front of her face. She rolled it around in her fingers, as if she was considering it. I'd seen her do it before.

"Why do you do that?" I asked.

She slipped the cigarette between her lips. "Do what?"

"Look at it, as if it's the last smoke you'll ever have?"

"Because that way, when I want to give up smoking, I can not only give up, but make all these tiny Shifts and not have smoked any. Neat huh?"

"Why don't you just Shift and not have bothered with the very first one? Wouldn't that be easier?"

"Well, some I might keep. Like the one I shared with Adam Jackson, for instance."

"Well, I don't think you should be smoking here. It's disrespectful," I snapped, feeling more jealous than angry.

"I think Heritage is beyond caring." She pulled the cigarette out of her mouth and put it back in the packet anyway.

I chewed my lip, feeling helpless and angry at the same time. In the space of a week I'd seen two dead bodies. More than that, I'd see the brains of two dead bodies. The image of the guy on the Tube kept haunting me. I was having dreams each night about him reaching out to me. But I couldn't help because when I looked down at my hands, they had become hooves and I had become a sheep. Warner would then laugh so hard that his head would explode, over and over. After seeing Heritage's mangled body, I wasn't looking forward to going to sleep tonight.

Besides the horror of it all, something else kept nagging at me. "Do you think the SLF did this?" I said.

"I don't know. After that bomb, I wouldn't put anything past them."

"I'm starting to think that Warner, the guy on the Tube, wasn't the bomber at all. I think they killed him too."

"You said he was in his thirties?"

"Forty maybe?"

"Doesn't sound like he was with the SLF to me."

I heard the sound of clanking from the kitchen. "Do you think there's anything we should do to help?"

"We'll only get in his way," Aubrey said, hugging her knees.

"We should probably check though."

Aubrey shrugged and gave me her hand to pull her to her feet.

In the kitchen, Heritage had been stripped of his shirt and shoes and there were dark purple blotches all over his chest. Kepple was bent over the body, prodding the open skull with a wooden stick. The brains were making slurping noises. In his other hand the doctor held a small recording device and was speaking into it.

"The victim has had the cranium removed. However, judging by limited blood loss to the area, this does not appear to be the cause of death. In fact, I believe the procedure was carried out post-mortem. Going by the distinctive purple bruising to the victim's chest, I would conclude that the actual cause of death was crush injuries." He leaned in closer to the gaping skull and lifted a flap of skin away. "There are teeth marks around the brain and part of his brain seems to be missing. I will have to get a cast of the marks, but there appears to be two sets of teeth marks present. One are clearly feline, but… the other may be human in origin."

Human? I thought. Someone has been munching on his brain?

"Have you seen anything like this before?" Aubrey asked.

Kepple looked up and blinked, as if only registering our presence for the first time. "Bluecoats, hmm? I hope you haven't contaminated the crime scene."

"We didn't eat his brain, if that's what you mean," Aubrey snapped, while I looked embarrassed and hoped he wouldn't notice where I'd thrown up.

The man harrumphed and went back to his examination. I stepped forward, trying to get a better look at the body. The initial shock had worn off and now it was like staring at a mannequin. Even the brains looked fake. Kepple was stroking Heritage's face with a cotton bud swab and I noticed a soft shimmer on the dead man's cheeks coming from what looked like a thin layer of dried slime.

"Is that from the cats?" I asked. Kepple grunted and carried on. "I guess not then." I looked at Heritage's hands and they had the same, soft sheen. As if they'd been coated in something gluey. Like saliva.

I shuddered and Aubrey looked up at me, her expression one of concern. I jerked my head to the side and raised my eyebrows. She got the hint and we both backed out of the kitchen silently, not wanting to disturb Kepple. Not that we should have worried. He was clearly a man who loved his work.

"What is it?" Aubrey asked when we were in the safety of the living room, only the cats to overhear us.

"I don't know. Just a thought. Did you see the slime

on his face?" Aubrey nodded. "Well, I bumped into this guy outside your flat, the day after we met. This fat, and I mean fat, guy." I stretched my hands out as far as I could to indicate just how fat I meant.

"What about him?"

"He licked me. Licked my hand. And said something about wanting to eat me up. He also almost crushed me to death. If I hadn't thrown up on him, I don't think I would have escaped."

"What is it with you and throwing up?"

"Hey, I've a delicate stomach. And you'd have been sick too if you'd smelt his stinking breath. It smelt like… well, it smelt like that guy in there. Like rotting flesh."

"You think your fat man did this?"

"Maybe, I don't know. It's the stuff with the eating of the brain. And the licking." I shuddered again.

"You should tell him."

"Tell whom what?" Kepple appeared in the doorway behind us, and we both jumped.

"Er, it's just that I was, threatened I suppose, well, he didn't actually threaten me verbally, but I felt threatened–"

"What Scott is trying to say is that he thinks he may have encountered Mr Heritage's killer."

Kepple's eyebrow raised a fraction. "Can you describe him?"

"He was pretty unforgettable."

"Then you should give your report to the Regulators when they arrive. I am done here. An ambulance will be arriving shortly to bring the body to the morgue. Good day." Without as much as a backward glance he left.

"Do you think he's going to do anything about the fat man?"

"Well, it's not really his job to go chasing after killers," Aubrey said.

I wandered back into the kitchen. Kepple had placed a white sheet over the body giving the man some kind of dignity. The cats were perched on the surfaces, looking annoyed at us for taking their snack away. I felt Aubrey lean her head against my back.

"Can they, you know, stop this? Can someone Shift so he doesn't have to die?"

"I don't know. They'll look at all the evidence. But we can't turn back time. We can only undo our own decisions. If someone was thinking of visiting Mr Heritage a few days ago, but changed their mind, then maybe. But it's not like you can go back with a warning or anything. As soon as you go back, the memory starts to fade."

"Not always though," I said, uncertain. I'd been worrying about why I was able to remember my old realities, when no one else seemed to be able to. "Sometimes it's like when you wake up from a dream and you can just hold on to it, right?" I really hoped that I wasn't alone in this.

Aubrey shrugged and shook her head. "I wouldn't know. I don't dream."

I heard the whoop whoop of a siren and a black, unmarked car pulled up outside. We wandered out to meet it.

The guys from the Regulators were efficient enough as they took our statements. They even weren't too condescending when I told them about my experience with the fat man.

"We'll look into it," they said. Before flipping closed their notepads. I assumed they'd do all that DNA stuff and track him down. That's if it was his saliva, and not just cat spittle that was stuck to Heritage's face. The ambulance Kepple had promised arrived shortly after and the body was carried away. Soon we were the only ones left in the house. Us and the cats.

"Who's going to look after the moggies?" I asked.

"Who cares? Evil things."

"Not the biggest cat fan then?" I'd always been rather fond of cats. I had one as a kid called Mr Tuffy that ran away. And I still checked every black cat I saw, just to see if it had a white spot on its nose, like mine had.

"They totally creep me out. It's as if they know," Aubrey said.

"Know what?" I asked.

"About the Shifts. It's as if they can see all the realities at once. And they're judging you for making the wrong choice. That, and they're so bloody smug."

She ran her fingers through her hair and sighed. "Come on. I'll have to write this all up. What did I tell you?"

"Fieldwork blows?"

"Sure does."

CHAPTER TWENTY-ONE

Watching Aubrey type was an exercise in patience. Her two index fingers hovered above the keyboard, making small circling motions, as she tried to hunt out the next letter. She pounded each key as if worried it would run away.

I sighed as she struggled to find the n.

"What?" she said, looking up from her notes.

"I can't believe you can't type."

Aubrey fixed me with one of her finest stares. Then started typing without taking her eyes off me. Words appeared on the screen without hesitation: "*Scott Tyler is a moron.*"

"You *can* type!" I said.

"Shudup,'" Aubrey hushed, and hit the backspace deleting her typing.

"But why pretend?" I asked, keeping my voice low.

"Because if they know I can type forty words a minute I'll end up with some ballache desk job after entropy. If they think I'm a complete luddite then I might be able to join the Regulators. So..." She pounded the *N*. I moaned again.

"You do it then." She pushed away from her desk and waved me into place. With two hefts of my chair I positioned myself in front of the screen. Aubrey had started typing up her report on Heritage's death. All she'd managed so far was to write his name, date of birth, date of death and one line.

> *In the course of my duty, along with First Class Shifter, Scott Tyler, I found Henry Heritage's body in…*

I looked down at her scribbled notes and flexed my hands over the keyboard.

"Is that an *R*?" I asked

She leant over to look. "It's a *K*."

"Your handwriting is terrible."

"Look, if you're going to be a dick about it, I'll do it." She pulled the notebook away and we played tug of war over it for a bit. I won in the end.

After a few minutes, Aubrey spun around on her chair, bored. "Do you want a drink?" she asked jumping out of the seat, leaving it spinning.

I nodded and continued to type. I was just about to hit save on the report when I got that weird, floating feeling I now knew meant a Shift was happening. I saw the words on the screen flicker and oscillate, like someone was switching between two channels on the TV. I focused in on one word, "murder", which kept being replaced by another: "suicide". The two words, the two realities, hung in place for a moment, fighting for dominance. And then the moment was gone. The Shift had taken place.

I looked at the screen and read the report. The report I knew I had written, just moments before, but it wasn't the one I remembered.

In the course of my duty, along with Scott Tyler, Shifter First Class, I found Henry Heritage's body in his kitchen. His wrists were slit and when Doctor Keppel arrived it was declared that he had committed suicide.

The new memory found its place in my mind. Aubrey and I had found Heritage's body splayed on the kitchen floor, a stained kitchen knife lying next to him. But I knew that wasn't how it had happened originally. Someone had made a Shift and I knew it wasn't me. Someone was trying to erase the truth. Erase the old reality. But why a suicide? If they could make a Shift, why let Heritage die at all?

I resisted the new reality and tried to hold on to the thread of the old one. I felt it slipping away from me. Hands shaking, I grabbed Aubrey's notebook and a pen and turned to a clean page. Before the last grain of the reality fell away I scrawled a note.

Heritage was murdered by the fat man.

I underlined it. And then circled it for good measure.

A feeling of paranoia crept over me. I looked around at my fellow Bluecoats who were all engrossed in whatever they were doing. I tore the page out of the notebook, slipped it into my pocket and looked over at Aubrey.

She was in the kitchen in the middle of a conversation with a red-haired girl. They were standing, heads close, and their voices low. It looked like they were sharing some particularly juicy gossip. But whatever the girl was saying was nothing with what I had to tell her.

Aubrey paused in talking, as if she'd forgotten what she was about to say. It was only a brief hesitation. She looked up and away, then shook her head and went back to listening to the girl. I glared at her, trying to catch her eye, willing her to know what I knew. I risked a peek at the note again. The new reality was fighting hard to take hold, and if I didn't keep a tight grip on the old one I knew it would slip away.

I hit save on the report and strode over to Aubrey.

She paused mid-sentence as I approached. "This is Scott," she introduced me to her friend.

I nodded briefly and then grabbed Aubrey by the arm. "Sorry, but there's something I need to, er…" I didn't even bother with an excuse as I pulled Aubrey away. "We need to talk," I whispered.

"Yeah, I guessed that," Aubrey said. "Sara was just about to tell me all about her date with weird-hair guy, so this had better be good."

I pulled her back to her desk and pointed at the screen.

"Well done, you've finished the report," she said.

"Read it."

She sighed and sat down in front of the screen. Her eyes darted across the lines.

"You've spelt *Kepple* wrong."

"And that's the only thing that seems off to you?"

"Well," she hesitated. "I'm not sure. Something seems wrong, doesn't it? A man as neat and tidy as him, slash his wrists like that. Seems a bit weird."

I reached into my pocket and handed her my note. She read it. And read it again. She stood up and pulled me into the corridor, leaving the soft clatter of the office behind.

"Scott, what are you on about? It was a suicide."

"Not five minutes ago it wasn't."

"But we found him three hours ago."

"Didn't you sense it? Sense the Shift?" She looked blankly at me, so I carried on. "I was typing up the report. Your report. About how we found him lying on the kitchen floor with the top of his head missing. That wasn't a suicide. Unless it was the most elaborate one ever. But now, there's this other image where he did kill himself."

"Someone Shifted?" She sounded uncertain and confused as I was.

"Yes!" I said. "Please remember."

"I remember us going in and seeing the blood. And he was lying there. And the cats."

"Yes, the cats! They were licking at his brains."

"And you were sick." She pointed at me, her eyes wide. "Oh god, I can sort of remember."

"Like a dream, right?"

"I wouldn't know."

"Yeah, you don't dream. But look, someone is trying to cover this up."

"The murderer maybe?"

"We should tell Morgan. Actually, forget him, I'm telling Abbott. He's the only one with any sense around here."

"No," Aubrey said sharply. "No," she repeated, softer this time. "We need to think about this more. No one can know that we know." She had that same scared look in her eyes I remembered from the time ARES came to take me away from her flat.

"You don't trust Abbot?"

"It's not that I don't trust him, Scott. It's just…" She sighed. "It's just that he was the one who took me away from home. He told me that everything would be OK and I believed him."

"Oh, but I'm sure he meant–"

"Who is the fat man?" she said, cutting me off and looking down at the note again. It shook in her hands.

I told her about my run in with him outside her flat.

"And you didn't tell me about some Shifter-hunting crazy on the loose?" Aubrey said, thumping me in the arm.

"Ouch! Yeah… sorry. I sort of forgot about him. All I could think about was making sure my sister was alive."

Aubrey shook her head at me. "You're sure it was

him?"

"It was the saliva on Heritage's face. It just made me think that maybe–"

The door opened and we both jumped. A girl walked into the corridor and we looked at her, and she looked at us. We must have looked pretty suspicious as her eyes narrowed.

"Look, I'm very flattered," Aubrey said. "But you're not my type."

The girl smiled and looked at her feet. "Excuse me," she said as she walked past.

I waited till she'd gone. "What did you said that for?"

"It worked, didn't it?"

"You could have said, Yes, you'd love to go out with me. That would have worked just as well."

"Yeah, right," she said, and snorted.

I threw my hands up in despair. Aubrey ignored me and reread the note. "Heritage must have got himself into some serious trouble to have been killed by a Shifter. First there's your guy on the Tube and now this."

"Both were seen with the SLF and both were left with half their heads missing," I said.

"We need to find out what is going on."

I wanted to protest. Wanted to point out that if we went sniffing around this mess then maybe we'd wind up as mysterious suicides as well. But I knew that Aubrey would think me a coward. So I kept quiet.

"Can you remember what the fat man looked like?"

"He was pretty unforgettable," I told her, a vague memory of saying the same thing to Dr Kepple earlier, before the Shift changed our conversation.

"Good," she said and walked away.

"Where are we going?"

"To do a little digging."

"So you believe me?" I caught up with her.

"Of course I believe you, Scott. We're partners. Now stop gaping. We're got a fat man to find."

CHAPTER TWENTY-TWO

"Bigger," I said. "Even bigger."

"You're kidding?" Carl, the E-fit operator, said.

"Think of the fattest guy you've ever seen and double it."

Carl punched a few keys and the photofit face expanded to fill the screen.

"Now make his eyes really, really small. And make his chin even weaker... Him. That's him," I said, pointing at the face.

Carl hit P and the printer nearby started churning out paper.

"Thanks, C," Aubrey said.

Carl looked up at her, all puppy-eyed and pathetic. Seriously, I thought, get a grip. He had no chance. He was a classic IT geek: in his thirties but still dressing like he was sixteen. He wore a brown Tasmanian Devil T-shirt that was at least one size too small for him and he'd pulled his balding hair back into a lanky ponytail.

Aubrey took the page off the printer and handed it to

me. The likeness was impressive. I almost sensed those beady eyes staring at me, and that turned-up nose sniffing me out.

"Shame you can't capture his smell," I said. "That's what I'll never forget."

"You want me to run this through the system and see if anything pops?" Carl said.

"No, I want to keep this off the radar, you know?"

"Okey dokey, Aubrey," Carl said, irritatingly. "But anything else I can do, just let me know."

"Well, there is just one tiny, tiny thing." She held her hand up, thumb and forefinger barely an inch apart, to show just how small a thing she was asking.

"But it's a little…" she said, moving her hand to her chest. "A little upsetting."

"What is it?" Carl asked, taking her free hand in his. I rolled my eyes.

"It's this Heritage case."

"The suicide?"

"Yes. And you know it was me who found him?"

"Oh, Aubrey. That must have been awful."

"You have no idea," she said. She covered her mouth as if holding back her sobs. I caught her eye and shook my head. She had this poor guy eating out of her hand.

"I can still sense him, watching over me."

"Displaced spirits often attach themselves to sensitive souls," Carl said.

"Yes, I think that's it. It's like he wants me to complete

something. Oh, this sounds so mad, doesn't it?"

"Not at all, Aubrey. I've read all about this sort of thing."

"Oh you have? Then you understand. You can understand why I feel the need to finish what he was working on." Carl nodded dumbly as Aubrey continued her brilliant performance. "The only thing is, I don't know what that was."

"Do you want me to get into Heritage's files and find out?"

"Could you, Carl?" She was laying it on thick and he was lapping it up.

"Of course I could, anything to help you Aubrey," he said. "Just give me a day. If there's anything going on around here, I'm the man to find it."

"Oh, you're like my knight in shining armour." She kissed him on his forehead and he blushed all the way to his hairline.

"I'd better go. Can't keep you from all your important work."

Aubrey nodded at me and I followed her out. She waved her fingers back at Carl and then pushed through the door.

"What was that?" I asked as soon as the door to Carl's office shut.

"What was what?" Aubrey asked, all innocent.

"All that 'Oooo, Carl. You're my hero,'" I said in a squeaking voice.

"That is called using my feminine wiles. I've been told

they are very effective." She flashed her eyes at me.

I coughed. "Well, maybe on some men."

We walked through the Regulators division. This was totally different to what I now thought of as my division, a floor above. The Regulators were full of intense older teenagers and young men and women who seemed ever-so-serious about their jobs. Huge TV screens flickered in every corner, broadcasting all the news channels at once. Their floor bustled with energy, like each member had a clear purpose and wasn't going to let anything stand in their way.

I banged into a tall girl, who scowled at me. "Sorry," I mumbled.

"Don't worry about it," said Aubrey. "They're all pissed off up here. It's because most of them are in the last stages of entropy. Apparently it's like PMS, all the time."

"PM what?"

Aubrey looked at me and shook her head. "I thought they educated you out in the real world."

"Oh!" I said, realisation dawning fast. "PMS. No, it's, I thought it was another acronym. Like ARES. Or SLF. Or…" I stopped trying to dig myself out.

We reached the lifts and Aubrey pushed the button.

"Where are we going now?" I complained. I seemed to spend most of my life these days not knowing where I was going.

"I think after your first day of fieldwork you deserve a drink."

I remembered the first time I'd had a drink with

Aubrey. It hadn't gone that well. The ping of the lift doors hid my groan.

It was 6pm and Copenhagen's was mostly empty. A couple of red-eyed gamblers were trying their luck on the roulette wheel. Not that they had a chance of winning in this place. They didn't even register our presence as we headed for the back room.

Shipley was standing behind the bar. He grunted as we approached. "What can I do for ARES today?" he asked Aubrey, ignoring me.

She handed over the printout. "Do you know this guy?"

Shipley squinted as he took the paper from Aubrey's hand. He examined it, looking down his nose then sniffed and seemed to give up.

"That'll be a no then?" I said

Aubrey raised her hand, telling me to wait.

Shipley hadn't finished with the fat guy yet. He pulled out a drawer behind the bar and rooted about. I saw papers, scissors and a black thing that I really hoped wasn't the butt of a gun. Finally he pulled out a tiny pair of brass-rimmed pince-nez and perched them on his bulbous nose. He glared at me, his eyes made larger behind the small lenses, and dared me to make a comment. I didn't. Shipley didn't strike me as the kind of guy who liked being laughed at. He coughed and held the photofit up to the light.

"Oh, yeah. This guy. I've seen him about. Had to kick him out once."

"Why?"

"He kept sniffing people."

Aubrey and I both shuddered.

"And he broke a chair. Yeah, he was really freaking some of the kids and wasn't even playing any of the games, so I asked him to leave. But he just grinned. I couldn't budge him myself not even with five guys helping me. He finally just up and left himself. And I haven't seen him since."

"Do you know his name?" Aubrey asked.

Shipley pulled the glasses off his nose and looked up, thinking. Finally he clicked his fingers. "Benjo. I remember because I thought it sounded like a dog."

"Benjo what?" I asked.

He handed the paper back to Aubrey. "No idea. Not many of my customers bother with surnames here. Or names at all, for that matter."

Aubrey folded the picture up and slipped it inside her jacket, looking disappointed. A first name wasn't much to go on.

"Why don't we just go to Abbott with this? It would be so much easier," I said. Not to mention the fact that we wouldn't have to be interrogating scary casino owners.

"No," she said sharply. "We've only just started."

"If you wanted to know where to find this man," Shipley said, "you could ask Rosalie."

"Rosalie? Don't tell me, she's a hooker with a heart of gold right?" This was getting more like a bad detective movie by the second.

"She's a hostess," Shipley snapped. "And as sound as they come."

"You think she'll know this Benjo guy?" Aubrey said.

"Maybe. I remember one night she was talking about a job she'd just walked out on. She ordered a double gin to try and block it out. But said that she didn't think there was enough drink in the world to wash away his stink."

"That's definitely him," I said.

"And where could we find this Rosalie?"

"I'm right here, darling," said a voice from behind us.

She was a couple of years older than me, with golden brown skin, dark, wavy hair, gathered up into a loose bun, and large chocolate eyes that looked familiar, although I couldn't place from where. She wore a tight pencil skirt and heels that were even higher than my mum would wear, but which Rosalie carried off without a hint of my mum's wobble. The words High Class came to mind. She smiled.

"You're the croupier?"

"And would you like to play?" she said, her voice dripping with suggestion.

"Can we have a word?" Aubrey asked, nodding towards one of the booths.

We took our seats and Shipley brought us over some drinks; Aubrey had ordered a beer, Rosalie sipped on a martini and I'd stuck with a Coke.

"So, how can I help you?" Rosalie said, sucking on an olive.

"We're looking for this guy," Aubrey said handing over the photo.

Rosalie visibly shuddered and swallowed hard, like she was trying to stop herself being sick. She quickly recovered her poise. "Mr Greene. I had hoped I would never see him again. What do you want to know?"

"You know him then?" I said, stating the obvious as usual.

"I wouldn't say I know him. We had a business arrangement. One which I... I had to renege on." Her voice was like maple syrup: sweet, dark and smoky. "Why are you looking for him?"

"Just after some information, is all."

"Well, little ones, let me give you some advice. I would not go after Mr Greene without some back-up. I only got out of our arrangement thanks to the help of a little friend."

"What friend?" Aubrey asked.

Rosalie raised her knee above the table and, with a hiss of material, she slowly hitched her skirt up to reveal the top of a stocking. Rather than a garter belt holding the stocking in place there was a thin leather holster. And nestled in that was a small pistol. She tucked her leg back under the table and brushed her skirt back into place.

"But you're a Shifter," I managed to say when I got my voice back. "I thought that guns were kinda redundant."

"Not always, sweetie. Shifting, as I am sure you know, is about finding the little point of pressure that leads to the best possible reality. And sometimes my Jennings .22 is just the pressure a girl needs." She shrugged an elegant shoulder. "Besides, why waste energy Shifting when you can just pull a trigger?"

"So you shot Benjo?" Aubrey asked.

Rosalie sipped at her Martini and licked her lips. "I'm afraid to say I did. Not that it had much of an effect. That tiny bullet of mine might still be lodged in his flesh, for all I know. But it helped me make a point."

A silence settled over the three of us as we examined our drinks. Were we seriously trying to find someone who didn't even notice when he was shot?

"Where can we find him?" Aubrey asked.

"Are you sure you want to?"

"Not really," I said.

Aubrey threw me a look. "Yes, we want to find him."

Rosalie sighed and looked down at the photo lying in the middle of the table. She dragged it towards her with a perfectly manicured finger and turned the photo over. Then she reached into her small black handbag and pulled out a bright pink lipstick, scribbled something on the page, and slid the paper back. She twisted the lipstick back into the holder and put the lid back on.

"But don't forget," she said returning the lipstick to her bag. "Bring back-up."

Aubrey nodded and finished her drink. "Thanks for your help," she said and slid out of the booth.

I hesitated for a moment, watching Rosalie. She tilted her head and looked at me, an amused smiled playing about her lips.

"Why?" I said.

She looked surprised. "Why what, darling?"

"Why do you do…" I hesitated. "What you do?'

"Ah, you mean why, when I can undo every decision, would I moonlight as an escort?"

I flushed and nodded.

She drew me in with a bent finger and whispered. "Would it help if I told you I never actually sleep with any of my clients? There are other ways to show them a good time." She winked.

I coughed, my throat suddenly very dry.

Rosalie laughed, a surprisingly girly laugh. "Although for the right price I might be persuaded to change my mind." She tapped my hand. "And should you ever make enough money, make sure you come and see me." With a flick of two fingers she produced a slim business card. Aubrey snatched it away before I had a chance to reach it.

"Thanks again," Aubrey said, grabbing me by my collar and pulling me away.

I heard Rosalie laugh as we left.

CHAPTER TWENTY-THREE

A faded sign on the front of the building read *Grouber & Sons Upholstery*. The windows were either boarded up or smashed.

"Seriously, no one would actually live in there," I said, looking at the abandoned factory. "Even him."

"Just wait," Aubrey said.

She'd been saying that ever since we arrived at the address Rosalie had given us. We were sat in the window of a café on the other side of the street and had been watching the building for hours. I was on my fourth cup of coffee and feeling twitchy.

"I reckon Rosalie was having us on," I said, twisting a wrap of sugar in my shaking hands. The wrap burst open, spilling sugar all over the table. The waitress leaning over the counter rolled her eyes at me.

"Wait," Aubrey said this time with real urgency. The door to the building jerked open and Benjo Greene squeezed through the doorway. It looked as if it took a lot of effort. He got one leg through and then had to struggle to get the other one free. I ducked away from the window, afraid that he might see me.

"Oh my god," Aubrey said.

"What? What?" I asked, panicking.

"He's so fat."

"I told you."

"But I mean, like, huge."

"I know. You see why I never wanted to run into him again."

"He's crossing the road," she said.

I risked a peek over the table. Benjo stepped off the pavement, not even bothering to look. A truck screeched to a halt in front of him and I didn't blame the driver. I reckon in a collision with Benjo the truck would have come off worse.

"Please, please don't come in here," I prayed as he reached the other side of the road. I ducked back under the table and hid. I didn't care about the weird looks I was getting from the waitress. She could tut and roll her eyes as much as she liked. Let her deal with him. A shadow passed over the window, blocking out the light, and then it moved away. Aubrey kicked me and I crept out. Benjo waddled away down the road, ignoring the people who stopped to stare as he passed.

"Come on," Aubrey said standing up.

"You've seen him now, can't we go home?"

Aubrey drained the last of her mug and headed for the door.

"Come on," I said racing after her. "You're not really

serious about going in there?" I pointed at the crumbling factory. "What if he comes back?"

"He walks at a metre an hour. We can be in and out before he's even turned around."

"But what if it collapses on our heads?"

"Do you want to find out what's going on or not?"

"If I said 'not really' you'll give me one of your looks, right?" She gave me one of her looks anyway. I sighed. "All right then."

We darted across the road in a break in the traffic. Aubrey stepped up to the front door and tried the handle. It didn't open.

"Shame,"' I said, not really meaning it.

Aubrey wasn't put off. She gestured with her head for me to follow her down the alley running alongside the factory.

Crumbling crates were stacked on top of each other, each stamped with the factory's logo. Aubrey started climbing up.

"Hang on. I should probably go first," I said, years of chivalric conditioning giving me a nudge.

She turned and looked at me. "Because you're a boy?"

"Well…"

She shook her head and took another step up.

"Rock, paper, scissors?"

She stopped mid climb. "You want to play rock, paper, scissors to see who goes first? With me?"

"Oh, yeah. I guess you'll just Shift if you lose."

She jumped down to the ground again, grinning. "Go

on then. I promise I won't Shift." She clinched her hand into a fist and stretched it out.

"On three?" I said.

She nodded.

"One."

I focused my mind, thinking about the three options I had. Just because she'd promise not to Shift didn't mean I couldn't.

"Two."

I'd go with paper. No one ever thinks you'll go with paper. But if I was wrong, then scissors it was. I held both choices in my mind, so it would be simple thing to flip to the alternative.

"Three!"

I flattened out my hand readying my mind to undo the decision.

Aubrey had a single digit raised. Her middle finger. I guess the bird beat everything.

"OK. You go first," I said, slipping my hand into my pocket.

She shook her head. "Boys," she said, and resumed her ascent.

The wood cracked under her weight. I flinched, expecting her to fall to her death at any second. But like a cat, she leapt from crate to crate and pulled herself up on the windowsill. She kicked the board covering the window and it fell through to the other side with a crash.

"Wait," I said, just as she had slipped one leg through the empty frame.

"What now?" she snapped.

"I want to think about this. Properly consider what we're doing. So that when it all goes wrong I can Shift and never have bothered going through that window. That's how it works, right? As long as it's a real decision?"

As an answer, Aubrey disappeared through the window.

"Right, as if I have a choice!" I said and climbed up on the crate.

My journey to the top wasn't as graceful as Aubrey's. I had to Shift three times to stop myself from falling and I was sporting a large graze on my arm by the time I made it through the window. Something crunched wetly under my feet as I landed on the floor on the other side. I'd just stepped into a box of rotting Chinese take-away. I shook my foot free, resisting the desperate urge to squeal. My free foot then crunched through the carcass of a chicken. I looked up. The entire factory floor was covered in empty food packets, crumpled plastic bottles and decaying food. Flocks of flies buzzed happily around the discarded remains.

The room stretched out and up, about thirty feet by thirty feet. You could hold a decent game of five-a-side football in here, if it wasn't for all the machinery in the way. What I assumed had been mechanised looms were now dustbins while fraying ropes and rusting chains swayed in a draught. The old factory, which would have once hummed with industry, now lay silent, apart from the buzzing of flies and the crunch of plastic.

Aubrey picked her way across the floor and started rifling through an old wooden desk.

"Found anything?" I whispered after a few minutes, really hoping she had and we could leave. She didn't reply. I followed her path, dodging pizza boxes and cardboard take away containers, and tried again. "Anything?"

"Just looks like stuff from the factory," she said showing me a pile of yellowing pages. She closed the drawer. "I wonder where he actually lives?"

"Call this living?" I wiped an unidentifiable sticky substance off my hand.

"Over there," Aubrey pointed at a cast iron staircase that spiralled up to a mezzanine level.

"Wa…" I didn't even have time to finish before Aubrey was climbing up it, two steps at a time. I glanced at the door out onto the street, said a silent prayer that Benjo was still heading in the opposite direction, and followed her, careful not to touch anything. I was starting to get really jumpy. Every creak and groan of the old building made me start, certain we'd been caught.

From the walkway at the top of the stairs I could see across the whole of the factory floor. Only a low guard rail, running around the edge of the platform, stood between me and the concrete floor twenty feet below. My head started spinning. I didn't think I suffered from vertigo, but maybe it was the height combined with the fear that was making me feel faint.

Aubrey laid a hand on my shoulder and I jumped, grabbing onto the rail to steady myself. "Relax," she said. "Anything goes wrong and you can Shift, just like in training."

"Sure, but in training there was less chance of me actually being killed," I said, reluctantly letting go of the rail.

Something banged loudly from below. We both hit the ground, pressing ourselves into the wooden boards of the upper level. Slowly, Aubrey dragged herself to the edge of the platform, while I stayed still, not even breathing.

"It's nothing," she said, standing up. "Just a pigeon."

A large grey bird was flapping around the roof, making the ropes and chains clang against each other. It settled on one of the large beams and started preening itself.

"I'm just going to lie here for a bit," I said, rolling over on my back and waiting for my pulse to slow down after the shock. The roof had once been all-glass but now was covered over with corrugated sheets of iron, blocking out the elements.

"Are you going to lie there all day?" Aubrey asked, stepping over me.

I pulled myself to my feet, dusted myself off and followed her down the narrow walkway. It opened out to a large area.

"So zis is where ze creature sleeps," I said, in my best Van Helsing impression.

Benjo had taken over this level and certainly made it his own. A large, sagging sofa bed sat in the middle of the floor. Next to it was a small fridge and in front, resting up against the guard rail, was an old-fashioned TV. It was markedly cleaner up here. I imagined Benjo sat on the sofa, stuffing his face, and hurtling the empty packaging onto the floor below.

Aubrey opened the small fridge and instantly closed it, wincing and covering her nose.

"What's in there?" I asked, covering my mouth in sympathetic horror.

"Moulding jars of mayo," she said, stepping away.

Behind the sofa, pressed up against the whitewashed walls, were a row of wooden cabinets. Aubrey opened the first one and gasped.

"More mayo?" I asked, joining her.

She shook her head.

Inside the cabinet was a row of surgical tools, which glistened in the dim light. Scalpels, steel clamps, a small circular saw and something that looked like a mini-crowbar were all lined up neatly. Some of the tools looked as if they were covered in dried blood.

"I think we should call the Regulators," I said, a cold panic creeping up the back of my spine. "We're in way over our heads."

"Speak for yourself," Aubrey said.

"Bull," I said, pointing at the blades. "This is some seriously messed-up stuff. And I don't care how brave and smart you want to play it, Aubrey, but I'm cacking myself here and I want to get out." I didn't care that I looked like a total coward. I was frightened. More frightened than I had ever been in my life. It was one thing to find a dead body, or have a guy explode in front of you. But to see the instruments used to actually kill someone, that was a whole world of nightmares right there.

Aubrey looked at me and her face softened. "OK. Five more minutes and then we call in the Regulators. I just want to make sure we've got everything we need before they start stomping around." She started tugging at the door to the next cabinet. I decided that the quicker she found what she was looking for, the quicker we could leave, so I tried to tug at it too. But it still wouldn't open.

I didn't hear him come up the stairs. Impressive considering how huge he was. I knew I was in serious trouble when I smelt a stink of rotting flesh. Before I had a chance to turn around I felt a damp cloth over my face, and then everything went black.

CHAPTER TWENTY-FOUR

When I started to wake up, my first thought was that it must have been a bad dream. I was still at home, waiting for my alarm to go off. I wondered, vaguely, if Mum would make me French toast for breakfast if I asked nicely. A pain in my wrists and shoulders started to penetrate the dream.

"Leave me alone, Katie," I mumbled, thinking my sister was giving me one of her famous 'Tyler burns'.

I opened my eyes and, instead of seeing my annoying sister, I saw, swinging twenty feet beneath me, a floor littered with rubbish. I snapped my head back up. I was hanging by my wrists from fraying ropes, dangling from beams in the factory roof. Aubrey was hanging next to me. She was awake already and thrashing about, trying to swing herself to the safety of the mezzanine level in front of us.

"Don't try and struggle, my sweetness. There is no escape." Benjo appeared behind the guard rail and stood level with us. Aubrey kicked out her legs, aiming for Benjo's head. But she was nowhere close.

He turned his head to me. "My fresh Shifter. So kind of you to find your way to me. The last time we met, you had to run off so quickly." He giggled, and then covered his red mouth with his chubby hand. He had the faintest hint of an accent, something harsh in the way he pronounced the letter w.

"What do you want with us?" I said, not really wanting to know the answer.

"I want to play." He grinned, showing his rotting, black teeth.

"Let me out of here and I'll kill you," Aubrey spat.

He giggled again. "I'm afraid that I have the upper hand here, my little Bluecoat."

That gave me an idea. "ARES know we're here," I said. "They'll be along any second now, and it's not going to look good for you if they find us like this."

"Don't be a big silly. ARES don't know anything about you being here. You're all alone and you're all mine." He grinned.

I squeezed my eyes closed and tried to focus on Shifting. I thought back to the alleyway and tried to decide not to follow Aubrey. Or when we were in the club and Rosalie had handed us the address, I could have just walked away. I had never wanted to come here. So I just had to find that point to tip reality in the opposite direction.

Nothing happened.

I opened my eyes and looked at Aubrey. "I can't Shift either," she said.

"Of course you can't," Benjo laughed. "That's because I don't want you to. And I'm the more powerful Shifter here."

"You're a Shifter? But you're… old."

Benjo posed, his fist disappearing inside the wads of flesh on his hip. "Actually, you'll find I have the body of a man in his prime."

"Locked up in your cupboard?" I muttered.

I looked at him. He was ageless in that way fat people often are. He could be thirty, forty maybe. But way too old to be a Shifter.

Benjo giggled, his eyes glinting crazily, and then stopped himself. "I will be thirty-two this November." He giggled again and waved his arm as if fending off a compliment. "I know, I know, I don't look a day over twenty. But it's true, I am the world's oldest natural-born Shifter. Although when I say natural-born, I am telling an incy-wincy lie. I was cooked up in a petri dish by my father."

Benjo shuffled away and returned with a photo frame. He showed it to us. The photo was of a thin, sharp-faced man, with a tiny moustache and cold, evil eyes. Benjo hugged the frame to his massive man-boobs. "My father was a genius geneticist. He had been a Shifter himself, but after entropy set in, he dedicated his life to finding ways to preserve our power." He gazed at the picture again and then placed it back on the table next to the sofa. "His primary investigation was into senescence – the deterioration that results in death. I can tell, my little ones, that you think death is natural, inevitable even."

He tugged at the end of the rope holding me and sent it swinging. "Not surprising given your… current circumstances. But it's not. Did you know that some turtles and amphibians don't age? No one really understands it. They are trying. Hundreds of scientists are beavering away trying to unlock the secrets of life and death. My father made huge advances by studying the genetic makeup of the blowhead whale. They live to be over two hundred years old, you know. Well, my father took the genes from the blowhead and–'

"You're part-whale?" I said, just about managing to keep up with his chatter. "Well that explains everything."

"I am special!" he roared, stamping his foot. Dust shook from beneath the platform. He stroked at the greasy strands of hair that coated his scalp and calmed himself. "Thanks to my father's brilliance, I don't age at the same rate as you pathetic people. And if you don't age…"

"You don't go through entropy," Aubrey said, pausing in her wriggling to stare at Benjo.

The fat man clapped his hands together. "Exactly."

"But if they could do that, we'd know," said Aubrey. "ARES would know about it."

"Would they? And even if they did know, would they really tell you?" He smiled, showing his tiny, pointed teeth, and for a moment he looked almost sane. Then the mad gleam was back in his black eyes.

"My father said I was one of the most powerful Shifters he'd seen. And that was before I found ways to become even stronger. Even more–"

My arms were burning. It felt as if they were being torn out of their sockets. "Argh! Are you going to talk us to death?" I shouted, pain overcoming fear.

"Do not be so impatient," he said, looking at me with his dark, empty eyes. "You'll get your turn."

I jerked in my ropes, trying again to loosen the grip. Even if I released my hands, it would mean falling to the floor below. But anything would be better than hanging here like Benjo's puppet.

"As for your friend…" Benjo waddled over to stand in front of Aubrey and started pulling on a rope, winching her, inch by torturous inch, towards him. He reached out a podgy hand and stroked her forehead. Aubrey kicked and writhed, trying to shake him off. When that didn't work, she resorted to spitting in his face. Benjo smiled and wiped the spittle off his cheek, then licked it off the palm of his hand.

"Get off her!" I shouted, suddenly taking him very seriously.

"As for your friend," he said again, taking a lock of Aubrey's hair and twirling it between his fingers. "I'll add her to my collection."

He let go of her hair and turned towards the cabinet we'd been trying to open when we'd been caught. With his little finger, he tugged on a chain around his neck and from somewhere under his stained T-shirt a small key emerged. He inserted it into the lock, giggled at us over his shoulder, then threw the doors open and stepped back proudly. I paused in my thrashing for a moment to see what was in the cupboard. I wish I hadn't.

Inside was a row of large, upside-down test tubes. Perched on top of each tube was what looked like a wig. But as I looked closer I saw dried crusts of blood. They weren't wigs; they were scalps. Five tubes and five scalps. The two on the right looked tiny, like they'd been taken from children. The one on the end looked the freshest and had tufts of red hair. Heritage. Benjo ran his hand over each scalp, lovingly.

"You sick freak!" Aubrey shouted. "You sick, twisted, fat freak!"

He stopped smiling when she called him fat. "It is so difficult when people fail to understand the brilliance of what I am doing here." He sighed and plonked himself on the sofa, as if all this talk of killing people was exhausting him.

"Cutting off people's heads! How is that brilliant?" I said.

The grin appeared again on his purple lips. "Well, let me tell you. You probably don't know that the power of a Shifter resides in a small area in his frontal lobe."

"Of course we know that, you slobbering excuse for a human." Aubrey was trying to make him angry – perhaps hoping to goad him into killing us quickly.

Benjo ignored her. "I came upon it as an accident really. After my father died, I was given a job. Carrying out lobotomies on Shifters who didn't... play by the rules. And I loved my job." He smiled, as if remembering fond times. "One day, I was examining the brain of an especially powerful Shifter, a child of only thirteen, and I thought, 'What if?' There had always been tales of tribes possessing some of the strength of their enemies by consuming their bodies. So what if I could possess the power of a Shifter?"

"You ate their brain?" I said, not really knowing why I was so shocked.

"Fried it up with some sliced onion," he said, plumping up one of the cushions next to him. "A bit chewy, if I'm honest. But I've perfected my technique now. Just a quick flash fry, not more than a minute, and it is quite delicious. Especially with mayo. But I find eating it hot and raw the most... satisfying." He licked his lips. "As soon as that first morsel had entered my stomach I felt the energy flood into me. That was just the beginning. Now I am more powerful than even my beloved father could have imagined."

"So you're going to eat our brains and take our power? Well, I really don't have enough power to bother with." I sounded like Billy Goat Gruff, trying to bargain my way out of being eaten by the troll. But I didn't have a big brother coming over the bridge. Aubrey and I were alone.

"Enough talk!" Benjo snapped. "Time to die."

It would have been more commanding if it hadn't taken him three tries to get out of the sofa. When he was finally upright, he pulled out a small circular saw from the cabinet of tools. With the press of a button, it started whirring. He brought it towards Aubrey's head, so close it made her hair blow back. She stopped trying to struggle and hung there, as if she'd accepted her fate. She didn't even close her eyes. Just stared straight at that blur of metal coming closer and closer to her face.

"No! No!" I screamed, tears flowing down my face. "Do me first. Not her. Please!"

"Don't worry," he shouted above the screeching of the saw. "Your time will come."

With the saw in one hand he brushed Aubrey's fringe back with the other. Then he pressed the blade against her forehead. She screamed as blood splattered over the blade.

I was begging now, pleading for her life. I didn't even know what I was saying, anything that came into my brain that might make this nightmare stop.

The blade stopped spinning. Benjo looked at it confused. Then he started jerking, as if electricity was racing through his body. His eyes went dull and he dropped the blade. He fell to his knees and, like the air coming out of a hot air balloon, toppled over the guard rail and down to the level below. He landed with a crash.

Only then did I see who was standing behind him. A small kid with sandy-coloured hair, big brown eyes and what looked like a taser in his hand.

"Jake," I said, stunned. "What are you doing here?"

"I'm back-up."

CHAPTER TWENTY-FIVE

Jake released the ropes and slowly winched us back down to the ground floor. Once there was enough slack, I twisted my wrists out of the straps holding them. My arms screamed as I dropped them to my sides and I shook them, trying to get some life back into the muscles. Aubrey hit the ground next to me and her knees buckled under her. I ran over and tried to hold her up. Blood trickled down her forehead but the cut wasn't too deep. Jake had arrived just in time.

I removed her hands from the straps and picked her up. Her eyes rolled back in her head as she lay in my arms like a rag doll. I pulled my sleeve down over my hand and wiped away the blood.

"Aubrey?" I said gently. Her eyes snapped into focus and locked on mine. For a moment she looked lost, as if I'd woken her from a deep sleep, and then she was back.

"I'm fine," she said, pushing me off her and getting to her feet.

"That was kerr-lose," Jakes said with an exaggerated sigh.

"Yeah it was, thanks," Aubrey said, gingerly touching the cut on her head. "But who are you?"

"This is Jake," I said. "He's another of the Fresh Meat Brigade." Jake mimed doffing a cap to Aubrey.

"Well, thank you," she said hitting him with her full, one hundred watt smile. Jake blushed. "We owe you our lives." She rolled her shoulders and rubbed at her wrists.

"Still reckon we're not out of our depth?" I said, looking up at the swinging ropes.

"What was all that about not being able to live without me?" Aubrey countered.

I gulped. I had no memory of saying that, but I knew I'd been screaming all sorts of desperate stuff. "I was, erm, just trying to stop him."

She raised an amused eyebrow and then winced at the pain in her forehead.

"What the hell are you doing here, Jake?" I said, trying to change the subject.

"Exactly what I would like to know," said a treacle voice from behind us.

I turned around to see Rosalie sashaying across the room, delicately picking her way through the detritus. She stepped up to Jake and grabbed him by the arm.

"You told me you were going to stay at home!" she hissed through clenched teeth.

"I thought Scott might need my help, so I followed him."

"You're impossible, do you know that?"

When I saw them standing next to each other I knew where I'd seen those chocolate eyes before.

"She's your sister?" I asked Jake. He nodded.

"Unfortunately for me," said Rosalie. "Yes, he's my stupid little brother who is always getting into trouble. Isn't that right, Jakey?"

"Sis," Jake groaned.

"We'll talk more about this when we get home."

We all turned our attention to the mass of blubber lying on the floor. One of his arms was bent underneath him, the other stretched out and was cupping a rotting bread loaf, like it was a teddy bear he'd brought to bed. He wasn't moving.

Rosalie bent down and pressed a long finger against his neck. Judging by her expression, you'd think she was sticking her hand up a cow's backside.

"Is he…?" Jake asked, chewing his bottom lip.

Rosalie shoved her hand deeper into the folds of flesh. "No, there's a pulse." She retrieved her hand and wiped it on her skirt. "He probably didn't even break anything in the fall with all that padding to protect him. As you're here, make yourself useful, Jake. Pass me my bag."

A very relieved-looking Jake skipped over the body and grabbed his sister's bag off the floor. I guessed that his dreams of being the big hero had not involved actually killing anyone.

Rosalie pulled a black case out of her bag. It was about twelve inches long and looked like a small flute case. A double clunk of the silver clasps and she opened it to reveal a long syringe and two glass bottles nestled in grey foam. She drained one of the bottles with the syringe and pressed the plunger, releasing a bead of cloudy liquid.

With two fingers she pulled up Benjo's T-shirt to expose a cavernous butt crack. Raising her fist high above her head, she brought the syringe down into his backside and pressed the plunger.

"Will that kill him?" Aubrey asked, a dark, angry tone in her voice.

"No. It's just a psychotropic drug."

"So it will make him forget?" I asked hopefully. I didn't like the idea of Benjo remembering anything about me.

Rosalie returned the syringe to the case and straightened up. "Not forget, exactly. It will make him unable to distinguish between dreams and reality. So he will awake and believe his finest fantasy to have come true. He will believe you dead and killed, no doubt, in the most satisfying manner."

"Clever drug," Aubrey said.

"A friend gave it to me. It comes in handy. A tiny drop and my clients will have had a night they will never forget. While I can catch up on my reading."

So that was how she showed her clients a good time without having to actually do anything. It was impressive, in a really messed-up way.

Aubrey walked towards the slumbering Benjo. "Doesn't seem fair. He should suffer for what he's done."

"Oh, he will," Rosalie said. "Just not yet."

"Why not now? He's here." Aubrey said, nudging his bulging stomach with the toe of her boot.

"We've been following him for some time now, slowly drawing him in. If we move too soon he will simply Shift and all our hard work will be for nothing. He really is quite powerful."

"But he's unconscious. Doesn't look like he could Shift his way out of a paper bag at the moment. Why don't we just, you know… do away with him?" I said.

"First of all, he has information we need. Information we can't get from him until he is willing to give it up. And second, even if we killed him here and now, he'd only Shift."

"How can he Shift if he's dead?" I asked, baffled.

"Really powerful Shifters can operate even on a subconscious level. When their brain senses a threat, when their functions start to shut down, they Shift. It's like a defence mechanism."

"Are you saying he can't die?" This was a disturbing thought. That a creature like the one lying in front of me would keep coming back. Like a zombie. Or the Terminator. Unstoppable and bent on the single thought of munching on my brains. I shuddered.

"He can die. We just need to manoeuvre him into a corner. A bit like checkmating in chess. You have to eliminate all avenues for escape. And currently, he still has options."

I stared at his mass. "And he got that powerful from eating all those brains?"

"Possibly. We have people looking into it."

Benjo snorted in his sleep and we all jumped back.

"Well, if we can't kill him, then let's get the hell out of here." Aubrey nodded and we turned to go. "So now can I tell Abbott?" I said.

"I suppose." Aubrey looked defeated. Ashamed even. "We should have gone to him at the start."

"No," Rosalie said. "You can't tell anyone at ARES about this."

"What? Why not? Aren't you from ARES?" I asked.

Rosalie laughed. "Of course not," she said. "I'm with the SLF."

CHAPTER TWENTY-SIX

It's amazing the rage that three letters can inspire. The SLF were the very people I'd set myself against. The people I was sure were behind Heritage's death and Benjo's brain-munching. The same people who'd blown me up.

"Come on then," said Jake, rocking back and forth on his heels, eager to leave.

I didn't move.

"Is there a problem?" Rosalie said.

"Er, yeah. Considering your lot tried to kill me."

"What are you talking about? We just saved you."

"Well, I doubt saving me was on your mind when you blew up that Tube."

She looked confused. "The SLF have never blown anything up."

"Your fearless leader Zac had coffee with Warner. The man I watched explode not one minute before the train went up."

"Zac would never..." She didn't sound too certain.

"Zac will do whatever it takes," Aubrey said, with

feeling. She came to stand next to me. "He has something to prove and he doesn't care who or what gets in his way. He uses people to get what he wants and then throws them away. Trust me. I know."

Rosalie went pale and looked at the floor.

Aubrey took a few steps towards the older girl. "And you think those stims that he's dealing are harmless? You think once those kids get a taste of those other possibilities they don't want to try them for real? He's messing with people's lives. I guess that's where you got that drug from," she said, pointing at Rosalie's bag. "But do you really know what it does?"

A heavy tension hung between the two girls. I looked from one to the other and saw something similar between them. Physically, they were totally different. Aubrey was small, blonde and looked like a pixie that might tear your head off if you looked at it wrong. Whereas Rosalie was tall, dark and graceful like a ballerina. But they shared a certain something. A way of carrying themselves. Pride.

"It's more complicated than you understand," said Rosalie, finally. "And we don't have time for this right now. I'll explain everything, I promise. But we have to go."

Benjo snorted on the floor and pulled his bread loaf closer to him. "Now!" Rosalie shouted.

She pushed Jake towards the door. I hesitated, looking from Rosalie to Aubrey to Benjo. He twitched. Aubrey sighed and started to run and I followed her. Jake opened the door and we all piled out. The freshness of the street was a relief after the stench of the warehouse.

A beat-up white van screeched to a halt in front of the factory and Rosalie opened up the back doors. Jake hopped in the back.

"Get in," Rosalie said.

"We're not going with you," I said, standing between Aubrey and the van. She laid a hand on my shoulder, moving me out of the way.

"I'm afraid I will have to insist," Rosalie said. I remembered the .22 Jenning – the 'little friend' – she carried in her handbag and decided this was not a woman to be argued with.

"It's OK," whispered Aubrey in my ear. "Let's find out what they're up to."

I wasn't convinced. But I guess this is what being a member of ARES was all about. Putting yourself in danger for the greater good. I stepped into the van and helped Aubrey in behind me. We sat on the floor as the doors shut and the van pulled away.

Jake was sitting on the wheel arch, all grins and twitching energy. "That was cool right? You were all like, 'Nooo!' And I was like *Zap!* And he was like, 'Aaarrggghhh!' *Slam!*" He continued to chatter away for what felt like about fifteen minutes. Telling us all about his sister's friends and how cool they were. As infectious as his enthusiasm was, I felt sorry for him. The friends he was talking about were a bunch of terrorists. He was a traitor and he didn't even know it.

The van rumbled to a halt and moments later the doors were thrown open and we all stood up to leave.

"Just Jake, please," Rosalie said, reaching out a hand to her brother. Jake shrugged at us and leapt down out of the van to join his sister. The doors were closed again leaving us alone.

We waited in the near-darkness, listening as footsteps moved away from the van. A steady Doppler whoosh of cars passing suggested we were somewhere near a main road. The clicking of the engine cooling seemed unnaturally loud, like a timer counting down.

I was running scenarios in my head. Once they opened the doors, I could charge them and run for it. Or I could go along with them and wait for an opportunity to escape to present itself. I tried to think of a Shift I could make. But I was too worried about finding myself stuck in Benjo's web.

"Do we have a plan?" I whispered to Aubrey. I was never very good at making decisions at the best of times and stuck in the back of a terrorist van was hardly what you could call the best of times.

"We find out what they want," Aubrey said.

"But what if what they want is to kill us?"

She looked at me. "If they wanted us dead, why would they bother saving us from Benjo?"

"So they didn't miss out on the fun?" I said, my voice squeaking slightly.

"Stop being such a pussy, Scott. They're anarchists not sadists."

"How do you know they're not both?"

Before she answered the doors were opened again. A

big guy wearing green combats and a black T-shirt stood outside. It was the ape from the club. The one Aubrey had beaten.

"Well, what have we here? A couple of imperialist scumbags?" He had a strong Northern Irish accent and a crooked grin.

"Who you calling scumbag, you bog-farming, potato-sucker?" Aubrey said jumping out of the van and shoving him in the chest. I didn't even know what that meant, but it sounded good.

His grin widened. "Looks like we have ourselves a little firecracker. Better watch ourselves, hey Rosie?"

"It's the boy you need to be careful of, Sean," said Rosalie. "Jake says he's the best fighter he's ever seen."

I stepped onto the pavement trying to hide my smile of satisfaction. I tugged my blue jacket, and brushed some dust off the arm. I was trying to play it cool, but my hands were already shaking.

Rosalie and Sean herded us off the street, up some steps and into an abandoned church. I glanced at a cracked statue of Mary gazing down on us, before being pushed through two large wooden doors. I whacked my elbow on a stone font as I tumbled through.

The nave was about thirty feet long, lined in black, square tiles. Half of the tiles were missing or cracked. All the pews had been pushed to the side and lay stacked up on top of each other against the walls. I felt a nudge in my back and started to walk forward. Multi-coloured light spilled in from the stained glass window, which showed a picture of a saint riddled with arrows. I really hoped it wasn't trying to tell me something.

As I got closer to the front I saw Jake, sat on the altar with his legs swinging. He waved and I ignored him. There were four or five other people standing around. They looked relaxed, as if they'd gathered for rehearsal or something – not a meeting of an underground terrorist cell. Every face was turned in the same direction. I followed their gaze to see Zac standing in the pulpit, with his hands resting on the wings of a carved golden eagle.

He smiled. "Good to see you again, Brey. We're making a habit of running into each other."

"Screw you too, Zac," she said in reply. A ripple of amused laughter passed among the group. Rosalie was standing with her arms over Jake's shoulders, watching Zac through tight eyes.

Zac vaulted over the edge of the pulpit and landed on the floor in front of us, sending up a cloud of dust. Show off, I thought.

"What's this all about?" Aubrey asked.

"Yeah," I said following her lead. "And if you wouldn't mind explaining why you tried to kill me, that would be great."

Zac's thick eyebrows lowered and he looked across at Rosalie.

"He thinks you blew up a Tube," Rosalie said, an uncertainty in her voice.

Zac threw his head back and laughed. The rest of the group picked up his cue and laughed along, although they didn't look so amused. When Zac recovered he looked at me. "The SLF don't go in for such barbaric displays of strength. We choose more subtle forms of eroding the state."

"Like what? Getting young Shifters hooked on dreams they can never have?" Aubrey asked, bitterly.

Zac paused for a moment, interrupted in his speech, then started strolling back and forth in front of us, like an actor. A bad actor at that. "We want people to question the forces of control. Guide them towards seeing that government is not necessary for civilization and that it is nothing more than a parasite eroding our very humanity. The powers want us to conform, obey, to give up our youth and slot into their little boxes, with a job, a house, crippling debt. We want people to have fun. To play! To stay young."

"'We don't stop playing because we grow old. We grow old because we stop playing,'" I quoted. "You spray painted ARES HQ?"

"Yes, that was one of mine. But you mustn't tell anyone. I am doing a good job of remaining anonymous." He winked at me and smiled to the rest of his gang, who were gazing at him, hanging on his every word. "So you see, we would never be so obvious as to blow up a train. Although we could. Sean here is an expert in explosives."

Sean held open his long jacket and revealed a wad of what looked like plasticine strapped to an inside panel.

"Plastique?" Aubrey asked. "I thought you said you weren't violent."

"Sean will only be allowed to use his experience as a last resort in bringing ARES to its knees."

The SLF members clapped and I just knew Zac was doing everything he could to stop himself from bowing at their applause.

"Look, I've had a pretty crappy evening and I'd really like to just get home. So if you could just tell us why we're here."

"Why so eager, brother?" he asked, laying a hand on my shoulder. I shook it off.

"I'm not your brother," I snapped.

"We are all brothers here," he said, raising his arms out and spinning around.

I looked around at the statues and the paintings of saints and sinners. I felt their eyes on me. "I'm surprised, Zac," I said. "I never thought you'd be a God-botherer."

"God?" Zac laughed and the sound echoed off the domed roof. "We don't believe in God. We are the only gods here."

"So what do you believe in?" Aubrey asked, impatient.

"Freedom." He let the word sink in. A couple of the gathered members whooped in agreement. "Freedom from those who want to crush anyone who questions their authority."

"I think you give them a little more credit than they're due, Zac" Aubrey said.

Zac stepped in close and stared into Aubrey's eyes. "Who do you think controls the stock market?" he said, softly at first. "Them. Who decided which political party gets into power? Them. Who goes to war? Them! Who wins? Them, them, them!"

"That's crap!" I shouted. "The First Law: Shifters can only change their own reality."

"And they have Shifters in every level of government, in every country. On the board of every major corporation. Delicately manipulating their reality until it aligns with ARES' image of the 'Ideal Reality'," Zac said, a sneer on his face.

Aubrey looked at the other members of the SLF and shook her head. "And governments and armies are taking advice from a bunch of kids now are they?" she laughed.

"Not all Shifters are kids. They've worked out a way to stop entropy. I know it. I just don't know how yet. But there are adult Shifters and they're the ones pulling the strings. Controlling everything." Zac had a dangerous gleam in his eyes. "We've been talking with someone who has evidence–"

"Henry Heritage by any chance?" I cut him off, remembering the photos.

Zac looked surprised for a moment and then recovered. "As a matter of fact, yes, he told us he has vital information that will bring ARES down."

"Well, I don't think he's going to be doing much talking, given that he's dead."

His eyes widened and his mouth formed a perfect "O". Rosalie and Sean both flinched and took a step towards Zac. "How?" he said.

I had been about to blame them for his death. But judging by the expressions of shock on the faces of Zac and the rest of the SLF they'd known nothing about it. "Well, we're pretty sure that it was Greene who did the actual killing. And eating."

"Eating?" Zac asked.

"He eats people's brains," Aubrey said. "He said he can consume their Shifting energy."

"So he definitely *is* a Shifter?" Zac said, looking over to Rosalie.

"Seems we were right," Rosalie said, smiling, standing up from her seat on the pew.

"I knew it!" Zac slammed his fist into his palm. "Don't you see? Entropy is a lie, a lie to keep us down!"

"Come off it," I said. "Greene is completely barking mad."

Rosalie left her brother and came to stand by her leader's side. "Just because he's mad doesn't mean he's lying, Scott. He might be the key we've been looking for." Rosalie looked up at Zac, her eyes burning with that same fire. He smiled at her and then turned to Aubrey.

"ARES have been lying to us all our lives, Brey. They only tell you the truth when they know they've brain-washed you enough so that you will do everything they say. Why else do you think they threw me out?"

"Because you broke into top secret files!" I said. This guy was seriously unhinged. He thought he was some kind of saviour. Great, I thought, two dangerous nutters in one day.

"It was what I found in the files that scared them," he said, taking another step towards Aubrey and ignoring me. "They've been running programmes dedicated to stopping entropy. I tried to tell you, but you wouldn't listen to me."

Aubrey was looking up at Zac a confused look on her face. She wasn't seriously buying any of this stuff, was she?

I threw my hands up in the air. "You know what, I don't care. I've had enough of this wannabe Che Guevara stuff."

I turned to leave and Sean gripped my shoulder. "You don't want to do that," I said, looking down at his tattooed hand. Small shamrocks were inked into his knuckles.

Sean tightened his grip and smiled. It took me two moves and he was lying on the floor in a heap groaning. I hadn't even needed to Shift. I looked at the others, daring them to take me on.

"Let him go," Zac said. "He won't tell anyone we're here. Not as long as Aubrey is with us, isn't that right, Scott?"

"Aubrey?" I said. I looked at her confused. "Let's go."

"Scott," Aubrey said, in a hushing tone.

I looked at her. "You're not... You don't believe him, do you? You're the one who said he couldn't be trusted." I pointed at Zac who stood perfectly still, his chiselled face turned to a beam of light, looking like another statue of a saint. I wanted to punch him.

"Scott, I don't know what to believe after what Benjo

said. And if ARES were really running these programmes. If there's a chance that we don't have to…"

I didn't even bother letting Aubrey finish. I stormed away, disgusted, and headed for the doors. They shut behind me with an ominous thud. The statue of Mary gazed down at me. She looked as if she was about to cry.

"What are you looking at?" I snapped and slumped down the stairs and into the drizzle-filled night.

CHAPTER TWENTY-SEVEN

"Afternoon, Scott," a brisk voice said.

I jumped, spilling the can of Coke I was nursing. "Afternoon, Mr Morgan," I said, righting the can and trying to mop up the spill with a sheet of paper.

I hadn't slept all night. I'd wandered the streets for hours, rage and worry chasing themselves around my head like moths around a light bulb. I was angry with Zac for, well everything, really. Annoyed at Aubrey for buying Zac's crap. And disappointed in myself for leaving her there. I should have stayed. On top of that, I was battling with the fact that I should tell Morgan or Abbott exactly where they all were. But Zac had been right. I wouldn't. Not until I knew Aubrey was well away from them. I'd tried calling her four times today, but she wasn't picking up. When I asked one of the other Bluecoats where she was, I'd been told she'd called in sick.

"Everything all right?" Morgan said. "You're looking a little pale."

"No, sir. I'm fine. Just a little tired."

"Well, I have some news that should perk you up." He flashed me his toothiest smile. "Abbott and his team have tracked down the SLF's HQ. They're going to raid it at 6pm today."

His hearty slap on the back disguised my gasp of shock.

"There," Morgan said. "You've got more colour in your cheeks. I knew the thought of catching those Tube-bombing bastards would cheer you up. Carry on." He slapped me on the back again and wandered off to go and push some paper, or whatever he did all day.

I pulled out my phone and selected Aubrey's number. After three rings it clicked through to her voicemail.

"Hi, this is Aubrey. You know what to do."

"It's me, Scott. This is really important. You have to call me as soon as you get this." I hung up and dialled again. It went straight through to the voice mail. "This isn't about them, I promise. Well it is. But you have to call me."

I fired off a text to her number, just in case. It was 4pm. Only two hours before the Regulators descended. Not that I cared about what happened to the SLF, they deserved to get locked up as far as I was concerned. The only person I cared about was Aubrey. I had to find her.

I pushed my head around Morgan's door. "Sir, I'm not feeling that well after all. Is it OK if I go home?"

He looked up from his screen. "Sick, Scott? You didn't strike me as a sickie sort. You know, I have never had a sick day in my life. Not one. But if you have to..." He grinned at me, showing a full row of his too white teeth.

"Just make sure you fill in a sick form tomorrow."

"Sure," I said, letting the door swing closed. I grabbed my coat from my chair and walked to the lifts. I punched the down button and waited. The lifts were taking forever. I punched the button again and again, in that stupid belief that letting a machine know you're in a rush will somehow make it hurry up. After the sixth impatient punch, I headed for the stairs.

The stairwell smelt of bleach, and the steps were slippery having been recently washed. I skidded and almost went hurtling down the steps three times, once knocking into the cleaner. He shouted muffled abuse at me as I raced on, taking half a flight in one leap.

Once out on the street, I waved down a taxi and leapt in. I gave them Aubrey's address. If I was lucky she might be at home.

I wasn't. Thirty-five infuriating minutes later I arrived at her place and got no reply from the buzzer. I tried calling her phone again and still it went straight through to voicemail. The first time I'd heard her answer message I'd thought it was really cute. Right now, I hated it.

She must be still at the church. But the problem was, I couldn't remember exactly where it was. I'd made my way home in a haze of bitterness and misery, jumping on the first Tube I'd come across. All I knew was that it was somewhere near Holland Park.

The cab I'd got here was in the middle of trying to perform a three-point turn, which was slowly becoming a seven-point turn. The cabbie was swearing at a rubbish truck blocking his path in one direction and the mass of mopeds blocking him in the other. Before he straightened out, I ran after him, flailing my arms like a drowning man. He was doing a good job of ignoring me, but when I threw open the door and flung myself in he didn't have much choice but to acknowledge my existence.

"Do you know a church near Holland Park?" I said, breathlessly.

"There are about fifty churches around there, mate," he said, "mate" clearly being cabby short hand for "moron".

"It was an old, white church. Abandoned now."

"St Sebastian's?" he suggested.

"Yeah. That one. Drive." I didn't know if it was the right one or not. But at least if he got me to the area I might remember something.

I watched the meter tick closer to £20 – all I had left in my wallet. I might have to stop before we even got there. Thankfully, it was still at £19.20 as he pulled into a street I recognised, with tall, double-fronted houses and expensive cars parked outside. I saw the church up ahead.

"Here! Thanks." I threw him the £20 note and jumped out. I raced up the steps, ignoring the sad look on Mary's face, and charged into the doors. They were firmly shut and I landed flat on my backside.

I dragged myself up, shaking my spinning head and started banging on the doors. After a few minutes, I heard a gruff voice from the other side. "Password?" it said.

"What is it with you lot and passwords?" I shouted.

"It's me, Scott. I need to speak to Aubrey."

I heard a muffled conversation, followed by a rattling of bolts and chains and the doors opened. Sean waved me in. Rosalie was sitting on one of the pews, looking back at me. Zac and Aubrey were standing annoyingly close to each other, next to the altar. There were four other faces I recognised from last night and a couple of new ones huddled over some papers. Jake was nowhere to be seen, hopefully safe back at ARES, which was a good thing. The kid didn't need to get caught up in the mess.

"Aubrey," I shouted, walking towards her.

"What do you want, Scott?" Aubrey said, her voice carrying down the length of the aisle. She sounded annoyed.

I didn't have time to answer before the doors behind me were kicked open and ten members of the Regulators poured in, screaming and shouting. They had their guns raised, covering the group of kids. Sean put up a fight and took one of them down before they got the cuffs on him. Their first man neutralised, the Regulators turned to the rest of the group and started walking slowly towards them.

I looked back at Aubrey, Rosalie and the others. Their initial expressions of shock had been replaced with looks of concentration. Yes, I thought, willing them to Shift. If they Shifted, none of this need to have happened. I could have banged all day on the locked doors and there would be no one here to answer. I'd not stopped for a second to think about what I was doing, so the Shift would have to be down to them.

One by one, they looked up, then at each other and finally at the Regulators walking towards them. I saw the little wrinkles appear on Aubrey's forehead that meant she was confused. Nothing was happening. None of them could Shift.

The Regulators reached them and started shouting at them to get down. I started to run towards Aubrey as one guy pushed her heavily to the floor. But a hand on my shoulder stopped me. It was Abbott. I looked up at him, hoping that he would explain what the hell was going on.

"Thank you, Scott," said Commandant Morgan, appearing through the doors. He had a manic grin on his face. "You brought us right to them." Morgan clapped his hands together, and started rubbing them.

I opened and closed my mouth, like a grounded fish gasping for air. "I... I..." was all I finally managed. Abbott threw me a pitying but warning look that said, "Keep your mouth shut."

Every member of the SLF believed I'd betrayed them. That I had set them up. I was caught between wanting to scream the truth, and not wanting Abbott to think that I had anything to do with them. I looked at Aubrey who was being dragged to her feet, willing her to understand. To somehow read my mind. I hadn't meant this to happen, I had come to warn her. She stared straight through me. I could do nothing to help, but I couldn't understand why they couldn't help themselves.

"Don't bother trying to Shift," said Morgan, looking

at his fingernails. "You know how this works. I'm a Fixer and I don't want you lot going anywhere." He grinned.

I'd forgotten that Morgan was a Fixer too. But I still couldn't believe that a jumped-up prat like this guy was really the most powerful Shifter here. Stronger than Aubrey? Than Zac? I'd never really understood why Morgan was the Commandant. I'd never seen him do any real work. And he can't have been far away from entropy. But whatever I thought didn't matter. He'd won.

Zac was being led away from the altar, his hands cuffed behind his back. He didn't even look at me. Rosalie was next. She paused for a moment and then started screaming at me. "You bastard!" She twisted out of the Regulator's grip and dove at me. I thought she was going to bite me. But it had all been a ruse. Before the Regulator pulled her off me she whispered in my ear.

"Look after Jake."

She was pulled away before I had a chance to reply.

Aubrey was the last to be taken. Her eyes were like fire and she was hissing like a cornered cat as the men dragged her down the aisle.

"Stop!" I shouted, and the Regulators, trained to obey any command from a Bluecoat, stopped. I turned to Abbott. "Please, she has nothing to do with them. It's a mistake."

Abbott looked at me, shook his head sadly, and then back at his men. He nodded at them to continue. Aubrey was dragged past, pausing only to spit in my face.

"Well, that's that." Morgan brushed his hands. "Abbott, you finish up here. I better get back to base and start the report. A good day." He dipped his fingers in the bowl of holy water and used it to slick back his hair. "Yep. A good day." He sauntered away.

The doors slammed closed, and the silence in the near-empty church was like lead. What had I done? I walked the length of the aisle and stared up at the stained glass image of the saint I now knew to be Sebastian. Tied to a tree and riddled with arrows, and yet he was smiling up at the beaming sun. What an idiot. But I was the real fool here. I'd allowed myself to be used in a game I didn't understand. And I'd betrayed my only friend in the process.

"I'm sorry we couldn't tell you, Scott," Abbott said after a while. "I wanted to. But I had my orders." He looked genuinely uncomfortable.

"You followed me here?"

He nodded and joined me at the altar. "We've had this building under surveillance for a few months but their security was too tight. Any time we tried to get in, they'd Shift and we lost them. But when you were seen coming out of here the other night we thought we might have found a way in. We just needed to get Morgan through the doors and then we had them."

"So, what Morgan said earlier, about the raid, that was all to get me to come here?" Abbott didn't answer, but I knew it was true. "So how come I'm not being dragged off in cuffs? How do you know I'm not one of them?"

"Because I know you, Scott. You'd never betray ARES."

"What do you mean I wouldn't? I did! I should have reported the SLF as soon as I knew where they were." My nails dug into my palms as I fought to control the rage.

"You would have in the end," Abbott said. "But we couldn't wait. The chatter we've been following led us to believe that the SLF had something big planned." He turned over a piece of paper on the altar. "Looks like we were right. Come see."

He pointed at the papers I'd seen Aubrey and Zac looking over as I came in. They were the blue prints for ARES' HQ and marked in red pen were the entrances and offices of key personnel. Next to that lay a sheet of A4 paper with some names written on. Heritage and Warner were top of the list. Looked like I was right, Warner hadn't been the bomber on the Tube, he had been their target. A third, large sheet of paper, was tucked underneath the blueprint. I pushed the other pages away to look at it. All I had time to see was a name written on the top in white pencil: "Greyfield's". Then Abbott pulled it away and started rolling it up. Another church they'd been planning on making their base, perhaps? Not that any of it mattered now. The SLF wouldn't be going anywhere for a long time.

"Seems they had more than a Tube bomb planned this time," Abbott said.

"Aubrey would never have stood by and let them hurt anyone. If we'd just waited she would have led you to them, I know it."

"We couldn't take that chance. Aubrey has a history of not playing by the rules. She might have been an undercover agent for SLF all along."

"Never!" I shouted and my voice echoed around the dome. "She hated them. She only wanted to find out what they knew." I stormed away from the altar and kicked over a brass candlestick. It clanged as it hit the stone floor.

"Scott, I can see how much Aubrey means to you. So I'll handle her questioning myself, OK? If what you say is true, and if she's willing to give evidence against the SLF then she'll get off with just a warning." He laid his hand on my shoulder. I looked up at him through clouded eyes. "Let's get you home."

CHAPTER TWENTY-EIGHT

The house was empty when I let myself in. I remembered with a cold, sinking feeling that today was the last Friday of the month. When Mum took The Tyler Friday Family Dinner out on the road. What I wouldn't give to be sat with Mum, Dad and Katie right now. I wouldn't even mind if Mum had chosen one of her "experimental' places, like the one she took us to last year – *Offally Good*. I looked at my watch. 8.30pm. Wherever they were, they'd be tucking into pudding right now. I'd missed the past four Tyler Fridays. One when I was pretending to be in Leeds but was really in hospital. The rest, I fed them some crappy excuse about training. The worse bit was I got the feeling they had much more fun without me moaning and whining all the time.

Hugo had been really pissed at me for not making Seb's party. I tried telling him about the explosion and how I'd been in hospital with a concussion, but he didn't believe me. And I'd been so carried away with my new life as a Bluecoat I hadn't bothered really trying to convince him. So all round I was a terrible friend, a terrible son and pretty crappy brother.

I plodded into the kitchen, opened the fridge door and stared in. Nothing in there looked edible. My body ached, but not as much as my brain. In the space of two days I had found a dead body, been tortured by a psychopathic cannibal, been responsible for the capture of a terrorist cell and lost my best friend. As weeks went, this one sucked big time. I made myself some tea, pushed some bread into the toaster and broke down in sobs.

Becoming a part of ARES had given me a sense of belonging. Focus even. The very thing all my teachers had always banged on at me about. But now I felt totally lost again. I was caught between the two worlds of authority and friendship. And didn't know which way to turn. I started to play over in my head all the decisions that had led me to running up those steps to the church tonight. There had to be a Shift I could make. When I'd finally got home and crawled into bed at five am that morning, I'd wanted to stay there. I'd wanted to hide under my duvet and let the world do without me for a day.

So why didn't I? If I'd not been at ARES, then Morgan couldn't have played me like a puppet, and I'd never have led them to the church. But then, would the SLF really have attacked ARES HQ like Abbott believed? Would Aubrey have gone along with them? Helped them even? I knew she resented ARES for taking her away from her parents. But I didn't believe she hated them. Not really. But was it a chance I was willing to take? Would I save my friend and risk the SLF hurting more people, even destroying ARES?

I lay my head on the granite counter top, trying to let some of the stony stillness flow into me. A knock at the door shook me out of my misery. I prayed it was Mum and Dad, home early after a huge row.

I threw open the door and looked down to see a sandy mop of hair. Jake stood on my doorstep. His usual grin was gone and his mouth was fixed in a thin, stoic line. His eyes were red and I could tell that he'd been crying too. The acid guilt bubbled in my stomach because I knew whatever pain he was in was all thanks to me. He spoke first.

"Rosalie's been arrested."

"Yeah I know. Come in," I said, standing aside and pointing him towards the kitchen.

He walked in like a robot, as if it was taking all of his energy just to put one foot in front of the other.

"Do you want a cup of tea? The kettle's just boiled." My mother always made tea whenever things went wrong, as if it could cure all of the world's ills. I think it would take more than tea to sort all this out.

We sat at the kitchen table, both staring into our mugs.

"I didn't have anywhere else to go," Jake finally said.

"Hey, no problem. But... how did you find me?"

"Hacked your files," he said, like it was the most obvious thing ever. I didn't bother asking him how. "What am I going to do?"

"I don't know, Jake." I couldn't lie to him. His sister was a terrorist and that meant she'd be locked up till entropy and he would be left alone. "Do you have anywhere to stay?"

He shook his head. "I could go back into the dorms. But I used to get nightmares. That's why they let me live with…" He couldn't even bring himself to say his sister's name.

"You can stay with me." I tried to sound upbeat, as if it would be a great adventure. I'd always wanted a little brother who I could play with and, if I was really honest, win against, because it had been a long time since I'd beaten Katie at anything. I didn't want to think about what my Mum would say when she came home to find a homeless kid in her kitchen. I'd deal with her when I had to. Worst case, I'd move out and find a flat and we'd both live there. Now I was a Bluecoat I was earning enough money. Maybe Aubrey could move in, too. That's if ARES let her go and if she would ever talk to me again.

"Did you know Aubrey was arrested too?" Jake said, looking up at me from behind his shaggy fringe. Had he known what I'd been thinking about?

"I heard," I said. "But Abbott said he'll try and get her off."

"That's good. Aubrey's cool."

"Yeah, she is." We both gazed back into our mugs. The tea had gone cold.

"I wonder if I'll see her again," Jake said, sadly.

"Aubrey? I'm sure you will, mate. Like I said, Abbott–"

"Not Aubrey. My sister." His bottom lip started to wobble. "I might not even get to say goodbye." Huge tears rolled down his face.

I hesitated for a second, and then decided to forget all the rubbish about manliness. I leant over and gathered Jake into a big hug. His tiny shoulders shook in my arms.

"Screw this," I said after letting him cry for a bit. "They can't stop you seeing your sister. I mean, prisoners have rights, right?"

He sniffed a bubble of snot back into his nose and his eyes brightened.

"We'll go to HQ first thing on Monday morning and demand to see her."

"Do you think we can?"

"Hey, I'm a Bluecoat. No one says no to a Bluecoat."

As it turned out, everyone says no to a Bluecoat.

Jake stayed with me over the weekend. I told Mum and Dad he was a kind of IT Savant who was studying at ARES, which wasn't exactly a lie. Surprisingly, Mum fussed over him and decided he needed feeding, while Dad got Jake fixing his computer, the one thing he never allowed me to touch. Katie pretended to ignore us but I kept seeing her glancing at Jake when they were in the same room. I teased her about fancying him and she threw an apple at my head.

On Monday morning, we'd started asking everyone we knew about Aubrey and Rosalie and were getting nowhere fast. They either acted as if they didn't know what we were talking about, or they told us to shove off. I'd even tried Shifting a few times, taking different tacks, the least successful of which had been when I'd tried to flirt with one of the girls in Analysis and got called a creep.

We were sat in the canteen, poking at our breakfast, feeling exceedingly sorry for ourselves. News travelled pretty fast around here. The place was buzzing with the news that the SLF had been caught. Although, luckily, no one seemed to know about my involvement. That wouldn't last long.

"I'll try Abbott again," I told Jake, pulling out my phone. Not that I thought it would do any good. I'd been told he was off site and he wasn't answering. Yet another person stonewalling me.

I threw my phone on the table. "Nothing."

"Oh," said Jake, his zombie expression was back. It looked like his belief that he would see his sister again was fading with each minute. But I wasn't even nearly ready to give up.

"We need to talk to someone who actually knows what's going on around here." I remembered something. "Come on. I have an idea."

I dragged him up two flights of stairs to the IT department. Carl was sat at his desk, a computer tower in bits in front of him.

"Hey, Carl. How's it going?"

He looked up from the tangle of wires and circuitry and squinted at me. "Sorry, do I know you?"

I tugged at my jacket. "I was here a few days ago. With Aubrey."

Her name worked better than my supposed Bluecoat authority ever could. He smiled at me. "Oh, yeah. You were the one after the fat guy."

"Yeah, that's me." I smiled and moved closer to him. Then I pulled up a chair and lowered my voice. "I need a favour. Well, not me. Aubrey. She told me that you were the only one she could really trust."

He leant in even closer. I smelt stale coffee on his breath. "It's so weird, because I've been trying to get hold of her all day. You know she asked me to do some digging into Heritage? Well I found something. Big."

"What?" I asked, deciding not to tell him quite yet about Aubrey being locked up and it being all my fault.

"Heritage was involved in a top-secret programme of ARES' and when I looked into it, Aubrey's name popped too."

"What was it?"

"That's the thing. I can't find out any more than that. Whatever other files they have aren't on the standard network. You'll need access to the private network."

"How do I get on to that?"

Carl laughed. "You don't. It can only be accessed by BCI."

"What's BCI?"

"Some Shifters can't be kept out of regular computer networks," said Jake. "Hacking passwords and whatever are just way too easy. We just Shift till we find the right combo, going through each variation in turn, and bam! We're in."

"Exactly," said Carl. "So we created a different way of storing and accessing information, with an interface that picks up brain signals. Brain Control Interface."

"You just think 'open' and the file opens. It's pretty cool. We were shown how to use it last week." Jake was sitting on one of the desk, playing with a mouse shaped like a car.

"Hang on, does it look like a skullcap thing?" I said, remembering the stims Zac used at the casino.

"The old models were. Now, the receptors are implanted into the brain of the operators just under the skull. There's less interference that way. But you might still be able to use one of the old stim sets to access the network. It wouldn't be as quick of course."

"OK, so we just need to get an old BCI thing and we can access the secure network?"

"Whoa!" Carl held up his hands, as if blocking me. "There are only three BCI receptor points in the building. In Sir Richard's office, but that one's never been set up as he refused to have the implant..."

"And where are the other two?"

"In Mr Abbott and Commandant Morgan's offices."

"Do you have an old model we can use?"

"Well, sure but it won't do you any good. The network

is designed to recognise the operator's brain waves. So you'd have to get Morgan or Abbott to access it for you. Or at least have them in the room with you."

I turned to Jake. "Do you still have your sister's bag?"

Five minutes later we were standing outside Morgan's office.

"You ready?" Jake nodded and I knocked and opened the door without waiting. "Excuse me, Commandant."

Morgan span around in his chair so fast it almost spat him out. I'd clearly interrupted him in spinning it round and round and he was looking a little flustered. "Well, hello, Scott. No hard feelings about last night's raid, I hope? All in a good cause."

"Of course, Commandant. Glad to see those SLF scum where they belong." I walked in slowly, trying to cover Jake who was crawling in behind me and hoping he hadn't registered Morgan's comment. I would have to tell him it had all been my fault soon enough. But first, we had a job to do.

I coughed and carried on. "The Regulators did a great job. Which is what I wanted to talk to you about. I know it's early to be thinking about what I do after entropy, but I have to look to the future. Like you kept telling us in Integration classes."

Morgan's face lit up. "Well, I'm glad to hear it, Scotty. Of course, I knew you had potential when I first met you. But you're not getting any younger, believe me, and your Shifting days are numbered." He stood up and gazed out of his large window. "So many Shifters only think about shaping their past. We need to think about shaping our future. Of course, once entropy hits I will move to become head of the Regulators and Mr Abbott can finally retire."

I decided not to say anything about Abbott only allowing that to happen over his dead body. He sighed. "I remember when I was your age…"

"Wasn't that like three years ago?" I asked, and Jake hit my leg to shut me up. But Morgan wasn't listening anyway.

"Tempus fugit. Tempus. Fugit," he said, just as Jake pounced. Morgan only had the time to squeal as the syringe entered his thigh and the drugs took effect. He slumped into his chair, a huge dopey grin on his face.

"Nice work,' I said, high-fiving Jake. "Now, let's see if we can get an answer out of him."

He was spinning around in his chair, giggling to himself. "Mr Morgan?" I said, trying to get him to focus on me. His eyes were rolling in his head and his tongue was hanging out of his mouth. He was well gone.

"OK, forget him. Do your thing," I said pointing at Morgan's monitor. "Carl!' I shouted.

Carl opened the door an inch, then stepped inside. "What have you done?" he said, staring at the drooling Commandant.

"Don't worry about him. Help Jake."

Carl rubbed his face. "I'm going to get in so much trouble."

"Do it for Aubrey," I said, giving his shoulder a squeeze. That seemed to work.

"OK," Carl said. "Push him in front of the screen and let's see if this will work."

I wheeled Morgan under his desk and slapped his hands away as he started stroking my face. Carl placed a skullcap on Jake's head and stuck the receptors in place. A single wire, ending in an electrode, trailed out of the back and Carl pressed it against Morgan's temple.

"This should pick up his signal and then you can piggyback it, I think," Carl said, stepping back.

Jake stared at the screen, his eyes glazed. It blinked into life.

"I'm in. What do you want?" Jake said, sounding distant.

"Look for Aubrey's file," I said.

A second later a document popped into existence on the screen and opened with a little whoosh. I scanned it. Aubrey's birth date, entrance to ARES' training programme, promotion to Third Class. The last entry said "Volunteered for the Ganymede Programme."

"What do you think Ganymede is?" Jake asked.

"I don't know, but I don't think Aubrey is the volunteering sort," I said.

"That's the name of the programme I was telling you about," said Carl. "Total security blackout. So I couldn't find any more than that. But now... Try and find anything on Ganymede, Jake."

Jake blinked and a file called Ganymede whooshed open. Inside were three documents. "Overview", "Volunteers" and "Candidates."

He opened the Overview file first.

PROJECT GANYMEDE
CLASS FIVE PERSONNEL EYES ONLY

Inception date:
12/10/86

Project Remit:
Investigation into: The origins of the ability known as "Shifting'; the nature of entropy; the potential to militarise the power.

Project Leader:
Dr Michael Lawrence, MD, PhD, DoR

TOTAL CLEARANCE:
APPROVED

"Well, that doesn't tell us much," I said, reading it for the second time. "Open Volunteers."

The Volunteers file was a list of names and dates ranging back to the 1980s. Aubrey's name appeared top of the list.

"Rosalie's name's not there," Jake said, shaking the monitor as if it would reveal its secrets that way.

"Don't worry, Jake. We find Aubrey, we find your sister. Try Candidates."

The file was almost identical to the previous: a list of about twenty names and corresponding dates. But next to the names it said either "In active service" or "Retired".

I scanned the list and the first name that jumped out at me sent a shiver down my spine. "Henry Heritage. Retired," I whispered. Six names above him was another name I recognised. "Clive Warner. Retired. That was the man from the Tube."

There were five other names marked Retired.

I rubbed my face and stared out the window, ignoring Morgan's jabbering next to me. Two men, who ended up with their brains missing, on the same list. Both candidates for some programme that involved experiments into sustaining Shifting. I thumped the glass. Zac had been right. ARES were up to something and Aubrey had got caught up in it.

"Er, Scott," Jake said pointing at the screen. I looked back and followed his finger to see a third, all-too familiar, name on the candidate list.

"JON CAIN. IN ACTIVE SERVICE."

CHAPTER TWENTY-NINE

"To what do we owe this pleasure, Mr Tyler?" Cain said, smiling as I entered the training room. "It's not often we have a Bluecoat in our midst." The group laughed and some of the kids waved. Distracted, I waved back.

"Sir, I need to–"

He held a hand up. "Sergeant Cain now, Scott. I think I have to call you "sir"."

"Sergeant Cain," I tried again, more urgent this time. "I need to speak to you."

Cain hesitated, looking me up and down. "All right. Class, carry on sparring. But don't think you can slack off. I might not be watching, but I'll know." He pointed to his foggy, 'all-seeing' eye. Then he led me to a corner of the room.

"Is this about Ms Jones? I heard that you've been trying every which way to get in to see her. I'm afraid I can't help with that."

I shook my head. "No, sir, I mean, sergeant." I swallowed

hard. I knew that what I was about to reveal could get me in some serious trouble. "It's about Project Ganymede."

Cain's face was totally expressionless, which in itself was a pretty big giveaway. He should at least be looking confused. "Go on," he prompted. Clearly he wasn't going to let anything slip till he knew where this was going.

"I know you're a part of it. One of the candidates."

He couldn't hide his feelings this time. Blood rose red in his cheeks and his jaw clenched so hard the tendons fought to escape his skin. For a second I was worried his head was about to explode.

"I don't think that is any of your business, Mr Tyler," he said when he'd recovered. "Now, I have a class to get back to."

"They're dying." I said to his turned back. He stopped. "The other men on the project. Seven of them are already dead."

He spun around, slowly. Blinked twice. And then spoke. "Tell me what you know."

With a glance at the sparring kids, I pulled Cain to the side. "I found the files on Project Ganymede. Don't ask how, I just did. And there was a list of candidates. Your name was on it and next to six of the other names it said 'retired', and we're not talking the pottering around in your garden wearing slippers kind of retired. It's the dead kind of retired. Head exploding dead."

"What are you on about, Tyler?"

"The explosion on the Tube. The guy they say was the

bomber – Clive Warner – he was on the list. Only he wasn't the bomber. Because I was on the carriage when it blew up and minutes before I watched him have a complete breakdown and then his head exploded. Only after that did the carriage blow up. He had nothing to do with it."

"They said it was the SLF who were responsible."

I kicked at the floor with my shoe. I really didn't want to say what I was about to say, because it meant that I was starting to believe Zac. And that meant that me being responsible for getting them arrested was even worse than I'd first thought. "I don't think it was them. They're a bunch of vandals who like to play at being tough guys. But the only brain damage they're interested in is their own." Our heads were inches apart now as we struggled to keep our voices unheard. "I think this is bigger than them. Then there's Heritage."

"Henry?" Cain said, sounding sad and angry at the same time. "He killed himself."

"No he didn't. He was killed. I found his body, but then someone Shifted and... well, anyway. It was no suicide."

Cain leant away, as if trying to distance himself from the information. He rubbed at the folds of flesh at the back of his neck and took a deep breath. I guess he knew Heritage. Probably from the Project and here I was telling him his friend had been killed. "So what do you want me to do about it?" he said.

"Help me get Aubrey out."

"Jones? What's she got to do with this?"

"She's been volunteered for the programme."

Cain smiled a little and shook his head. "I think you're mistaken. Only adults are on the project."

"No. The adults were listed as the Candidates. There was a second list called Volunteers and all the names on that list were kids."

His smile slipped away and a look of cold realisation spread over his patchwork face. "They're using kids? I mean… They wouldn't." His jaw clenched. "We have to find her."

"Yes!" I said, getting excited. "Only…"

"Only what?"

"Only I have no idea where she is. I think it might be in a hospital called Greyfield's but I don't know where that is," I said.

"Leave that to me. Oh, and Tyler, I should warn you. We'll be up against some serious firepower. Grown men, trained and ruthless."

I wasn't worried. "That's OK. I can Shift."

"That's the thing," Cain said looking me straight in the eye. "So can they."

"What? But adults can't Shift."

"Some of us can," he said.

I walked after him and then stopped as I replayed what he'd just said over in my head. "Hang on," I said. "*Us?*"

Cain stopped and turned back to me. "I thought you knew. That's what Project Ganymede is," Cain said. "A secret group of adult Shifters. There are only about twenty of us, as far as I know. But if they're dying, maybe less now."

"So there are adults who can Shift?" The weird world I'd found myself in over these past three months tilted and yet again I was totally lost. "Why has no one told us about this?"

"What bit of top secret don't you understand, Tyler? As far back as the Thirties they've been trying to find ways to stop entropy. During World War II they really stepped up the research. An army of Shifting soldiers – you can imagine why they were so keen. Of course there were units of Shifters. The Germans had the Hitler Youth and we had our Scouts. The Nazis got furthest, carrying out sick tests on Jewish Shifters."

"Did they work?" I asked.

"Not as far as I know. But they learned a lot about how the Shifter brain worked, because they weren't limited by anything as inconvenient as morals. They put their victims through horrific experiments, just to see what would happen." Cain's eyes tightened and his fists clenched. I imagined if there were any Nazis around he'd happily carry out a few experiments of his own on them.

"After the war," he continued, "the experiments were shut down. But then the Cold War started up. Shifter spies is what they were after this time. And at the end of the Eighties they cracked it. They worked out how to re-ignite the ability to Shift in a full grown adult."

"How?"

Cain looked uncomfortable. "I didn't ask that many questions. I was twenty-one and had only been without my power for a couple of years and I missed it, bad. So when I was told I could get it back, I jumped at the chance. We all did.

"All I know is I had an operation and when I woke up, I could Shift. Not as powerful as before, but it was there. And so I was put to work. First in Russia and later in the Middle East and Yugoslavia. Shifting saved my life more times than I can tell you. But I got too cocky. And pushed it too far." He pointed at his milky eye. "I got this from a land mine in Sarajevo. So I was sent here. To teach. I was made to sign some papers saying I'd never Shift in public."

"So why do you think they, whoever they are, are killing the men on the project?"

Cain looked over my shoulder and I knew he wasn't really with me for a moment. He was back there, with his memories. "I saw one guy in Afghanistan who lost it, bad. He started talking about being a god. How the petty humans should bow to him. He killed seven civilians before we could bring him down."

"Sounds like what happened to the guy on the Tube."

Cain blinked and looked back at me. "I thought it was just a one-off. The stress of what he'd seen. What we'd been forced to do. But maybe…" He didn't finish.

"What do you think they want with Aubrey? Do you think they want to make her into a spy?"

Cain shook his head. "She's too young. We were told only those post-entropy could go through the process. And as far as I know all of us were taken from the military. You said her name was on a list of volunteers? I can't believe that they would…" He stared back into the distance, lost again in whatever images were haunting him.

"Cain?" I said trying to snap him out of it. "Cain, what are they going to do to her?"

"We may not have much time," he said suddenly. "And we're going to need as much help as we can get." He strode back over to the freshers who'd been sparring the whole time.

"Right class. We're going on a field trip."

They all cheered.

CHAPTER THIRTY

Greyfield's hospital was a red-brick Victorian building. More mental hospital than your modern NHS complex. Cain, the freshers and I had scaled the walls surrounding it, and were now hiding in the bushes, peering through the leaves. Something scrabbled behind us and we all jumped. It was just Jake back from his recce.

"There are two guards on five-minute rotation," he whispered to the group. They all nodded like they knew what this meant. Which was good because I didn't have a clue. I hadn't been keen on Jake or any of the kids coming. But Jake had moaned and said he'd only follow me. Plus, Cain assured me none of them would be in any danger. That job came down to me and him.

"Good job, Jake," Cain said. "What about cameras?"

"One there and one there,' Jake said, pointing them out. "And a light sensor about three metres from the front door."

"OK. Listen up. This is a lesson in evasion. You're to try to set off that light sensor and then get out of there.

You get caught, you Shift. And it's the next person's turn. You know the drill. Focus on your decisions. Don't react…"

"Anticipate," the group said as one.

"Good, now get out there."

The first boy, Max, stood up, flexed his fingers and ran.

"They'll keep the guards busy," Cain said.

"But if the guards are Shifters?" I said.

"No, they're just regulars. No problem for these kids." He smiled and his eyes were huge in the dull light. I was worried he was enjoying this a little too much. I just hoped he didn't freak out on me and blow up. But he was my only way in. And he wanted to find out what was going on in there as much as I did. After all, his life depended on it.

He crept away and I followed him, trying to keep my body low to the floor. Cain moved like a panther, fluid and strong. He was pure instinct and this was just another of the thousands of missions he'd been on. I was less cat-like, and after five minutes my back was starting to ache.

He stopped suddenly and pressed himself flat up against a wall. I copied him, pushing my cheek into the rough brickwork and instantly regretted going in face first. I coughed as I breathed in a mouthful of dust. I heard footsteps coming towards us and my heart started to pound in my chest. The footsteps came closer and I started to wonder if I could really go through with all of this. I'd had a few months of training and now I was expected to break into some military facility, get past Shifting adults and rescue my friend. The thought of Aubrey washed away all doubt.

I stepped out from the wall and had a second to enjoy the surprised look on the guard's face. Then a chop to the throat, a side kick to the knee and an elbow to the back of the neck and he was lying face down on the pavement. Out cold.

Cain raised an eyebrow and nodded, looking impressed. High praise indeed. "Hide him in the bushes," he said then pressed on.

I struggled with the deadweight of the guard, pulling off one of his boots in my attempts to get him out of sight. Eventually I dragged him into the shrubbery and threw a handful of leaves over him.

Cain was peering out from behind a small bush when I caught up with him. Just ahead of us was a door leading into the hospital. An orange glow spilt out of the hatched window creating a pool of light. Cain crept out and headed for the door, clinging to the shadows. He tugged at the door. "Locked," he mouthed and joined me back behind the bush.

We huddled together, peering through the leaves. "What shall we do?" I said.

"If we force it, we'll set off the alarms."

The door clicked and a woman dressed in a white nurse's uniform walked out carrying a blue bin bag. I dropped to the floor, wishing myself invisible. It seemed impossible that she wouldn't see us. The nurse opened a dustbin, threw in the bag and walked back through the door, ignoring us completely. I popped my head up to see the soles of her white shoes disappearing through the doorframe. This was my chance. I dived forward and threw out my hand. The metal door closed on my fingers and I had to stop myself from shouting out in pain.

Cain crept up behind me and patted me on the back. When he opened the door I yanked my throbbing fingers away and held them under my armpit. Muttering to myself, I stepped inside the hospital.

It was quiet apart from the soft clicking of heels echoing through the tiled corridors and a gentle bleeping from one of the rooms ahead. Like every hospital it stank of bleach and desperation, as if the decades of pain and death had seeped into the very bricks.

"God, I hate these places," I said.

In response, Cain pointed to the room ahead and darted forward. I followed him through the door. The room was dark and smelt of mothballs and even more bleach. As my eyes adjusted to the light, I saw a row of large armchairs all facing a wall with a small picture of a boat on it. Three men sat in the chairs, dressed in tatty dressing gowns. They stared at the picture, their eyes hardly focused. I crept up and waved my hand in front of their faces. No reaction.

Cain ignored the comatose men and looked out the doorway. He darted back in as we heard the sounds of footsteps coming closer.

"They're getting her prepped up on the third floor.

She's dosed up now so shouldn't be much hassle," a male voice said.

"I hope not. The little cow bit me you know?" a female voice said. Their chatter faded away down the corridor.

"That sounds like Aubrey," I said to Cain.

He nodded, took a quick glance out of the door and moved out. I looked back at the dribbling men and moved to the doors. Cain was already at the exit to the stairwell. He waved me forward. A quick check to see no one was around and I ran. The stairs seemed never-ending, spiralling up and up. There were large floor-to-ceiling windows in the stairwell, looking down on the ground below. The trees and bushes grew smaller with each level. I saw a tiny figure below, being chased by a guard. I saw the ripple of a Shift and then the kid was running alone. Nice work, I thought.

Finally we reached the third floor. I listened for sounds and couldn't hear anything. I pushed the fire door open and entered an identical corridor to the one below. The lights were dimmer here and nothing stirred in the gloom. I stepped into the corridor. My trainers squeaked loudly on the lino floor and I hushed at them to be quiet. Cain too put his fingers to his lips, hushing me. I raised my hands, asking him what I could do. It wasn't my fault this place was so clean.

I crept on, walking on the tips of my toes, trying to stop the noise. I felt like a burglar from a bad cartoon. All I needed was a stripy shirt and a bag that said "Swag" on it.

Two blue doors faced each other across the hall. I stopped, focused on my decision and chose the left door. The room held a neat row of four metal-framed beds. In each lay a child, ranging in age from eight to about sixteen. Two of the kids had angry red scars running across their temples and were wide awake, staring at the ceiling. They didn't react as I walked into the room. Their eyes rolled in their heads and most of them were drooling just like the men we'd seen downstairs.

In the last bed lay a small dark-haired girl. She had a tube coming out of her nose and seemed to be fast asleep. No scar disturbed her pretty features, but even so it took me a moment to recognise her.

"CP?" I said. I stared at the sleeping girl not quite able to believe what I was seeing. She was supposed to be dead. But here she was, tucked up and snoring away. She even had a small teddy bear tucked under her chin. "Mr Cain, it's CP." I looked at him, expecting him to run over and share in my astonishment. He was standing at the foot of one of the beds, frozen, watching the child with the dead eyes. Slowly, inch by inch, he raised his hand up to his head and gently stroked his own scar. A mirror of the scar the kid had. The truth behind Project Ganymede was clear.

"I have a daughter, you know?" he said, with a dead voice. "She is so beautiful. So smart, smarter than me. And she has this way of laughing that sounds like bells ringing. Her mother won't let me see her any more. She says it confuses her now that she has a new Daddy. She'll be seven next month." A single tear rolled in a zigzag following the jagged path of his scars.

I watched him wondering if I should say anything. But what can you say to a man who's just realised the only reason he'd been able to escape war zones and dodge bullets was because someone cut up a kid's brain and gave a bit to him? I left him to his agony and turned back to CP. I tried shaking her, but she just flopped about and made no response. The tube in her nose was attached to a metal tank standing on the floor. I tugged at it, slowly pulling it out of her nose and waited. A few minutes later she started to stir. Her eyes blinked open and she looked at me, her eyes red and unfocused.

"CP," I said softly. "It's me, Scott. I'm going to get you out of here."

I helped her sit up but she was too weak to stand. So I scooped her up along with her teddy bear and carried her in my arms. She curled herself around me like I was her daddy carrying her to bed.

Cain still hadn't moved. "Sergeant!" I hissed. He jolted and looked at me. It was the face of a man so utterly broken he was hardly a man any more.

"We have to find Aubrey and the others and get out. There's nothing we can do for these kids now."

"Yes, there is." His voice was cracked.

"What?"

"Revenge." He looked up and smiled and a shudder went through me.

"Cain, don't," I said. But he was beyond hearing me. He was beyond everything now. He turned slowly and headed out of the room. Cain had his job to do, and I had mine.

I readjusted CP's weight in my arms and walked into the corridor. The door opposite was open a few inches and I pushed it with my foot. The same sight greeted me; a row of lobotomised kids. The last bed was empty, although the ruffled sheets told me that someone had been in it recently. I walked up to the pillow. A bleach-blonde strand of hair lay across the crisp white of the pillowcase. With my spare hand I picked up the pillow and brought it to my face. It smelt of vanilla mixed with smoke.

I was too late. They'd already taken Aubrey in for her operation and she'd end up like these kids. I wanted to scream. I wanted to tear this place down around me. I threw the pillow away and squeezed my arms around CP, hoping that if I held on to her it would stop me from crumbling away.

Then I felt a tap on my shoulder.

CHAPTER THIRTY-ONE

"What the hell are you doing here?" asked Aubrey.

I stared at her through foggy eyes. She wore a pale blue nightdress with small white dots on it and had a plastic strip around her wrist, like the ones you get at gigs, although I don't think this was a tag Aubrey would be keen on wearing for months to come. Her feet were bare and the blue nail varnish had been cleaned off her big toe. Her hair was a mess and the makeup smeared around her eyes made her look like a panda. She was the most beautiful thing I'd ever seen.

"Rescuing you," I said, finding my voice again.

Aubrey laughed. "You idiot. I can look after myself."

My mouth bobbed open and closed while I tried to think of something to say. I failed. This was not going as I had imagined it. I had planned on being the big hero, storming the castle to save the damsel. I had hoped Aubrey would throw herself into my arms and be forever in my debt. She was right. I was an idiot.

"Who's that?" Aubrey said, pointing at the girl curled

up around my neck.

"This is CP Finn. The fresher girl we thought was dead. I wonder how many other kids have been sent 'down under'."

"Cleopatra Finn?" Aubrey asked.

"Cleopatra?" I said. "Her name is Cleopatra?" I looked at the girl in my arms, and couldn't wait till I could tell the others I'd found out her secret.

"That's what it said on the nurse's board. She was scheduled to be operated on today."

We shared a look that said a lot about near-misses and evil nurses. "Did you see the other room?" I asked.

Aubrey nodded. "It was awful. All those kids. What's happened to them?"

"Seems Zac was right. ARES have found a way of stopping entropy."

A scream of rage echoed through the corridors, followed by what, if I wasn't very much mistaken, was a security guard being thrown against a wall.

"What the hell?"

"That will be Cain having his revenge."

"Cain? Sergeant Cain! What is he doing here?"

"He was one of the candidates for Project Ganymede."

"And that is?" Aubrey said impatiently. I don't think she liked not being the one to know everything.

"This is," I said indicating the hospital. "This whole thing is."

I filled her in on what I found in the files in Morgan's office and what Cain told me. Her face went even paler than usual.

"So that's what they're up to! Zac knew something was going on here, but never this. Cutting out kids' brains and sticking them in adults. And Cain was one of them?"

"Yeah, but this is all new to him too. And I don't think he's too happy about the fact."

Another crash and a wet scream came from outside the room. We winced.

"Doesn't sound like it," Aubrey said.

Alarms started wailing and the lights in the room turned red giving everything a weird, hellfire glow.

Aubrey and I looked at each other. "I guess they know we're here."

So much for the swift "in and out" Cain and I discussed. We were going to have to fight our way out now. The guards didn't seem to be too much problem. Even the freshers had been able to outwit them. It was the other members of Project Ganymede I didn't want to have to come up against. From what Cain had said, there would be at least four of them stationed here.

"We have to get CP out of here. I'll carry her–"

"I can walk," said a muffled voice close to my ear.

"You're awake," I said looking at her. I brushed her fringe out of her face.

"And you wear too much aftershave," she said, wrinkling up her nose.

"Remind me to introduce you to my sister, CP," I said. "You two would get on."

I put CP down. She was unsteady on her feet but able

to stand. She blinked in the red light and looked around. "What's going on? The last thing I remember was being told my Ma had come to see me. And then some weird woman gave me a drink and then I woke up here. And what the hell is this?" She said looking at the teddy bear in her hand. She threw it to the floor.

"I'll explain later," I said. "If there is a later," I added under my breath.

Aubrey moved to the door and looked out. She pulled her head back in a second later and shook it. No way out.

"The window," she said.

I tugged at the sash window. It was locked.

"Out of the way." Aubrey picked up a gas tank by the side of one of the beds and hurled it through the glass. The tank hit the ground below with a thud. We poked our heads out of the shattered remains of the window and looked down. It was thirty feet to the grass. An electricity pole stood in front of the window and a large tree behind that. Perhaps, with a running jump someone might be able to make it to the nearest branch. Or they might just crash onto the concrete below. There had to be another way.

I looked at the beds with white sheets and neat hospital corners. "I've seen it work in movies," I said. "But I don't know if it works for real."

Aubrey followed my gaze. "Let's find out."

The kids didn't even make a sound as we pulled the sheets out from under them. They just allowed themselves to be turned over. Rage bubbled up in me as I looked at their blank faces. They'd had their lives stolen and for what? So adults could steal their power and stay in control. Somehow, I was going to make them pay.

I tested the rope of sheets. It seemed strong enough. I threw it through the broken window. The wind had picked up and was blowing hard, tossing the rope about. Along with the sirens blaring it was hard to hear myself speak. "The rest of the freshers are out there somewhere causing chaos," I shouted, helping CP get onto the windowsill. "Find them and then get the hell out of here. Oh, and they might be surprised to see you. They thought you were in Australia."

"What?"

"Never mind. Just get going."

"You're coming too, right?" CP asked.

"Not just yet. I have to find some other people and help them out," I said looking at Aubrey.

"You think Zac and Rosalie are still here?" she said.

"I hope so, or it's going to be a really long night."

"It certainly is," said a very welcome voice from the doorway.

CHAPTER THIRTY-TWO

"Mr Abbott!" I said, so happy to see him. "I've been trying to get hold of you all day. You would not believe what's going on here." I helped CP down off the window ledge. Now that Abbott was here there would be no need for dramatic exits. He'd sort everything out.

"Really," he said walking into the room and looking around. Two guards followed him in. They wore black uniforms, different to the guards outside, and both had scars on their foreheads. A silver *S* shone in their collars. Shifters. They raised their guns and pointed them at us.

"And what is going on? Exactly?" said Abbott.

He smiled and I shuddered. Gone was the warm, caring expression and in its place was a smile like a shark. The wailing alarms stopped and the lights switched back to normal. The alert was over. They'd found their intruders.

"You know," I said. "You knew all along."

Abbott gestured to the guards. "Wait outside please. I have them covered." He pulled a small handgun out from inside his jacket and pointed it at us. With a look of hesitation, the two men lowered their weapons and left the room. Abbott turned his attention back to us. "Of course I do, Scott. Nothing goes on in ARES without me knowing. Unlike that imbecile Morgan. I found him spinning around in his chair, with his tie wrapped around his head. That was your doing, I suppose? That man never fails to disappoint me. You know all that stuff about him being a powerful Fixer when we took the SLF down? Nonsense. Complete and utter tripe. You were the most powerful Shifter there, Scott. You." He smiled at me. "That was why it was so important we sent you running off there without thinking. How else could we have captured them all so neatly?"

"You bastard!" shouted Aubrey. "How could you?"

Abbott gave her the briefest of glances. "Ms Jones, still causing trouble I see. I should have volunteered you for the project years ago. But as they say, better late than never."

I heard a roar and a few heavy thuds and Cain appeared in the doorway. Blood poured down his face and he was grinning so wide I thought it would split his scars. He made a move for Abbott.

"Oh, I wouldn't do that, Jon," Abbott said, pointing the gun at Cain. With his spare hand he reached into his pocket and pulled out a phone.

"What you gonna do? Call your mother?" Cain spat.

"This, I have been told by the boys in IT, is an app." He punched a button on the phone's screen with his thumb and an image of Cain appeared. "An app which remotely controls the cortex bomb we placed in your brain twenty years ago." Abbott's thumb hovered above the red button on the screen. "All I need to do is push this button."

"That's what you did to Warner," I said. "You killed him and then blew up the carriage to hide the evidence."

"So you had been on the train? Yes, you are as powerful as I suspected. Such a shame we didn't find you earlier. Unfortunately you are too old now. The operation is a little tricky, so we prefer to use younger, more adaptable subjects. Such as Ms Jones and Ms Finn there. I see you're out of bed, CP. Tut tut. We shall have to get you tucked back in quickly."

"You're not touching her," I said, pulling CP behind me.

"Let the kids go, Abbott." Cain took a step forward.

"Make me,"' Abbott said, holding the phone out as if it was the bomb.

"I'm dead already," Cain said from between clenched teeth. "CP. The poles."

CP turned to the window and got that look I'd seen on her face before. Utter concentration. She started running for the window, her thin arms pumping, just as Cain dived at Abbott.

Abbott's gun blazed and I saw the bullet aiming straight for Cain's chest. Cain Shifted and the bullet missed, slicing instead through the top of his shoulder. He didn't even flinch. He reached Abbott just as CP dived out of the window, her arms outstretched as if she was diving into a pool. She made it to the electricity pole and pulled herself up. I was watching her steady herself on the top of the pole, just like she had in class, so I didn't see the struggle. But I heard a sickening flat popping sound. I'd heard it before. I looked around to see Cain staggering away. Blood running from his nose and ears. The scar on his forehead had peeled open like a fig. His knees buckled as if finally receiving the message from his head and he toppled forward into a growing pool of blood. I glanced back to see CP leap safely into the tree. I was just glad she hadn't been here to see this.

Abbott took a steadying breath and slipped his phone back into his pocket. He turned and pointed the gun back at us.

"Please, let's not have any more fuss."

My mind was racing through the decisions I'd made tonight, coming here, finding CP and Aubrey, looking for something to undo. I should have persuaded Cain to stay out of it and come on my own. I grabbed Aubrey's hand and closed my eyes tight, willing on that flipping feeling, focusing on telling Cain he couldn't come. But nothing. I couldn't Shift.

I heard him before I saw him. The slap slap of flesh on flesh. Benjo walked into the room, followed by two new Shifter guards, and I understood why we couldn't get out of there.

He looked from the crumpled bodies outside the door, to Abbott and then finally settled his piggy eyes on us. "But I killed you," he said, pointing a stubby finger at Aubrey and me.

Abbott looked momentarily confused. "You've seen these children before?"

"We tracked him down after he murdered Heritage," Aubrey shouted. "After you told him to."

"Murder?" Abbott said, innocently. "But your report clearly states suicide, does it not?"

"Someone changed that," I said. "When we first got there, Heritage had been killed and his brains eaten by that fat freak! And you told him to do it!"

Abbott looked at Benjo like a master looking at a naughty dog. "Oh, dear, oh dear, Benjo. What did I tell you about getting carried away?"

"But I got hungry. And I fixed it all up afterwards."

"Never mind. We can discuss this later." He turned back to us. "Heritage proved a problem. Not only was he starting to show signs of psychosis, he was helping the SLF get a little too close to uncovering the truth about Ganymede and I couldn't have that. So, I had Benjo deal with him. I knew Morgan would delegate the responsibility of checking on Heritage to you – if there's one thing that boy can do, it's delegate. Combined with the photos I had taken of Heritage meeting with Zac, I knew it would start you on the trail that would take you to the SLF. Which in turn would allow me to capture them. I might not be a Shifter any more, Scott, but in my time as a Mapper, I became exceptionally good at understanding the nature of consequences."'

I couldn't believe what I was hearing. The man I had so much respect for, coolly discussing how he'd arranged for a man's murder. "And Warner? You killed him because he was going to tell the SLF?"

"No, I had to dispose of him because he was going to tell Sir Richard."

"And the Director of ARES doesn't know about your sick experiments?" Aubrey said.

"Sir Richard chooses to remain ignorant of the precise details of the project. He leaves the running of things up to me and stays out of it – as long as he sees results."

"If he did know–" I started.

"If he did know," interrupted Abbott, anger rising in his voice for the first time, "I doubt he'd be able to show his face in his fancy clubs. From the start Project Ganymede was designated black ops – totally deniable – because men like Sir Richard Morgan do not care to get their hands dirty. They leave that to men like me. Which brings me back to you two. Sergeant," Abbott said to one of the guards. "Take Ms Jones here away and get her prepped for surgery. And do it properly this time."

I punched the first man who stepped close in the stomach and tried to take the other one out with a roundhouse. But before I connected, the guard Shifted and smacked me in the face with the butt of his rifle. I fell to my knees, dazed. Lights spun before my eyes and blood poured from my nose.

Aubrey put up a good fight, elbows and knees flying. But they were too much for her alone and in seconds she was handcuffed. Not that they needed it with Benjo in the room. Whatever freak experiments they'd done on him, he was more powerful than any of us, and his version of reality held sway. What made it worse was it was clear the bastard was able to stop us from Shifting, while letting the guards do whatever they wanted.

They started to drag Aubrey away and I pulled myself to my feet, trying to stop them. Another smack to the face and I hit the floor again, my head reeling.

"Cuff Mr Tyler here and take him to the basement. He is going to help us in our research," I heard Abbott say before I blacked out.

CHAPTER THIRTY-THREE

I came round to find myself strapped to a cold metal table. I yanked at the bindings on my wrists and ankles. They were buckled tight. Overhead was a large round bulb, which burned an afterglow image into my retina when I looked away. Benjo was standing in the corner of the room, next to a table covered in green cloth. He clapped his hands, as if delighted a show was about to start. Abbott stood beside me, his head tilted and a look of concern on his face. For a minute, I thought he might be here to help me. And then I remembered. It was him who put me here in the first place.

I thrashed around, trying to get free so I could strangle him.

"Shush," he said, stroking my shoulder. I tried to bite his hand but he pulled it away too fast.

"There is so much we don't fully understand about Shifting," he said, walking around the table. "Why do only certain children get it? What triggers it? And of course, why does the ability fade after adolescence?" He stopped pacing. "We tried what is known as the Greene process – after our friend here." Benjo smiled and nodded. "We fed the brains of Shifters to our first subjects. But it never worked. It seems that only Benjo is able to process the ability that way thanks to his unique genetic code. Anyway, as you have learned today, we found our own way. We mastered the process of transplanting the area of the brain that controls Shifting into an adult host. A crucial breakthrough, as Shifting is simply too powerful to leave in the hands of children."

He stroked my forehead, like he was soothing me back to sleep after a nightmare. "I decided to forego having the treatment myself, so that I can remain impartial in these investigations. And, as you have seen, there are some unfortunate side effects. Paranoia, delusions of grandeur, even psychopathic tendencies. But we have learned how to take care of those as well, although the idea of placing the cortex bomb only came to Dr Lawrence in phase two of the project. So there are some of our Shifters that we had to take care of... personally. Such as Mr Heritage. Such a shame, he was a good analyst but it was in his nature to ask questions." Abbott looked so pleased with himself. "So you see, we are so close to mastering the power completely. And once we do, we will go public and the whole world will finally know who is truly in control."

"You're mad, you know that? You think this is going to make you famous or something? It will bring the world down on top of Shifters. You said yourself that the world wasn't ready to know about us. It never will be."

He ignored me and checked the straps holding me were tight. "However there is one element that we have yet to fully understand. And that has been the primary focus of my investigation." He walked behind me and I heard the rattling of metal. I twisted my head around to try and see what he was doing. "Have you heard of the hypnic jerk?" he asked.

"The only jerk I know of is you!"

He chuckled and continued. "The hypnic jerk is the twitch you get sometimes just as you're falling asleep. It's the brain's response when it perceives the body to be dying. The twitch is a reflex used to keep the body functioning. To make sure you're not dead. Shifters have their own version of this feedback system. If the brain senses it is dying, it sends a desperate signal to Shift. A survival mechanism. It is so powerful that our clever cuffs can't override it. Not even a more powerful Shifter can stop it."

"Are you saying you can't kill me?" I said, hopefully.

"It's not easy, but there are ways. Instant explosion of the brain is particularly effective. Removing the frontal lobe while the subject is still alive works also. But I want to try another, more artful approach." He walked back into view pulling a machine behind him.

I didn't like the sound of this. I looked up and saw Benjo pull off the green cloth to reveal a row of surgical tools lined up on a tray – the same ones I'd seen in his cabinet. He stroked them with his fat hands, as if they were a collection of dolls. He picked up a scalpel and licked the edge of the blade. It left a red mark on his tongue.

"I want it to be the Shifter's choice to die," Abbott said, from behind me.

I laughed and dropped my head back down onto the table. "You want me to choose to die? No way."

The machine Abbott was fiddling with had wires curling out of it. He untangled three of the wires and held them up to me. They each ended in a white disk. Like a stripped back skullcap. "Have you used a stimulator yet, Scott? 'Live out your fantasies, consequence free,' isn't that what they say? Well, I've made a few modifications." He started placing the receptors onto my head, the way I'd seen Zac do to that girl in the club what seemed like a lifetime ago. "With my machine, you won't live out your best realities. You will experience your worst possible realities. And it will send you quite mad. I give you five minutes before you're begging to die."

I shook my head, trying to dislodge the electrodes. I saw Abbott reach a hand up to the machine. He paused, his wrinkled face taking on a look of pained concern, then flicked a switch. The world Shifted.

Images, no they were memories, raced through my mind. Me as a child in the playground, at home with my parents, playing and laughing with my friends, at kick boxing with Katie, at school trying to pay attention. But each memory was somehow distorted. Crooked and broken. The machine was taking each moment in my life and unravelling it, and tearing me apart in the process.

I clenched my teeth so hard I felt my teeth crack. But still the memories came. Every terrible thought I'd ever had, became solid. The thoughts you bury deep because you feel so guilty that they even flicker across your mind floated up and started to morph into reality. Each time I'd idly ever wondered if stabbing someone in the hand with a pen would stop them humming happened. Every time I thought about pushing a friend off the edge of a bridge, I did it. Over and over. I did unspeakable things to my family. I killed Katie a hundred times in ever more horrible ways and laughed at my parents' agony. Then I killed them. Stabbed Mum in the eye with her stupid stiletto heels, strangled Dad with his tie. And these weren't fantasies. They were real.

I don't know if I was screaming or laughing. Anger and anguish coursed through me. And hate consumed me. Everything I'd once loved I now despised. My parents were weaklings, my sister a freak, my friends were parasites.

And Aubrey. My mind turned to her. I should hate her. I'd come to try to save her and she had laughed in my face. I should punch her and punch her and see how hard she laughed then.

But I couldn't. Not Aubrey. I wouldn't.

I heard Abbott's voice as if coming from another room. "Ten minutes, surprising. Normally they can't take more than five."

I'd lost all sense of who I was. My parents meant nothing to me. No family or friends had ever mattered.

Except her. I knew that a minute more and they would strip that from me too. Make me hurt her. I would rather die than that. In the dark storm that my life had become, Aubrey was my anchor and if I lost her, I would lose everything.

"Do it!" I screamed through cracked teeth.

Benjo leaned over me, his knife glinting. And I died.

CHAPTER THIRTY-FOUR

The darkness came quickly and the pain stopped. In the last fleeting moments I was myself again. All the fragments of my life had been put back into place and I had the strongest sense of relief. My parents and Katie were safe and all my friends unharmed. I knew that everything would be all right now that I was dead.

I'm sorry to say that there wasn't a tunnel of light. I didn't float out of my body and see myself below. No grandparents or old pets came to greet me. Just darkness and peace. Like falling asleep after a really long day. And that was it.

OK, I know what you're thinking: he can't be dead. How could he have written this whole account if he were dead? But I was. Dead. Deceased. Gone.

For a full ninety seconds.

Then it happened. It was like a light going on, on an old fashioned TV set. A flicker and then bam! Everything came on, sound, light, smell. All my senses kicked back in as if someone had jolted me with one of those defibrillator things. A whole body reboot.

I was still strapped to the table and wired up to the machine. The light overhead burned into my eyes and I blinked trying to understand what the hell was going on. I heard Abbott speaking, "Eleven minutes. Very impressive."

I sensed the prickling of electricity on my skull, sending tendrils of power through into my brain. But the machine wasn't working. The scenarios had stopped playing out and I was myself again. But only more so. They say what doesn't kill you makes you stronger. Well I was strong. Impossibly so. I knew I was the one in charge now.

"I'd like to get out now," I said softly.

The men paused to look at each other and then, as if it was the most natural thing in the world, Abbott reached over and unbuckled the straps holding me down. I reached my hand up and pulled the electrodes off my head. I sat up like Frankenstein's monster awakening on the slab.

There was a metallic clang as Benjo dropped his scalpel. Abbott was staring at his hands as if he didn't recognise them.

I placed my bare feet on the cold floor and wriggled my toes. My trainers appeared back on my feet. I looked at the surgery gown I was wearing. That won't do, I thought. I closed my eyes and I was wearing my clothes again. In this new reality that I'd brought into existence, Abbott simply hadn't bothered undressing me. That is what had happened, because that's how I wanted it to have happened.

The two men backed away from me, their eyes wide in shock. I turned first to the fat one. His rubbery lips flapped about as he struggled to speak.

"You look hungry, Benjo," I said. "And those tools look so tasty, don't they? Why don't you tuck in?"

Benjo reached for the tray with a shaking hand, his black eyes darting around trying to find a way to stop himself. But he couldn't resist my command. Not only was I back in control of my decisions, I could control his too. I turned my back to him as I heard the first wet, crunch of him biting into the blade.

"Mr Abbott," I said, smiling at the man I had once thought was my friend, my teacher. The man who had destroyed the lives of the children in the ward, those men in the armchairs staring at a boat that would never come in, and I didn't know how many others. "I think it's time you tried out your little invention for yourself. That's right, put the electrodes on."

Abbott climbed up onto the table and obediently placed the electrodes on his head. Only his eyes betrayed that he was fighting a battle to regain control over his mind.

And that's what this had all been about. Control. Over us kids with the power. Over the world. Well, I was the one in charge now. I reached the machine and flicked the switch. I didn't know how the stimulator would work on non-Shifters. All I knew was that after two minutes he was screaming and sobbing. I left him to it.

The guards outside fell asleep with a single look from me. Energy radiated out of me like I was the bloody Ready Brek kid. I saw the ripples of reality pulsate out of me and they were only going one way. My way.

Aubrey was gowned-up and already unconscious when I found her in the operating room on the first floor, her pale arms dangling over the edge of the metal table, her sleeping face soft and empty of any expression. But that's not how I wanted it. The merest blink of a thought and she was awake and struggling with the anaesthesiologist. I grinned as Aubrey kicked the man in the balls and sent him flying. I didn't want to make this too easy for her, after all. The rest of the medical staff stood around looking confused.

I raised my hands. "It's OK everyone. You all just need to have a nice nap." One by one, they stretched out their arms and yawned, lay down on the floor and started to snore.

"Scott," Aubrey said, running to me and wrapping her arms around my neck. "I thought I'd lost you."

I breathed in the scent of vanilla. "For a while there, you did," I said. "But I found my way back."

She looked up at me through eyes blackened with smudged mascara. I brushed a strand of hair away from her face. I could have anything I wanted now. I could bend everything and everyone to my will without them ever knowing. I looked at Aubrey, her lips parted and her eyelids already closing.

"Stop," I said. She blinked and pulled away. "Not

like this."

I sighed. I was passing up on the chance to do what I'd wanted to do from the very first moment I'd laid eyes on Aubrey Jones. The very thing I laid awake at nights thinking about. But some stupid moral code was stopping me. I know, you don't need to tell me. I'm an idiot.

"Let's get out of here," I said, letting go of her.

"What about Abbott and Benjo?" she said.

"They've been taken care of. Let's find Rosalie and the others, get the kids out of here and then," I paused and took her hand. "We're going to blow this place to fuck."

By the time we'd found Rosalie, Zac and the others, locked up in a cell in the basement, I felt the power draining out of me. It was like after going for a really long run, when your body starts to give up and it's only your mind that keeps you going. My hands were trembling and my head span. I steadied myself on a wall as Aubrey started to work at the lock.

"You OK?" she said, looking worried.

"Yeah, I'm fine," I said, shaking off the fatigue.

"Of course, he's fine. We're the ones locked up," Zac said, yanking at the bars.

"Do we have to let him out?" I asked.

The lock opened with a heavy clunk. "Afraid so," Aubrey said, stepping aside.

Zac charged out, followed by Sean and the rest of the gang. Rosalie came out last. She looked tired and pale, but she smiled as she saw us. "Is Jake OK?"

"He's fine. He's outside."

She squeezed my arm as she passed.

"Right, let's bail," Zac said, looking around frantically. Despite all his big man talk, it was easy to see he was terrified.

"Hang on. There's a bunch of kids who need your help first. And you, Sean, you need to get your explosives."

He looked from me to Zac. "I would, if I knew where they'd put them."

"You'll find them in the Guard's Office on the first floor," I said, not bothering to explain how I suddenly knew. Even if I could explain it.

Sean ran off and the rest of us headed back up to the wards. We wheeled all the kids and the men from the lounge out onto the front lawn. The medical staff and guards I'd passed were still sleeping, curled up on the floor. Zac was all for leaving them here after what they'd done. But I'd seen enough death for one day. I shook them awake and without any protest they slumped down the stairs.

Cain's body still lay on the floor of the children's ward, lying face down in a pool of congealing blood.

"What shall we do with him?" Aubrey asked.

I turned him over, so he lay face up. His eyes were closed and if it wasn't for the hole in his head, you might think he was sleeping. I wondered if he was at peace now, free from all the horrors he'd seen. I guess I'd never know.

"He had a daughter, you know? He didn't even get to say goodbye," I said. I crossed his hands over his chest, not really sure why, but it seemed the right thing to do.

Aubrey laid a hand on my shoulder. "She would be proud of him."

I stood up and my knees gave way, I hardly had the strength to stand any more. Aubrey pulled my arm over her shoulder and led me outside. With every heavy step the power faded more. I paused in front of a huddle of wide-eyed nurses. "Look after the kids," I said to the two women.

The buzzing energy was fading fast and don't know if I'd made them do it, or if their caring instincts simply took over, but they quietly walked over to check on the lost children.

"We're on," Sean said running out of the building, his face flushed and a manic grin showing his teeth. "I added some bleach from the caretaker's cupboard. Just for good measure." He looked at his watch. "In five, four, three…"

The hospital exploded before he reached two. A deafening boom and a ball of fire took out every window on the ground floor.

"It must have been a lot of bleach," Aubrey said, shielding her face from the heat of the flames.

"Oh, and I set the bomb next to the gas cooker."

"Nice work, Sean," Zac said, knuckle-punching his friend.

We left the hospital grounds and stood on the other side of the road, where CP and the rest of the Fresh

Meat were watching the flames take over the building. Every now and then there would be another, smaller explosion. Abbott's dream of the adult Shifters really was going to make him famous.

"So what now?" Aubrey asked.

"I don't know. I don't know whether to believe Abbott that no one else at ARES knew what was going on here. I don't know whether to trust Morgan or his father, but we have to tell someone."

Jake laughed. "Let's just hope he doesn't remember what we did to him."

"I'll tell you later," I said to Aubrey who was looking up at me quizzically.

I felt a thud in my arm, and on auto-pilot I Shifted to block Zac's gentle punch. "Guess you're not too bad, Tyler," he said.

"Yeah, but you're still a dick."

He laughed. Then turned to Aubrey.

She held up a hand before he could even open his mouth. "I know, I know you don't have to say it."

"I hate to say I told you so..."

"Come off it, Zac. You love saying I told you so."

"Well, I guess. So, are we friends again, Brey?"

I didn't like the way he said friends.

"We'll see," Aubrey said.

Zac smiled, then clicked his fingers and faded with the rest of the gang into the night.

"You'd better get back too," I said to CP and the rest of the Fresh Meat. "Before anyone at ARES realises you're not in the dorms. And you might need to come up with an explanation for why CP's back. Can you find your way?"

"Find our way?" CP said with a shake of her tiny head. "Who do you think we are, Scott? You?"

The kids laughed and CP moved to go, then tuned back and hugged me.

I returned her hug and said, "Go on. Get home. Before I put you all in detention."

With another laugh the kids raced away, CP in the lead.

Rosalie hadn't stopped hugging Jake since they'd been reunited. She stood next to me, her arms wrapped over Jake's shoulders, watching the flames as Jake watched the rest of his class disappear around a corner. I turned to see her smiling.

"Thank you, Scott," she said, planting a kiss on my lips.

I blushed as Jake laughed and whooped.

"We'd better be going," Rosalie said.

"Yeah, sure," I croaked.

"Yes, bye, bye," Aubrey said, waving the brother and sister away. She looked pleasingly annoyed.

Now it was just the two of us, watching as a fire engine screeched down the road. Firemen jumped down from the truck and started hosing down the building. They were quickly followed by black vans with ARES written on the side in white paint. The Regulators piled out, followed by a dazed-looking Morgan. He blinked up at the flames. Now he had some real responsibility, it looked as if he didn't know what to do.

A large silver car, with blacked-out windows glided through the open gates and pulled up next to Morgan. I saw him lean down and talk to whoever was inside. His bottom lip was wobbling when he straightened up and I thought he was going to cry.

"I think we should probably go."

We stepped back into the shadows, slipped down an alleyway and started to walk away from the burning building.

I felt a warm hand in mine. "Back there," Aubrey said tightening her grip. "I had this overpowering desire to kiss you. Like if I didn't, the world might end or something."

I coughed.

"That was you? You can affect other people's decisions?" she said, stopping. I didn't know if she was impressed or scared. Both probably. The idea of another person blocking you Shifting was bad enough. But someone being able to actually control what you did, that was terrifying.

"Not any more," I said. "It's gone. At least I think it is. It's just me again." I still sensed the power, but now it was just a faint presence in my mind. Like the forgotten lyrics from your favourite song. You knew you'd remember them eventually.

"Let's find out," Aubrey said, taking a step closer.

"What?"

"Kiss me," she said.

I looked at her and swallowed hard. Her pale skin was glowing in the flickering streetlights and there were flecks of brown in her green eyes I'd never noticed before.

She smiled. "Hey," she said. "If it doesn't work out, you can always change your mind."

I leaned in to kiss her, knowing this was one decision I was never going to change.

ACKNOWLEDGMENTS

To say I never dreamed I'd write this would be a lie. I've dreamed about writing this ever since I was a kid, scribbling stories about two-headed monsters. While other girls practiced Oscar acceptance speeches, I was writing pretend acknowledgements. What I genuinely never dreamed, however, was just how many people there would be to thank. Don't believe anyone who tells you writing books is a solitary thing.

So, first off, a huge thank you to my incredible editor, Amanda Rutter, who saw something in *Shift* from the first page and helped make it the best book it could be. Your passion and energy has been a revelation. To Sam Copeland, my agent, whose charm and humour made navigating the publishing game that much easier.

To my early readers, Sandie and Samantha Dent, your input was invaluable. To Mark Jervis, for his advice on quantum physics, even if I didn't understand it. To my "cheerleaders": Kathy Martin; Miranda Dickinson; Judith Kinghorn; Victoria Morley; Sarah Terkaoui; Nick

Hollin; James Smythe; Liz de Jager; Rob Perham, Regan Warner and my old colleagues at Frontroom. You guys kept me going.

To my sisters, who never made me feel that giving up my job to write was a bad idea. To Mum and Dad, who taught me the importance of following your dreams. And to Lisa "Kick Ass" Myers. Your faith in me, even when I'd lost all in myself, has meant everything. Know that this book would not be here if it weren't for you.

To my husband, Chris. You have been my anchor throughout this crazy journey. Words don't often fail me. But in this instance they do. I guess all I can say is thank you and I love you.

And finally, thank you! The reader. A story is only a story when it's shared. And it's been my enormous honour to have shared mine with you.

STRANGE CHEMISTRY

EXPERIMENTING WITH YOUR IMAGINATION

"With whip-smart, instantly likable characters and a gothic small-town setting, Bond weaves a dark and gorgeous tapestry from America's oldest mystery." — *Scott Westerfeld*

CASSANDRA ROSE CLARKE

the Assassin's Curse

STRANGE CheMiStRY

"Unique, heart-wrenching, full of mysteries and twists!"
— *Tamora Pierce*

"*Ghostbusters* meets *Sabrina the Teenage Witch* with a dash of *X-Files*. A magical spell with equal parts humour, adventure and surprise." — *Sara Grant, author of* Dark Parties

MORE WONDERS IN STORE FOR YOU...